DAWN'S PRELUDE

This Large Print Book carries the
Seal of Approval of N.A.V.H.

SONG OF ALASKA, BOOK ONE

DAWN'S PRELUDE

TRACIE PETERSON

THORNDIKE PRESS
A part of Gale, Cengage Learning

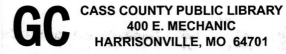
GALE
CENGAGE Learning·

Detroit • New York • San Francisco • New Haven, Conn • Waterville, Maine • London

GALE
CENGAGE Learning™

LIBRARY OF CONGRESS CATALOGING-IN-PUBLICATION DATA

Dawn's prelude / by Tracie Peterson.
    p. cm. — (Thorndike Press large print Christian fiction)
(Song of Alaska ; no. 1)
ISBN-13: 978-1-4104-2138-8 (alk. paper)
ISBN-10: 1-4104-2138-4 (alk. paper)
    1. Widows—Fiction. 2. Alaska—Fiction. 3. Large type books.
PS3566.E7717D39 2010
813'.54—dc22   2009037107

Published in 2010 by arrangement with Bethany House Publishers.

Printed in Mexico
1 2 3 4 5 6 7 14 13 12 11 10

Dedicated and thanks to

Bill and Carole Denkingeer, owners of
the Alaska Ocean View B & B in Sitka.
Your hospitality and kindness was much
appreciated.

To Bob Medinger, Director of the
Sitka Historical Society and
Museum. Your research suggestions and
history museum
offer me a great understanding of Sitka.
Thank you for answering my countless
questions.

And to the staff at the
Sheldon Jackson Museum
in Sitka for all your help.

CHAPTER 1

Kansas City, Missouri
Early April 1870

"I have no intention of Lydia inheriting any of Father's money," Mitchell Gray announced. "She's nothing to this family — an outsider imposed upon us after the death of our mother. She's entitled to nothing."

"Hush," his younger sister, Evie, replied. "She's just in the next room."

Sitting alone in the formal parlor that had displayed her husband's closed coffin only hours earlier, Lydia Gray rocked quietly. She allowed the hatred of his grown children to wash over her and numb any concerns or fears she might have otherwise given credence. With exception to Evie, they had hated her from the first moment she'd entered their home — not that Lydia could blame them. She'd hated nearly everything about her twelve years of marriage to Floyd

Gray. Nothing would change their feelings now.

And so she rocked.

I'm only twenty-eight, she reasoned. Twenty-eight years old, and nearly half of those years had been spent in an abusive marriage to a man who treated his horses better than he'd treated his wife. His *second* wife.

Lydia glanced up at the portrait of the children's mother. The oil painting had been commissioned at Charlotte Gray's request for her husband's Christmas gift in 1858. After presenting it to him in the morning, Charlotte promptly excused herself from her family's revelry and leaped to her death from the widow's walk. She had been thirty-seven years old and had left behind two grown sons, a twelve-year-old daughter, Jeannette, and four-year-old Eve.

The sorrowful gaze of the blond-haired Charlotte stared down from the wall. Her lonely expression had haunted Lydia since she'd first come to this house — it bore a look of pain that Lydia understood first-hand. It was almost as if the two shared a bond that crossed between the living and the dead. Many had been the time Lydia had come to this room just to rock and stare at the painting.

"The will can be read immediately, and

once we see what that has to say," Marston, Mitchell's twin, announced, "we can be rid of her. I can't imagine that Father would have left her anything. I believe we should give her until the end of the month to settle her affairs and leave. It's not like she has much to concern herself with. Father never gave her anything of her own. It all belonged to Mother. The jewelry, furnishings, and servants will stay here."

"Then why give her until the end of the month?" Jeannette Gray Stone questioned. Jeannette had resented the intrusion of her father's second marriage. It wasn't that she missed her mother all that much, but she didn't like her position as lady of the house being usurped by a stepmother — especially one only a few years older than Jeannette herself.

Lydia listened to them argue about how long they should give her to be gone from their lives. They had already established she should have nothing that had belonged to their father. No reward for enduring twelve painful years of marriage to a cruel and vicious man. No sympathy for all she had suffered.

She glanced up again. Charlotte's gaze seemed sympathetic, almost soothing. She seemed to silently suggest that only death

9

would ease Lydia's miseries.

And so she rocked.

Shadows danced across the elegantly flowered wallpaper. The diffused light of early evening gave them a specter-like appearance. Perhaps Floyd Gray had come back to torment her. It would be just like him.

"Less than a month hardly seems reasonable, and her father was killed in the same carriage accident that took our father," Eve told her siblings. "You don't want society saying we were heartless."

"She never loved our father, and she certainly isn't mourning the loss of him now," Mitchell declared.

"But what of her own father?" Eve asked. "She has lost him, as well."

Marston quickly countered, "They were never close."

"That's right," Jeannette agreed. "Not only that, but she made Father's life miserable. He told me so on more than one occasion. She was cold and indifferent to his needs."

Frowning, Lydia folded her gloved hands and sighed. She had tried to be the perfect wife to Floyd, despite being married against her will at the tender age of sixteen. The arrangement had been her father's idea, and his alone. He had betrothed her to Floyd Gray as a business arrangement; Lydia's mother had been appalled to see her only child wedded to a man who had been widower for two short months. She died the following winter after a bout of pneumonia weakened her heart.

"Perhaps we should wait to decide until after the reading of Father's will on Monday," Eve suggested.

Lydia didn't know why the young woman even bothered. At seventeen, Genevieve Gray Gadston had only been married six weeks herself. Her older siblings gave this no bearing, however. She was still a child in their eyes and would always remain so. Her comments were given little credence.

"I suppose a day or two can't possibly matter," Jeannette replied.

"Very well," Mitchell declared, thoroughly surprising Lydia. "We will wait to decide, but as soon as the reading is finished, we will dictate our wishes with the lawyer as our witness."

This was agreed upon in hushed murmurs before the foursome entered the parlor to address Lydia. She didn't bother to glance up from where she sat; she had no desire to see their hard, hateful expressions. She was unwanted and unloved by this family, but

11

very soon, she would be free of them.

"We have decided," Mitchell announced as the family spokesman, "that you will remain here until the reading of the will is complete. We are to meet with the lawyer on Monday."

Lydia picked lint from her black gown. "Very well."

"It would be prudent, however," Jeannette said, "to have the maids begin packing your clothes."

"Except for the furs," Mitchell interrupted. "Those will remain here to be given to our sisters and my wife. They were much too costly, and I'm certain Father never intended for them to leave the family."

Still Lydia rocked and refused to meet their eyes. "Very well."

"It would also be in your best interest," Marston added, "to inquire as to what options are available to you for your living arrangements. No sense waiting until the last minute to decide where you will move."

This was his way of informing her she would not be allowed to remain there. None of the Grays had ever been hard-pressed to deliver orders or unpleasant news, but for some reason, Mitchell and Marston seemed uncomfortable with actually commanding her to leave. Who could know their reasoning? Perhaps they did worry about what Kansas City society might say. Maybe they feared the newspapers would pick up the story and capitalize on their scandalous behavior.

"I need to leave for home," Jeannette finally announced. "I must see the children before Nanny puts them to bed for the night." She left the room without another word.

"Come, Marston, I'll drop you to your house on my way home," Mitchell said. "We can discuss how best to split up the business."

Only Eve remained as the men's voices echoed down the hallway until at last they exited the house. When Lydia finally looked up, Eve was watching her.

"I should be going, as well. Thomas sent the carriage for me some time ago. He'll wonder why I haven't returned."

"I understand," Lydia said. Only then did she still the chair's movement.

Eve seemed reluctant to go. She started to leave, then turned back. "What will you do?"

Lydia shrugged. "I don't really know. I've not had much chance to think about it. I'm still in a state of shock over the accident."

"It's hard to believe he's really gone," Eve admitted.

All of Floyd's children had known his harsh demands and heavy hand. Eve was certainly no exception to that. Many had been the time Lydia had watched helplessly as Floyd had backhanded his youngest child for the slightest infraction of his rules.

Rising from the chair, Lydia drew a deep breath. "But he is. He's gone, and he cannot hurt us anymore."

Eve's frown deepened as if she didn't believe her stepmother, but she made no attempt to correct the comment. "Good-bye, Lydia. I suppose I shall see you on Monday."

"I know it is rather soon to bother you with this," Dwight Robinson announced in greeting on Saturday morning, "but it was necessary that you see this before the reading of the will."

Lydia looked at her father's lawyer and then to the letter he extended. "Very well. Please come in."

Thunder rumbled outside and rain began to pour in earnest as the butler secured the door against the wind. Lydia led the way to a smaller, informal sitting room. She suppressed a yawn. All through the night she had tossed and turned, listening for Floyd's footsteps in the hallway. Then she remembered he was dead and could no longer hurt her. She had fallen asleep sometime around four in the morning, only to be awakened some four hours later to start her day.

"Please be seated. Should I ring for refreshments?" Lydia asked. "It's rather chilly in here; perhaps you'd like some coffee?"

"No. I'm fine." He gave her a sympathetic smile. "I suppose this has been very hard on you."

Lydia shrugged. "No more so than anything else." She took a seat on the richly upholstered silk sofa while Mr. Robinson settled himself on an ornate Baroque-styled chair. The piece had been one of Mr. Gray's favorites.

Again Robinson extended the letter. This time Lydia took it. "What is this?" she asked, turning over the folded pages in her hand.

"It's from your father. He left it with me some months ago, with instructions that should anything happen to him, you were to be given this missive."

Lydia frowned. Her father had barely spoken two words to her since forcing her into marriage. She tried to imagine what he could possibly have to say to her now.

"I think you will be . . . well, perhaps comforted by the words," Robinson said, giving his thick mustache a stroke. The rather portly old man studied her for a moment, then added, "He had me read the letter."

"And what does it say?"

"Why don't you simply read it, and then we can discuss any questions you might have. It isn't all that long."

She had thought to read it later in the privacy of her bedchamber, but seeing that Mr. Robinson had no intention of leaving until they were able to converse about it, Lydia nodded. Unfolding the pages, she drew a deep breath at the sight of her father's large script.

My dearest daughter,

For so long, my heart has been burdened with the mistakes I have made. I caused you great misery in forcing your hand in marriage to a man I knew to be ill-tempered and harsh, and all for the sake of financial security.

I pray you find a way to forgive me. So many times I desired only to come to you and plead my case, but deep in my heart, I knew there was no excuse for what I had done. I was a greedy man, whose only purpose was to build a vast fortune. That it came at the expense of those I loved was not something I considered. I believed that in time, my choices would not only be understood but applauded. Now I see the truth of the matter and know that I have done you a grave injustice.

If you are reading this letter, then I have passed from this life into eternity. The purpose of leaving this missive behind is twofold. First, the terms of my will are complicated and were never intended to cause you grief, although they most certainly are destined to do so. Second, I have left money in trust with Mr. Robinson that no one else knows about. This money is for you. It is enough to help you get a divorce or whatever other living arrangements you might desire.

The rest of the letter repeated the request for forgiveness, but Lydia was too stunned to read further. She looked up at the lawyer and shook her head.

"I don't understand."

"Your father wanted to give you a way out of your marriage. He spoke to me about it on more than one occasion. We knew it would be most difficult to help you obtain a divorce; however, that is no longer an issue."

She silently refolded the pages. "I suppose I should be happy that he came to realize his mistake." It seemed too little, too late, but Lydia didn't wish to sound as lacking in feeling as her late husband.

The older man once again shifted his bulky frame. "Your father grieved his decision to see you married to Gray. He hoped that something — anything — could be done to change it. Of course, you know that your husband was a powerful man. Most were too intimidated by his ruthlessness to do anything but yield to his will. Your father found himself in that position."

Lydia wasn't ready to feel sorry for her father. She felt the boning of her corset dig into her waist and straightened. "He mentioned that the terms of his will were complicated. Might you enlighten me in this area?"

Just then, there was the unmistakable sound of someone in the foyer. No one had bothered to knock, so Lydia knew it must be one of the children.

"It would seem we have company," Lydia said, loud enough to draw the attention of whomever had entered.

Marston Gray looked into the front room

as he doffed his black hat. "Robinson? What brings you here?" he questioned, ignoring Lydia.

Lydia watched him cross the room to shake the older man's hand. Robinson had gotten to his feet and was clearly uncomfortable with Marston's appearance.

"I had business with Mrs. Gray."

"Truly?" Marston looked at Lydia in disbelief. "And what caused my stepmother to summon you?"

Robinson cleared his throat rather nervously and focused on the floor. Lydia hated to see the man take this stance. Marston loved to see people intimidated. He fed upon it, just as he did now. His expression turned almost cruel as he sneered at the older man.

"Surely in her state of . . . mourning . . . it would be appropriate to have the guidance of a family member in any legal matter."

"Mr. Robinson was just leaving," Lydia interrupted. She came to the man's side and motioned toward the foyer. "Allow me to show you out."

Marston wasn't going to stand for this. He blocked the doorway. "I'm only looking out for you, Lydia. Was there some question you had about your future?"

Lydia met his pale blue eyes. "If there were, I certainly wouldn't be asking you."

She saw the anger course through her stepson. If her father's letter was true, and she had no reason to think it wasn't, then she was free of this man and his siblings. She had no reason to fear him anymore.

Standing her ground, Lydia squared her shoulders. "Now, if you'll excuse us, Mr. Robinson has other important meetings, and I have a headache and intend to lie down."

Marston said nothing more. He pulled back, much to Lydia's surprise, and allowed them to pass. Lydia could feel the man tremble slightly beneath her touch. She felt sorry for him, knowing that he was embarrassed by the entire encounter.

"Oh, there is one other thing," Robinson stated as they reached the front door. The butler arrived with his hat in hand, then turned to open the door.

Lydia glared at the man until he took his leave. The servants were always trying to overhear her conversations. Seeing that she no longer required his service, the butler bowed stiffly and left them. "You said there was something else, Mr. Robinson?"

"I wish to accompany you to the reading of the will on Monday. As your father's lawyer, I have made arrangements with Mr. Gray's lawyer. We will both need to be present for the reading, due to those complications of which your father spoke."

"I see." Lydia glanced over her shoulder to find Marston watching her. She lifted her chin and spoke loudly enough for him to hear her. "I would be very glad for you to accompany me. What time shall I expect you?"

"I will arrive for you at nine-thirty. The reading is set for ten."

Lydia nodded. "Very well. I shall await your arrival."

As soon as Robinson had departed, Lydia hurried upstairs before Marston could stop her. She nearly ran for the sanctuary of her bedroom and locked the door behind her before allowing herself another glance at her father's letter.

If he had provided enough money, then Lydia knew exactly what she wanted to do. Her only living relative, Aunt Zerelda, lived in far-off Alaska in a tiny island town called Sitka. It had long been Lydia's desire to join her there.

Perhaps now I can do exactly that. After all, it would resolve all of her problems. Moving to such a remote place would put her well beyond the reach of her vindictive stepchildren. It would also allow her a fresh new start.

She went to her desk and took out pen and paper. It would take considerable time for a letter to reach her aunt. It would be best to get started and allow Zerelda knowledge of what had happened. She didn't yet know of her brother's death.

For the first time in years, Lydia felt a spark of hope. She glanced across the room to where her violin awaited her. Forgoing the letter momentarily, Lydia crossed to the instrument and lovingly took it in hand. She tested the strings and tuned it before drawing the bow.

Music filled the air and sent soothing waves across the stormy seas of Lydia's heart. Throughout her life, she had known no comfort like that of her music. For a moment she lost herself in the haunting melody of Bach's Mass in B Minor.

She had once thought of having this music played at her funeral. Now, however, her death seemed far away. A new future awaited her.

CHAPTER 2

Lydia sat uncomfortably between her twin stepsons. They seemed unhappy that she had been asked to be in attendance by both her father's lawyer, Mr. Robinson, and their family lawyer, Nash Sterling. Truth be told, Lydia wasn't at all excited about the humiliation of hearing her dead husband's will read.

At least Father considered my needs. For all the wrong he did me in forcing me to marry, he at least considered my situation. She held her gloved hands together so tightly that they immediately began to ache. Lydia wanted to relax her grip, but if she did, the entire family would see how hard she was shaking.

Mr. Sterling stood. "We have agreed to meet here today for the reading of two wills. That of Mr. Zachary Rockford, father of Lydia Rockford Gray, and of Mr. Floyd Gray, husband of the same Mrs. Lydia

Rockford Gray, and father to Mr. Mitchell Gray, Mr. Marston Gray, Mrs. Jeannette Gray Stone, and Mrs. Genevieve Gray Gadston." He looked up as if to take a silent roll call, then nodded at Mr. Robinson.

Lydia drew a deep breath as her father's lawyer began to read the content of Zachary Rockford's will. Marston and Mitchell were not going to like hearing that her father had left her a trust. They had taken such satisfaction in knowing she would be left without any provision whatsoever, and this would surely steal some of that joy.

" 'In agreement with the contract signed on March 10, 1859, at the marriage of my daughter Lydia Rockford to Floyd Gray, I do hereby leave all my worldly goods to Floyd Gray upon my death.' "

Mitchell and Marston both turned a smug face to Lydia, but she neither acknowledged their stare nor the words spoken by Mr. Robinson. She had known of the agreement. Her marriage had been a business arrangement. The wholesale purchase of a sixteen-year-old bride by an older man whose wife had committed the unspeakable act of suicide.

"However, there is also another point of reference written here," Mr. Robinson continued. " 'Should Floyd Gray precede

24

me in death, then all of my properties, including stocks, business interests, and monies, will pass to my only living child, my daughter, Lydia Rockford Gray.' "

Lydia couldn't figure out why in the world this point was being brought to light. She was surprised by it, but her father and Floyd had died as a result of the same carriage accident.

Robinson picked up a sheaf of papers. "I have the signed and sworn statements by three doctors, given before myself and Mr. Sterling, as well Judge Brewster, which confirm, as you know, that Floyd Gray died immediately at the site of the accident on April 2, 1870." He paused and lowered his glasses to the tip of his nose. "I believe both of the Gray sons were available to identify their father's body on the second of April, as well. Is this true?"

Mitchell stood. "It is, but I hardly see the purpose of this."

"Please be seated, Mr. Gray," Mr. Robinson requested. Mr. Sterling appeared rather upset and refused to look Mitchell in the eye. It was this small but important action that caused Lydia to take interest. Something wasn't right.

Robinson continued. "The purpose, Mr. Gray, will become apparent."

Mitchell looked at Marston, then took his seat. "Very well, please continue. But do remember the delicacy of my sisters. They needn't be burdened with comments about identifying the dead."

As if on cue, Jeannette began to sob. Lydia wanted to be sick. The girls had no more love for their father than she had.

Mr. Robinson lifted his papers again. "I have the same type of signed statement on behalf of Mr. Rockford, which in addition includes the papers that were completed by the hospital officials, where he was taken after the accident. As you are aware, Mr. Rockford died on April fourth. Given this and the obvious fact that Mr. Rockford outlived Mr. Gray," Mr. Robinson stated, pulling his spectacles from his face, "Mrs. Lydia Rockford Gray is the sole heir of her father's fortune."

Mitchell looked aghast. "That is hardly legal." He turned to Sterling. "It isn't legal, is it? Mr. Rockford's property was to go to our father."

Mr. Sterling shifted uncomfortably, not even attempting to answer.

Mr. Robinson peered over his wire-rimmed glasses at Mitchell. "Yes, that had been part of the agreement. However, as I stated, the will reads that your father would

26

receive Mr. Rockford's properties should he survive Mr. Rockford. Given that he did not, but rather died two days prior to the death of your stepmother's father, the will clearly passes the inheritance to his only direct descendant, Mrs. Lydia Rockford Gray."

"Is this right?" Marston demanded, staring hard at Mr. Sterling. "Our father shared a profitable business with Mr. Rockford. They owned the venture in a fifty-fifty share. Are you telling me that, even though she had nothing to do with the growth and development of this industry, Lydia will now inherit half of what we've worked so hard to build?"

"I think it would behoove us to hear the contents of your father's will before this discussion continues," Dwight Robinson declared.

Lydia felt a strange sensation of confidence rush over her. She had never held any power over these men, and now she did. Now she was truly free from their demands and desires. She sat a little straighter and nodded at Mr. Robinson. "Please do continue."

Marston glared at her, but Lydia was unmoved. In her mind, she began to plan for her future. She would go immediately to live with Aunt Zerelda in Sitka. She had posted the letter that morning. She would simply enlist the help of her father's lawyer and leave Kansas City forever. She wouldn't even pack her clothes — those ghastly provocative fashions chosen by her husband. There was nothing, save her violin, that she would even want to take into her new life. Giddy with the weight of oppression lifted from her shoulders, it was all Lydia could do to keep from giggling out loud.

Mr. Sterling began. " 'I, Floyd Gray, upon my death do hereby bequeath my worldly possessions to my partner, Zachary Rockford. Should he not survive me, then my goods are to be divided equally among my children as follows: To my daughters, Jeannette and Genevieve, I give equally the properties of their mother, including all jewelry, china, house furnishings, furs, and the like. To my sons, Mitchell and Marston, I leave all business ventures, investments of stocks and bonds, and the entirety of my bank accounts, which are detailed in this document."

Mitchell and Marston smiled at each other. Lydia could see they were pleased with the outcome. Knowing her stepsons as she did, Lydia surmised they were already making plans for their inheritance.

Mr. Sterling cleared his throat nervously and stood. "I find this most awkward and difficult," he began. "I must admit I have not ever been placed in this position before, and hope never to see myself here again."

Lydia couldn't imagine what he was rambling about. She wanted only to get up and leave the stuffy office. She looked at Mr. Robinson, who gave her a reassuring nod.

"What are you going on about?" Mitchell demanded. "I want to know if Mr. Rockford's will is going to be honored and the business turned over in complete to our handling."

Mr. Sterling met their gazes with a most panicked expression. "I'm sorry. You must understand that the terms of your father's will are legal and valid. I have already made inquiries on your behalf, and there is nothing to be done."

"Perhaps Lydia will sell you her portion," Eve called out from behind her brothers.

Lydia heard Evie's husband quiet her, but not before Marston gave her a withering look. He then turned back to the lawyer. "What exactly are you saying, Mr. Sterling?"

"You've heard the will for yourself." He cleared his throat again and picked up the papers he'd left on the table. "I'm afraid the situation is not what any of us expected. Your father created this provision, not only as a part of the marriage contract he and Mr. Rockford agreed upon, but he solidified the terms by putting them also in his business papers of partnership and his last will and testament. Therefore, upon his death, his possessions . . . everything . . . went to Mr. Rockford, who survived him by two days."

Lydia blinked hard at the words. She was beginning to see exactly what the man was saying. Her heart raced as she looked again to Mr. Robinson. Mitchell jumped to his feet in the same moment.

"Now wait just a minute," he declared.

"What's wrong?" Jeannette suddenly joined in. "What is going on?" She pulled at her husband's sleeve.

Marston glowered at Lydia. He knew exactly what was happening, just as she did.

Mitchell continued to rant. "Are you telling us that our inheritance was passed to Mr. Rockford, and in turn, he passed it to her?" His eyes shot daggers at Lydia, but instead of it causing her to shrink away as once she might have done, Lydia merely returned his angry glare.

"That simply cannot be," Jeannette declared. "It isn't possible." Her shrieking voice grew louder. "That can't be what he means."

Marston folded his arms and matter-of-factly replied, "That's exactly what he means."

Robinson met Marston's fixed stare. "Your brother understands it correctly. Mrs. Gray's father outlived your father. The carriage accident took both lives, but not at the same time. There is no disputing that Mr. Rockford survived your father in death."

"But he never regained consciousness," Mitchell protested. "That's not any kind of living, as far as I'm concerned."

"But legally, he was not dead," Robinson said. "His death did not come until two days after Mr. Gray, and therefore, he was Mr. Gray's survivor."

Mr. Sterling had taken his seat. He seemed only too happy to give the argument over to his fellow lawyer.

"I won't stand for this. She is not stealing our inheritance," Marston said, getting to his feet. "She was nothing to my father. He hated her. She made his life unbearable."

Lydia steadied her nerves and listened to the Gray children argue with the two lawyers. She wanted to smile at the uncanny manner in which the situation had played out. It was a sweet revenge. The fates had not been pleased with her circumstance, after all. Her mother would have said that God had looked out for her, but Lydia didn't believe God even cared about such matters. He especially didn't care about her. If He did, then He had some explaining to do as to why He would allow her such a heinous existence for twelve years of her life.

Marston and Mitchell, along with their sisters' husbands, had moved to the front of the room to discuss the news with the two lawyers. Lydia felt lightheaded by the knowledge that she now held control of the Gray and Rockford fortunes. Never again would any Gray man impose his will upon her.

She frowned as ugly memories came back to haunt her. Floyd had been a terrible husband without any affection or compassion. And while Lydia had grown used to his lack of concern for her comfort or interest in her desires, she had never been able to reconcile his brutal abuse in exercising his husbandly rights. When word came about the accident, she was unable to muster any concern whatsoever for his condition. When told that he had been found dead beneath the carriage, Lydia didn't shed a single tear. The shock of her liberty — her sudden freedom from the unbearable misery that had been her fate — was more than she could withstand. She had fainted dead away.

"Are you all right?" Evie whispered in her ear. "You look pale."

"I'm fine," Lydia replied. Evie had never allowed her siblings to see her get too close to Lydia, so her act of kindness was unexpected.

"Have nothing to do with her, Genevieve," Jeannette snapped and pulled her sister away.

"Then we will simply investigate the matter on our own," Mitchell declared, turning away from the table where the lawyers had delivered the bad news. He came back to his chair and took up his walking stick. "We will not allow our inheritance to be stolen from us. We will reconvene at my house."

Marston came to Lydia as Mitchell bounded from the room. "If you know what's good for you, you'll sign everything over to us and be done with it. Otherwise, you will never know a moment's peace."

Lydia got to her feet, pushed past him, and went to Mr. Robinson. "Would you please take me home? I find the day has been most taxing and would like very much to consider all that has happened."

"But of course."

She could feel the gaze of every other person on her as she moved across the room to the door. Mr. Robinson quickly caught up and took her by the elbow to lead her into the hall.

"You know they will torment you over this," Robinson whispered.

Lydia smiled ever so slightly. "They will certainly try."

"I'm not about to sit by and watch Lydia take advantage of this family," Marston declared to the small audience seated in Mitchell's parlor.

"What do you suggest we do?" Jeannette asked. "The lawyer said it was legal. I can scarcely believe it, but it seems to me —"

"Oh, shut up." Mitchell was not one to brook his sister's nonsense for long. "I don't care what it seems to you. The fact of the matter is, we are in for a fight. Robinson is obviously happy to stand on Lydia's behalf. After all, he will, no doubt, receive a tidy sum."

Marston paced, tightening his facial muscles as he often did when disturbed. "Do you suppose we could pay someone off? We have connections amongst the judges. Surely we can get someone to take up the case on our behalf."

"But even if you do," Evie's husband, Thomas, interjected, "she could do the same. The money will be tied up for years. You will be destitute by that time."

Mitchell got to his feet and motioned Marston to take a seat. "The way I see it, we will simply have to find a way to handle this ourselves. As far as I know, Lydia has no family, and certainly has not had time to draw up a will. Perhaps if she is . . . eliminated, the problem itself will go away."

"Better still," Marston said with a wicked grin, "she could leave her entire fortune to us."

"Exactly my thinking," Mitchell replied.

Jeannette and Evie's husbands appeared to be trying to mask their shock, yet they said nothing to suggest they wouldn't support such an idea. Marston reasoned that with a little thought, they'd know exactly how it would affect them, and he believed they would hope for any decision that might benefit their coffers.

Evie was indignant. "I can't believe you're sitting here so calmly suggesting the death of another human being. I understand wanting to reclaim what is rightfully ours, but to kill someone is an entirely different situation."

Marston turned to his youngest sister. "You are only seventeen. What do you know of life — or death, for that matter? Lydia has never liked any of us, so you can hardly hope that she would willingly right this wrong."

"We never gave her a reason to like any of us," Evie replied. "You were always scheming against her."

"She didn't belong in our family." Jeannette's voice was shrill and bitter. "She should never have married Father in the first place."

"I hardly believe she was given any say in the decision," Evie countered. "She didn't want to marry Father any more than we wanted her to marry him."

"But the fact remains, she *did* marry him," Marston replied. "There is absolutely nothing that we can do to change that now. What we cannot do is stand by and allow that woman to ruin our well-being. Can you really tolerate her taking all of Mother's jewelry and furs? Would you see Lydia sell off the family heirlooms to pad her purse?"

"She will do it, too," Jeannette said, hissing against her sister's ear. "She's only been waiting for a moment like this. I say we put her from our lives once and for all."

Evie could hardly believe her siblings' heartless comments. She moved to the parlor door, saying, "I'm afraid I have no stomach for this. I will retire to the music room until you have concluded this madness."

"Oh, for pity's sake, Evie. Sit down and do stop with your prattling."

Evie looked into the eyes of her husband. The man seldom had more than two words to offer her in any given day. Now he fixed her with a cold stare that left her feeling empty inside. Theirs, too, was a marriage of arrangement, set up by her father for the betterment of business. Her husband stood to lose a great deal in this situation.

"Yes, do sit down and be quiet," Marston ordered. "We haven't time for your delicate constitution." He and Thomas turned back to the gathering.

It frustrated Evie that they had dismissed her, knowing she wouldn't dare defy them. With a heavy sigh, she did as she was told — just as they had known she would.

If I had more courage, I would stalk from this room and give them all something of a shock. She frowned and looked down at her gloved hands. *If I had more courage, I would have stood up to Father and refused to marry*

Thomas Gadston. It isn't as if he cares about me or loves me.

No, love might have actually made the arrangement bearable. Even if the love had only been on Thomas's side, Evie might have learned to return his feelings. Instead, they both found the arrangement a misery. Thankfully, Gadston had never even attended her properly as a husband. He had never visited her room to consummate the marriage, and rumor had it, he never would. The household servants often whispered of unthinkable, unholy interests held by her husband, and while Evie found such ideas abominable, she was just as glad to be left to herself.

"You do make a good point." Mitchell's deep voice broke through Evie's thoughts. "If she were to be murdered, then everyone would suspect our family. It would have to look like an accident."

"Or a suicide," Marston suggested.

Evie cringed at the word. She was immediately taken back in time to when she was four years old. It was Christmas Day, and gifts had already been exchanged. Evie had received a pretty new doll and a handmade wicker perambulator. She loved her holiday dress and especially her kid-leather button-top shoes.

The morning had been a happy one, she recalled. Father had not raised his voice or his hand to any of them. Even Jeannette, who generally had a whining, weepy temperament, seemed content.

Still, that day became the worst in Evie's life. She had been a fearless child, often making her way in secret to the attic, where she would search through long-forgotten trunks and crates to see what treasures they might hold. On that Christmas morning, she remembered a particularly lovely hatbox that contained doll clothes and thought they might work well for her new baby.

The attic and its dark shadows had never frightened her. Here was the only quiet and peaceful room in the entire house. Here, Evie could sit and play and dream.

But that day there was to be no peace in her lovely hideaway — or ever again, for that matter. She had heard her mama's footsteps on the attic floor and hid away to avoid being chastised. Mama went to the small door that led outside to a railed walk. Evie had heard her call it a widow's walk. It was a wondrous place at the top of their mansion, where her mother could pace away her frustrations.

Evie watched her there on more than one occasion. Mama would walk and cry softly into a lace-edged handkerchief. Always, Evie wanted to go to her, but she never did. Even at her young age, Evie knew her mother would have been embarrassed that Evie knew of her misery and shame. But for Evie, it was a special kind of bond that knit them together in a way she knew none of the other children shared. Not only was she the one child who favored their mother's features instead of their father's, but Evie was also the one whose soul was intricately tied to Mother because of this secret.

Moving to a place in the attic where she could watch her mother out of a decorative oval window, Evie longed to go to her — to comfort her. It was cold outside, much too cold to be walking without a coat, yet her mother didn't have so much as a wrap.

How strange it seemed. Mama stopped pacing and stood at the rail doing nothing. She seemed to stare out across the landscape as if contemplating the future. Evie heard a disturbance behind her and ducked down just before her father entered the attic. He walked with determined steps to the widow's walk door and stepped outside to join his wife. Again Evie was drawn to the window, wondering if they would fight, as they so often did. To her surprise, however, Father embraced Mama. The sight caused

Evie to feel a surge of hope. Maybe her mother would learn to smile again and be happy.

Evie gripped the windowsill and watched with a sense of anticipation as her father lifted her mother in his arms and pressed his lips to hers. Then without warning, Father stepped to the far edge of the walkway and without so much as a word, threw her mama over the rail.

Evie's eyes widened and she barely suppressed a cry as her father hurriedly bound back into the attic and headed downstairs. Stunned, Evie sat for several moments, unable to move. Had she really just witnessed her father kill her mother?

But maybe Mama hadn't died from the fall. Maybe it was just done in jest. Evie bit her lower lip and summoned up her courage. Just then, she heard someone scream and knew her fears were realized. She raced from the attic and back to her second-floor bedroom, where she hurriedly climbed into bed and burrowed deep within the sanctuary of the covers.

What if Father found out that she'd seen him? Would he throw her from the roof, as well?

"Evie? Evie are you all right?"

For a moment Evie didn't recognize the

41

voice of her sister. She glanced up to find herself safe in her brother's parlor, with everyone watching her. Watching and waiting for some explanation of why she had failed to respond.

"I'm . . . sorry," she said, hesitating only a moment. "What was it you asked?"

Jeannette moved closer. "I asked if you were all right. You seem quite pale. You aren't with child, are you?"

Evie was shocked at the question. She would have laughed out loud at the lunacy of the idea had her husband not been fixing her with a most serious expression.

"I don't think so, Jeannette. I'm simply overly tired."

Her husband looked away with a thin smile edging his lips. "She has been far too busy of late. I believe I will send her on a trip for a rest."

With that they all seemed to forget about her and went back to their discussion of what to do with Lydia. Evie breathed a sigh of relief and folded her hands. She would have to be more careful. She had never told anyone of what she had witnessed that day in the attic, and she never would, for fear of what might happen to her. People with secrets did not bode well in this family.

CHAPTER 3

Lydia sorted through her jewelry, separating out what she knew to be Gray family heirlooms from the things her husband had bought particularly for her use. She had never cared for any of the pieces. All of them were ostentatious and tasteless, as far as she was concerned. Floyd Gray never did anything out of affection, but rather out of a need to impress those around him. The heavy necklaces of gold and sapphires, rubies and onyx, and diamonds and pearls had been designed in multiple tiers to capture the attention of others. Matching earrings, too, that dangled long and heavy. Lydia remembered getting headaches just wearing them.

Other pieces were ghastly for the combination of jewels used. They were Mr. Gray's attempt at creativity, but they were truly awful. One in particular was of amethyst, topaz, and emeralds. The jeweler had fash-

ioned the stones in a series of bizarre flowers that encircled the neck on a thick vine
of gold. Another piece was something Lydia
could only describe as a spider's web of
silver with large stones of varying colors
sprinkled liberally throughout. When worn,
it looked like a strange sort of jeweled chain
mail for the neck.

"Well, I certainly have no need of these."
She gathered the hideous pieces and secured
them in their cases. She would let Evie and
Jeannette have them, and if they didn't want
them, she would give them to Mitchell and
Marston — a sort of peace offering, along
with the rest of the home's furnishings.

She had no desire to take anything that
belonged to the family or had been given
her by Floyd. Certainly not the outlandish
clothes he had made her wear. No, she
would have several new, more serviceable
pieces made before departing Kansas City
and leave all of the rest behind.

"I'm starting a new life," she reminded
herself. In all honesty, it was more like she
was finally being allowed a life. She thought
about living in Alaska with her aunt and felt
awash in giddiness.

A knock on the door startled Lydia for a
moment. It was almost as if someone had
sensed her happiness and had come to put

an end to it. "Come in." She looked up to find a dour-faced woman nearly twice Lydia's age at her door. "What is it, Mary?"

"The Gray sons are here to speak with you."

Lydia had been expecting them. After all, it was already half past eight in the morning. It was amazing they had waited this long.

"Very well. Tell them I'll be down directly."

Mary looked at her a moment, then gave a huff and closed the door as she left. Lydia knew none of the servants had much use for her. She had never had so much as a single confidante in the entire staff. They were too afraid. They knew who paid their wages, and they weren't about to alienate the master by cozying up to the wife he despised. No doubt they were all confused as to who held the purse strings now.

Lydia stood and once again surveyed the display of jewelry on her bed. Should she tell Mitchell and Marston her plans? Would they be pleased or just further angered that she should dare to even pretend she had the right to divvy up their father's property?

Making her way downstairs, Lydia knew it would not do to appear nervous or weak. She squared her shoulders and lifted her chin. It would be hard to stand up to Floyd

Gray's sons, but she would manage it.

She found Marston and Mitchell huddled together in the same room where their father had been laid out for the funeral. Gone were all reminders of that hideous day, but Lydia could still envision the scene in her mind.

"You took your sweet time in attending us," Mitchell said with a scowl. "I suppose you believe yourself to be somehow in charge, what with the absurdity of the will in question."

"Is it in question?" Lydia asked, her voice strong and clear.

"You know it is. It's just a matter of time before we have this resolved in our favor. Father never intended you to inherit anything that belonged to him. You know that as well as we do."

"I know that your father never thought it possible that he would die."

"Don't act so smug," Marston said, taking a step toward her. "We will see the wrong made right."

"Despite your attempts to set the circumstance in your favor," Lydia began, "I still have no need to concern myself. My father has left me sufficiently able to care for my own needs."

She crossed the room and took a seat in

her rocking chair. She folded her hands together and looked up at the men who approached her. They towered over her for a moment, as if hoping to intimidate her. When she said nothing, Mitchell finally sat opposite her, while Marston continued to stand.

"The fact of the matter is you know full well you are not entitled to our properties and businesses, whether they were shared by your father or not. We expect you to accompany us to our lawyer to put an end to this farce."

Lydia could see that Mitchell looked rather nervous. He had a tick just under his left eye, and he shifted his weight continuously as if his seat were red hot. Marston, meanwhile, held his hands behind his back and watched her carefully. Lydia knew he was looking for some sign of weakness in her — some chink in the armor she had carefully fitted around her. She felt like prey being watched by a wild animal.

Imagining a strain of a Beethoven pastorale through her head, Lydia calmed. *They cannot hurt me anymore. They cannot take away my freedom.* She drew a deep breath and met their gazes once again.

"Mr. Robinson is handling all of my legal affairs for me. You may take up this matter with him."

"No. You will come with us," Marston insisted, stepping toward her. "Today."

"Oh, do sit down, Marston." She tried her best to sound indifferent to his approach, but in her mind, she could very nearly feel the blows he so obviously longed to deliver. "I will not be bullied by anyone anymore." The words gave her strength.

Marston looked at her oddly for a moment. He seemed uncertain — almost confused by her declaration. *Good,* Lydia thought. *The prey has fought back. If I can only manage to keep them imbalanced with my reactions, then I will have the advantage.*

"We hardly need Mr. Robinson to handle affairs for you," Mitchell finally stated. He motioned Marston to join him on the couch. "Mr. Sterling is far better equipped to deal with this situation. He has represented our father and the Grays' business dealings for the last twenty-some years."

"Perhaps for that very reason I prefer to have my own legal representation. To approach Mr. Sterling," she stated quite logically, "would seem a conflict to his position with you and your desires."

"Not at all," Mitchell interjected quickly. "Mr. Sterling can easily represent all of us. He can clear up the mistakes and see our

48

father's true intentions fulfilled."

"I cannot say what your father intended, except through the instructions he left behind." Lydia tilted her head as if considering the situation quite intently. "Your father was a brilliant man — a solid businessman, well known for his ability to manage his affairs. How could any of us suppose that this matter went unattended by him? Should I honestly believe that your father — my husband — had no understanding or knowledge of the law?"

"You play a dangerous game, Lydia," Marston replied, narrowing his eyes.

"I play no game at all," she responded. "I was there, you will remember, the day the contract was signed between my father and yours. My wedding day was no more of my choosing than the terms of the will were of yours."

Marston tensed. "It was clearly a mistake and you know it."

Lydia shook her head. "That is hardly a part of my understanding. That is why I have chosen to rely upon Mr. Robinson for assistance in this situation. I am a mere woman of twenty-eight, uneducated and ignorant, as you have so often pointed out. I was forced into marriage with your father as a means to benefit his financial standings. Now that he is dead, I am no longer obligated to such an arrangement."

Marston appeared ready to leap from the couch. "And neither should our father be obligated to that arrangement."

"Your father isn't obligated to that arrangement," she countered. "However, my lawyer assures me that the terms of the wills must be abided by, and I intend to take his counsel. Now, if you'll excuse me, I have a great deal to attend to." She got to her feet, not at all surprised that Marston and Mitchell jumped up to stop her.

"This dispute is not resolved," Mitchell protested.

She looked at him for a moment and nodded. "I am sure you are correct, but at this juncture, I can do nothing more. Mr. Robinson is the one to whom you should speak. He clearly has studied the wills and has approached the finest legal minds in the area for their counsel. I believe it would benefit you both to sit and discuss his findings at length with him."

With that, she left both men gap-mouthed. She'd never seen any Gray man at a loss for words, but it was clear Mitchell and Marston were confused by her reaction. The prey had managed to escape to live another day.

"I don't understand why this should be so difficult," Marston began. Nash Sterling seemed to wilt a bit in his chair. "We've bought off people before."

"That was before the politics of the town shifted. You know how hard it has been these last few years. Your father was always ranting . . ." He paused, as if realizing he was about to say something completely inappropriate. "Well, you know how it angered him. Anyway, all of that to say, there is little I can do. No one is willing to risk the wrath of those in charge."

"Cowards," Mitchell declared.

"Be that as it may," Sterling said, "it is what we are up against. We can tie things up for a while — have the legal documents reviewed and assessed for any inconsistencies. But in the end, I believe the result will be the same."

"All right. So if it can't be done legally," Marston began, "perhaps we can do it illegally."

"Bribing a judge and paying off people at the courthouse *is* illegal," Sterling countered. "What else do you have in mind?"

"I believe what my brother is implying,"

Mitchell said carefully, "is that people often change their minds when a threat or ultimatum is delivered. We have incriminating evidence and information on nearly every judge and lawyer in this town. We have sworn statements on dozens of powerful men, along with witnesses who will swear to whatever we ask of them."

"And you believe, after the well-known business affairs of your father and the very public announcement of his death and funeral, people are simply going to let this come to pass?" He shook his head. "Robinson is no fool. He has already enlisted the help of a great many people. He has taken the will quite seriously. He knew the details before I did."

"Then you are a fool," Marston replied in anger. "I blame you for not helping my father to see a way out of this mess."

Sterling frowned and tightened his expression. "If I were you, I would find a way to work with your stepmother rather than antagonizing her. Surely she has little desire to be the decision maker at a casket production company. She is quite young and may even remarry, and then she will be less concerned about her well-being."

"But that is exactly why we need to resolve this immediately," Mitchell declared. "She might very well marry, and then the Gray fortune will pass to her husband's control. We will never see a dollar returned to us. Once word gets out that she has a vast fortune at her fingertips, men will flock to court and woo her."

"As I said, perhaps the trick is to win her over. Show your concern. Explain to her that the weight of such a responsibility will only cause her misery. Maybe start by simply offering to oversee things for her. Tell her you'll report to her and let her know what's happening."

"I suppose it's worth a try," Mitchell said, looking to Marston for his opinion.

Marston knew it wouldn't work. Lydia had already started to show a bit of backbone. She was slowly but surely learning to stand on her own two feet. It hadn't been long since their father had died, but Lydia seemed to be transforming before their very eyes.

"We can only try," Mitchell encouraged. "Perhaps we can have Evie help us. Lydia has always liked Evie."

Marston nodded, not yet willing to share his thoughts on the matter. "It's possible. We shall give it consideration and see if a plan can be developed." Marston didn't miss the look of relief in Nash Sterling's dark blue eyes. Imbecile! If he'd done his job properly, they wouldn't be in this mess.

Leaving the office, Marston was in no mood for his brother's fretful conversation. "I have been careful with my own investments, but this may not bode well for my family. We might be forced to reconsider our standard of living," Mitchell confessed.

"Bah, please be quiet," Marston said as he climbed into the carriage. "Nothing is going to change. We simply have to find a way to fight back — to win." He eased his hat down over his eyes as if he intended to sleep on the ride home. "Lydia is not going to tell us what to do. She has no idea of our strength and resolve."

"Do you suppose she'll really want to remarry — after all she's been through?"

Marston pushed his hat back. "Why do you say that?"

Mitchell looked almost embarrassed. "Well, we both know our father was not the easiest man to live with. Maybe Lydia doesn't like being married."

"Women don't know what they like or dislike. They really have no mind for such things. They understand entertaining and raising children but are otherwise useless unless properly trained. Father was simply attempting to make her acceptable to society."

Shrugging, Mitchell fell back against the leather upholstery as the carriage merged into traffic.

Marston considered something he and Mitchell had discussed once before. "If I could force her to marry me, then there would be little difficulty in regaining control of our money."

"But wouldn't society frown upon such an arrangement? She is our stepmother."

"It would have to be dealt with carefully. Perhaps we could enlist the help of the girls. They could put it out among their friends and social circles that Lydia is distraught and unable to go on with life. My marrying her would be done purely out of a desire to see her safe and assured of her position."

Mitchell chuckled. "But one word from Lydia would put all of that nonsense to rest."

Marston gave his brother a smug smile. "But she has to be able to talk and to be out in public in order to share such thoughts."

His brother raised a brow and nodded. "And then perhaps in time, Lydia could simply do herself in — as our mother did."

"Why not?" Marston replied. "Weak

women do it all the time." He glanced out the window feeling hope for the first time in a long while. "I believe this crisis may resolve itself quite easily after all."

CHAPTER 4

Lydia could feel Dwight Robinson's gaze on her without needing to turn around. She stood at the window of his office, watching the Kansas City traffic bustle about.

"I have had several meetings with your stepsons. They are not happy, as I'm sure you know. They intend to see the inheritance returned to them, regardless of what they have to do." She could hear him shuffle papers. "They've petitioned to have the will set aside, but I can't see it causing you any difficulty. Once reviewed, a judge is going to see that the arrangement was contracted legally."

Lydia turned and met his gaze. "I honestly don't want their inheritance. To tell you the truth, there is nothing of Floyd's that I desire to keep. I'd just as soon give it to them and be done with it."

"But what of your future?"

Smoothing her dove-gray walking skirt,

Lydia crossed the room and took a seat in the high-backed red leather chair. "My future is fairly well set, what with the trust fund Father set up for me."

"And what of your father's furniture business?" Dwight asked, lowering his wire-rimmed glasses. "That is intricately tied to the casket business he created with Mr. Gray. Your father and husband owned equal shares of the latter."

She frowned. "I don't know that I even want to have my hand in the business at all."

"And the Gray family also had a freight business and two mortuaries. . . ."

She felt completely overwhelmed with it all.

"I suppose we could approach them to see if they would like to buy out your shares." Dwight reached for his pen and held it aloft a moment. "Is that what you would like me to do?"

"Is it feasible? Can it be done without my being here to handle the matter?"

Dwight nodded. "I can see to everything. Even the review of the will. You won't have to appear before the judge unless you want to."

"I most certainly do not." Lydia stiffened and folded her gloved hands. "I want nothing more to do with this whole affair than I absolutely must. I would be glad for you to handle everything."

Her lawyer jotted down several things before putting down his pen. He leaned forward and put his glasses aside. "May I be frank?"

Lydia nodded. What else had he been? They had talked about all the intricate details of her marriage to Floyd and the reason behind her father's decision to marry her off at such a young age.

"I fear for you, Mrs. Gray."

She felt her brows knit together as she narrowed her eyes. "I beg your pardon?"

Mr. Robinson got up and walked to the front of his desk. He leaned his stocky frame against the top. "I worry that your stepsons mean to cause you as much trouble as it takes in order to get back everything. I have heard stories about their dealings in the past. Given that their father was such an abusive man, I find it completely reasonable to believe them capable of the same."

He cleared his throat as if hesitant to continue. "They are men used to having their own way."

Lydia shook her head. "Exactly what are you saying?"

"I don't want to falsely judge them or

their motives," Robinson said. "And I certainly do not mean to speak indelicately, but I believe they will do you physical harm."

Lydia couldn't keep the surprise from her voice. "You do?"

"There are rumors that Gray and his sons have eliminated problems in the past. When people got in their way, there were times those folks simply . . . disappeared."

Her eyes widened. "Are you saying that Mr. Gray had people killed?" She knew she shouldn't be shocked by that thought, but she was. The man had been cruel, there was no doubt about that — but a murderer?

"Nothing has ever been proven, but the rumors are too numerous to be ignored. I have heard that Marston and Mitchell were involved in several situations where they intimidated witnesses against their father. Some men were beaten so severely they never recovered. One can't say if the actual job was done by the hands of one of the Grays or another's, but I'm willing to believe the order came from a Gray's mouth."

Lydia felt her breath catch. Her stomach churned and she shook her head. "I truly had no idea."

"I hope this won't seem too out of place.

I realize you hardly know my family; however, I discussed your circumstances with my wife, Rhoda. We would like to encourage you to stay with us until you leave town for Alaska."

Lydia felt at a loss for words. The entire situation took her off guard. "I don't know what to say."

"At least consider our offer. You won't be leaving for a week or two. I'm still making the arrangements for your trip to Sitka."

"Perhaps we can find a way to start my trip sooner. However, I am having new clothes made for the journey. Nothing I currently have is sturdy or simple enough for life in Alaska."

"I'd hate to see you stay in that house. You have no friends there, and the children — any one of them would have easy access to you. The servants could be bought off and even paid to do you harm."

Lydia had never considered such possibilities. So many times she had felt unsafe while Floyd was alive, but since his death, she'd known a new sense of peace. She supposed now that such feelings were foolish. She was never truly going to be free until she was long gone from Kansas City.

She was nearly ready to agree to Mr. Robinson's invitation when he added a further comment that changed her mind.

"We've prayed about this and truly believe that God would have us extend this invitation to you."

"I don't believe in prayer," Lydia said, stiffening. Why did people always have to say such things? As though stamping God's name on something made it more official or stressed the need to comply?

Robinson's expression changed to one of shock. "What are you saying?"

Lydia got to her feet. "I have endured far too much at the hands of a cruel and vicious husband to imagine God ever cared about me. My mother told me long ago that God loved me and watched over me to protect me from harm, but my marriage to Floyd proves that was not true. Now if you'll excuse me, I am late for my dressmaker's appointment."

Taking afternoon tea in her favorite teahouse, Evie listened to her sister drone on and on about how much the circumstances of the will had wreaked havoc with her health.

"I've suffered a headache every day since Father died," she told Evie. "I sometimes have to lie in a dark room for hours to find even a tiny bit of relief."

"I am sorry to hear that," Evie said absent-mindedly.

Jeannette touched her hand to her head. "Sometimes even my hair pains me."

Evie shrugged. "Perhaps you should cut it off."

"You are speaking nonsense. Does one cut off one's head just because it pains them? I'm merely trying to help you understand the degree to which I suffer."

Probably like I'm suffering right this minute, Evie wanted to retort. She remained silent, however. For several moments neither sister said a word. Jeannette stuffed her mouth with lemon tarts and motioned the waiter to pour more tea.

"Well, I know our brothers will not rest until this matter is resolved," Jeannette said after a long sip from her teacup. "I'm glad that they are working to see it made right. I can hardly sleep nights, knowing she is in our mother's house, probably stealing the very heirlooms that belong to us. I cringe when I think she might have already taken the sherry glasses that Grandmother Beecham gave Mother."

"Oh, be reasonable, Jeannette. Lydia never cared about the possessions our parents owned."

"You think not? I believe she played a coy

game with you. She might have seemed a friend, but she was conspiring all the time behind our father's back."

"Conspiring for what?"

"For the property — the money. She was never happy — never content."

Evie rolled her eyes and leaned forward. "Our father beat her and very nearly held her imprisoned in that house. How could you possibly expect her to be content?"

Jeannette's eyes widened and her mouth dropped open. "You shouldn't speak ill of the dead — it's bad luck."

"Bad luck seems to haunt this family." Evie set aside her teacup and napkin. "Nevertheless, I hardly believe Lydia wants to keep anything that belonged to our father. And she doesn't drink, so she'd have little use for sherry glasses."

"You are so naïve. You believe her to be a good woman, but she has caused nothing but misery and pain to this family."

"Like the misery and pain she caused when she nursed us back to health when we had measles? Or how about the time we muddied our Sunday dresses and knew Father would beat us senseless when he saw what we'd done? Lydia took the dresses and cleaned them before Father arrived home."

Jeannette sniffed into her handkerchief.

"She was always lying to him like that."

"She was not. She never lied to him at all. Lydia had the dresses completely repaired before Father returned, and he never knew the difference. Can you not even acknowledge her kindness?"

"I refuse to," Jeannette replied. "It was motivated by selfish ambitions."

Evie shook her head. "How does cleaning a child's dress reveal any type of selfish desire? Lydia was only trying to keep us out of trouble. You have always been the kind of person who seems to thrive on seeing people get their comeuppance, so I don't expect you to understand her desire —"

Jeannette gasped. "How can you say such a thing? I am your sister. You would side with that . . . that . . . greedy, conniving woman over me?"

"How is it that she's a greedy and conniving woman when the wealth she's been given has been placed at her feet by the actions of our father and hers?"

"But it was never intended to be that way, and you know it. My own husband finds the situation disturbing. He says that Lydia probably had something to do with all of this. Possibly she tampered with the will."

"Herman Stone is only disturbed because you stood to inherit a good portion of the money and stocks owned by our father. Honestly, Jeannette, I am not the simpleton you believe me to be."

Straightening her shoulders, Jeannette dismissed the topic. "The weather has been unseasonably warm. Mr. Stone believes we might anticipate storms."

"Mrs. Stone," a voice called from behind Evie. "How good to see you. I am surprised, however. Your father has not long been dead. Isn't it a bit early for you to be out in public?"

Evie recognized the shrill, accusing tone of Merdina Winchester. Glancing up, she found the older woman accompanied by her busybody friend Rhoda Sterling, wife of Nash Sterling.

Jeannette was clearly unfazed. "We made our dear father a promise not to spend our time in mourning. As you can see, we have even set aside the wearing of black at his request." She paused and sighed. "Of course, it was hard to do so. We did worry what society might think, but our father's wishes were far more important than what gossips and such could say."

Merdina raised her chin in a rather hostile defiance. "And how could your father have elicited such a promise? Surely he was unaware his demise was soon to be upon

66

him. Why in the world would such a topic even be discussed?"

Evie looked to Jeannette in expectation of what she might say. Jeannette was never at a loss for words, and this time was no exception.

"Our father was a practical man, as you well know. He, of course, did not realize his life would be required of him at such a young age. He was only fifty-four, you know." Jeannette seemed to ponder this for a moment while the two women waited for her explanation. Evie had seen her sister use this tactic on more than one occasion when she wanted to prove the point that she was well in charge of the conversation.

"But being a man of great wisdom, he knew his time would come one day," Jeannette continued. "He took us aside and told us in no uncertain terms that we were not to waste our life in contemplation for the dead. He wanted no mourning period — no funeral wreaths or gowns of black crepe. He requested that no social gathering be set aside on his behalf. And while it is hard to face the questioning of those who do not understand, the important thing is, we are doing his will." She gave a sniffle into her handkerchief as if she might burst into tears and then added, "Just as Jesus did His

Father's will."

Evie wanted to laugh out loud but instead bowed her head. It was as if she had uttered a silent amen to her sister's declaration.

"See now, you've upset my sister. There, there, Genevieve, you mustn't let the ill will of others disturb you so."

Merdina gave an audible huff, while Mrs. Sterling said nothing. Evie looked up and met their stern expressions but remained silent.

Rhoda Sterling patted her friend's arm. "Come, Merdina. We should leave them to their . . . mourning."

Evie didn't miss the sarcasm in her voice. She would have giggled had Jeannette not fixed her with a fierce stare. Once the ladies moved away from their table, Jeannette leaned forward. "Let's go. I will not sit here to be judged by the likes of them." She got to her feet and pulled her shawl close. "Oh, and would you mind paying? I'm afraid I forgot my reticule."

"Of course," Evie said, having already anticipated the request. Jeannette Gray Stone never paid for anything. It was her way of holding on to her allowance for secret vices, such as her love of brandy.

CHAPTER 5

A few days later, Dwight Robinson arrived at the Gray mansion to bring Lydia the tickets for her trip.

"It won't be an easy journey," he told her. "I've arranged for one of my young clerks to accompany you west to San Francisco. Complications can occur that make such trips uncomfortable, so I'm glad you won't travel alone on the train."

Lydia examined the telegram Robinson handed her. It contained brief information about her ship, the *Newbern,* a steamer owned by the Quartermaster Department.

"I'm told," Robinson said, "the ship is not all that large. It is used to haul supplies to Alaska and often carries a few passengers. This telegram is from a friend of mine in San Francisco, Ernest Woodruff. He assured me he could arrange your passage. He will have the ticket ready for you, but you must be in San Francisco by the twenty-fifth of

April, when the ship will head out."

"That gives us very little time," Lydia replied. Her sense of adventure and excitement mounted with each new announcement.

"Indeed, that is true. You will have to leave tomorrow in order to get to Omaha to catch your train."

"Tomorrow?" Lydia looked up in shock. She had been expecting at least a few weeks to set things in order.

"I know it is sooner than you had expected, but it was the best I could do. There really isn't that much in the way of transportation; the area has only belonged to the United States for a few short years, and the government is still uncertain what to do with it. Most people believe it an example of the poorest judgment that we even purchased it."

"My aunt says it's the most beautiful country in the world," Lydia countered, remembering incredible descriptions in Zerelda's letters. "I'm sure the purchase will prove to be wise in time."

"I seriously doubt it," Robinson said and then seemed to realize he'd spoken out of turn. "I only hope that you will be happy there. It seems harsh and isolated."

"But my aunt is there, and that will make

me quite content."

"Very well. My man will be here to pick you up at ten tomorrow morning. Can you be ready?"

Lydia thought of the things she had yet to arrange and suddenly realized that nothing was as important as slipping away from the Gray children and leaving this awful place. "I'll be ready." She glanced at the clock. "But you must excuse me. I'll need to get my shopping done in all haste."

"Might I make a suggestion?"

Lydia nodded, wondering what Robinson could possibly say. "I'm happy for any advice."

The older man smiled. "San Francisco is a large city. You can purchase anything you might need for your journey there. I would travel as freely as possible across the country and arrange for your necessities once you are there."

Lydia considered his words. "I have already ordered several outfits."

"Perhaps my wife could settle the account when they are complete, and I could have them shipped to you in Sitka."

"I suppose that would work. I could purchase a couple of ready-made suits instead."

"I think you'll be better off for it. Now,

one of my clerks, Mr. Lytle, will arrive in the morning to accompany you. He will have a sufficient amount of money for your needs. I will also arrange for money to be available for you at a bank in San Francisco. You might wish to take additional supplies to Alaska. I believe the ship can accommodate you in this."

"I hadn't really thought about taking supplies, but I am sure you are right. I should probably purchase food and other items that will ease the burden of my arrival." Lydia considered the various things she might need. She would also enjoy taking some gifts to her aunt. It had been years since she'd seen the woman, but they had been faithful correspondents.

"Well, if that is all," Robinson said, "I will be on my way. Be assured: I will take care of all legal matters. I will send any correspondence to you in Sitka in care of your aunt, and I expect to have the review of the will resolved in a few weeks. There is little reason to believe it will be settled in any other way than in your favor."

"Thank you . . . for everything." Lydia lowered her head slightly. "I know that I offended you in the office the other day with my comment about God. For that I hope you will forgive me and put aside any ill

72

feelings toward me. I had no desire to upset you."

"My dear Mrs. Gray, all is forgiven."

She looked up and smiled. "Thank you. I am afraid the past has made me quite bitter at times. But my hope . . . my hope is in the future now."

When Lydia returned from her shopping trip, she was stunned to find the Gray children rather formally assembled in her parlor for tea. The servants stood at the ready, and the family was already enjoying refreshments when Lydia entered the room.

"Where have you been?" Marston asked, getting to his feet.

Lydia found all faces had turned her way. "I didn't realize I needed to check my appointments with you."

Marston's eyes narrowed, then his expression changed. "You needn't take that tone with me; we were merely concerned for your safety. We have business to discuss." He waved away the servants and waited until they had departed before continuing. His tone was more congenial than Lydia could ever remember. "We would very much like to know your plans for the future. Are there areas in which we might lend assistance?"

Lydia thought of her plans to go live in

Alaska but said nothing, confused by Marston's gentleness. She understood their anger and resentment, but when one of the Grays attempted kindness, it was reason enough to be on her guard.

Instead of taking a seat to join them, Lydia stood at the back of the nearest chair. She clutched the ornate frame for strength and met each person's eyes before speaking.

"I can't think of any way in which you could assist me. However, you should know that I have no intention of keeping your mother's things," she said, looking directly at Jeannette. "The jewelry and furs are of no interest to me. Some time back, my father set up a trust for me, and I am quite comfortable. So whatever the outcome of having the will set aside and reviewed" — she now turned her attention to Marston and Mitchell — "I want you to take the contents of this house, and the house itself. I have already spoken to my lawyer, and he will make the arrangements once the will is settled."

Marston took his seat and reached for his coffee. "And what of the rest of the fortune — the businesses, stocks, and bank accounts?"

"My lawyer has advised that those are issues for the court to determine, and he will see to the matter."

"And what do you intend to do in the meanwhile?" Mitchell asked.

Lydia chose her words carefully. "My lawyer is arranging new living quarters for me. I hope to be gone from this house very soon. I desire to take only my violin and the few personal items I brought into the marriage."

"You aren't taking your clothes?" Jeannette asked in surprise.

"No, you are welcome to them," Lydia replied, knowing full well that Jeannette's stockier frame would never fit into any of the garish fashions.

Evie looked at her for a moment and smiled. Lydia could see that the young woman clearly understood. She wanted nothing of this life to serve as a reminder of the past. No trinket. No memento of her twelve years of fear and pain.

"I'm glad to see that you are being reasonable about this. It will be much easier on everyone. We will want to divide up the goods and sell the place as soon as possible," Marston stated in a businesslike manner. "As for the other, we want to discuss your plans. Mitchell and I both hold stock in Rockford and Gray's Casket Company. We have a vested interest in the future of that company and of the furniture business, as well."

"I can appreciate that, but I am honestly uncertain how the lawyer will handle the businesses. You may feel free, however, to discuss it with him at any time."

Marston put down his cup. "But can we not discuss it with you?" He surprised Lydia once again by softening his tone. "Lydia, you know we have worked hard to grow this business. Rockford and Gray makes the finest caskets in the country. We have a reputation to uphold. It's to your benefit, as well as ours."

"My father invested heavily in the business, as well. As I recall, when I married your father a great deal of money changed hands. My father was already making caskets on the side, as many furniture makers did. Your father saw his own business struggling. The arrangement benefited both sides. Unfortunately, I was forced to be in the middle of that affair."

"You benefited, as well —" Mitchell began.

Lydia held up her hand. "I will not discuss this with you any further than to say you all bore witness to the misery I endured. We all know the truth. You know it for yourselves, as well. Your father was overbearing. He was

76

harsh and uncaring. He beat you without cause, just as he did me." Lydia felt her anger increase. "I don't care what you think of me. I was a young girl when I married, and I did my best. I was terrified when I came here, but I leave feeling quite the opposite. I have endured the worst that any woman could ever suffer. I have miscarried my unborn children. I have lain awake at night, fearing the morrow. I am free of that now, and I will never allow myself to fall victim to that again."

"What a martyr," Jeannette said in a huff.

Marston turned to his sister. "Be still, Jeannette. Lydia is right. She has borne a great deal since coming to reside in this house."

Lydia felt a wave of shock wash over her at Marston's defense. He had never offered her any consolation or acceptance. He and Mitchell had treated her with cruelty and oppression over the years, and she had never expected any such support.

As if reading her mind, Marston turned back to Lydia. "I am particularly sorry for my part. I'm afraid I desired only to please my father, and because of that, I acted in a manner most unbecoming a gentleman."

Lydia frowned. She didn't know what to say and so said nothing. The others seemed taken aback by Marston's comments. They sat in silence, as if trying to figure out if this were some sort of game being played out.

"We are hoping you can understand our position," Mitchell said.

Releasing the back of the chair, Lydia gave a brief nod. "I think I understand it very well."

Marston got to his feet. "I believe we have imposed long enough." Mitchell and Jeannette followed him to the door, with Evie slowly sipping the last of her tea before rising.

Marston Gray had baffled Lydia completely. He had started out the conversation demanding as usual, only to apologize for twelve years of ugliness. Funny how people believed that casual words of apology could somehow erase all of the pain and suffering they had caused.

Lydia heard Evie approach and turned to face her. Evie had never been cruel to her but had often found herself forced to go along with her siblings. "I'm sorry that life here has been such a grief."

"I'm equally sorry for you, Evie. I'm sorry that you had to grow up without the love and affection of a mother . . . or father." She wanted to comment on knowing that Evie hadn't found these things in a husband's love, either, but thought it might be unkind.

Evie nodded and reached out to take hold of Lydia's hand. "I hope you will go far away from here. You deserve to have a happy life. I hope and pray my brothers will leave you in peace. It isn't as if they don't have plenty of their own money. They might have to reorganize their lives a bit and make new plans for their future, but honestly, neither one will suffer all that much."

"I am glad to know that," Lydia replied. "I hope the same is true for you and Jeannette."

"Oh goodness, my husband has more money than he knows what to do with, and while Jeannette may have to learn to curb her spending, perhaps she will still wear the latest fashions."

Lydia smiled. "And that is truly all that will matter to Jeannette."

Evie grinned in return. "Well, that and her social standing. I suppose if somehow it is determined that without Father's money she is less than desirable in the upper classes of this city, she will suffer most heinously." Evie walked to the door and pulled on her gloves. She turned and looked at Lydia as if realizing this would be the last time she would see her.

For a moment Lydia met Evie's gaze, uncertain what to say. She didn't want to share any detail that might cause problems for her departure the following day. "I hope you will be happy," she finally murmured.

A shadow seemed to pass over Evie's countenance and then was gone. She smiled. "I hope you will be, too, Lydia."

There was something of a farewell in her tone that made Lydia sad.

Gerald Lytle was a companionable sort of man. Standing only a little taller than Lydia, he was stout and well muscled and a good conversationalist.

"I am glad to meet you, Mrs. Gray. This trip is one I have often dreamed of taking." He paused and lowered his gaze just a bit. "I hope you don't mind my saying so."

Lydia was touched by his concern that he might somehow have breached etiquette with his comment. "Of course not. I'm quite happy for your company. I was uncertain how I would make the journey on my own."

"I've wanted to take the train west since the tracks opened last year." His animated tone actually served to excite Lydia. "Of course, there are still Indian troubles, but I do not want you to worry. I have brought my rifle, and should the need arise, I will protect you to the death."

"You are most kind." Lydia smiled and motioned to her few things. "This is all I'm taking." She reached for a case. "I gave my servants the day off."

"I can carry that for you," Mr. Lytle said, rushing forward.

"No. I would trust no other to handle my violin. It has been my only comfort and consolation for many years."

"I can well understand," he said as he collected the other things. "Music soothes the soul as nothing else can."

She smiled and nodded. "Yes, that is true."

They departed the house, and Mr. Lytle handed Lydia up into the carriage. He secured her bags, then took his seat opposite her. He seemed to sense her mood and said nothing more.

Lydia couldn't help but stare at the house. She wondered at the lost years there — of the time when she had been a prisoner of Floyd Gray. With a kind man, she might have had happy memories. Even though the marriage was not of her desire, a loving man might have changed her heart for the better. She might have known great joy and passionate love. Instead, something inside her had died and would remain buried there at the Grays' estate.

Her gaze traveled upward to the widow's walk, off of which she knew Charlotte Gray had thrown herself. She had no doubt longed for an escape, just as Lydia did. Floyd had probably neglected and abused her in the same manner he had Lydia, and in Charlotte's case, she had grown too weary to bear it.

Well, now we both have our escape, Lydia thought. *We are both set free, and I shall be set upon a new path of hope.* The carriage started down the drive, while Beethoven's Ninth Symphony built to a crescendo in her head. The words played out in her mind.

Oh friends, not these tones!
Let us sing more cheerful songs,
And more joyful.
Joy! Joy!

And more joyful! Joyful! The word pierced her heart. She would be joyful and happy. Truly happy for the first time in her life.

CHAPTER 6

May 12, 1870

The journey to Sitka had been an arduous one for Lydia. Having never traveled so far, she suffered during the seemingly endless miles of train soot and smoke, only to discover that the ocean voyage was worse. Now, as the *Newbern* stood anchored in the harbor off Sitka's shores, the gentle rocking of the waves made her sick.

Please, just let us get ashore, she thought, pressing a scented handkerchief to her nose. The sweet scent of lavender calmed her momentarily.

Miss Sophia Cracroft stood not far away on the deck with her aunt, Lady Jane Franklin, who was searching for some memento of her husband, Sir John Franklin. He had died some twenty-four years previous while trying to discover a northwest passage from the Atlantic to the Pacific. Lady Franklin, a delicate but sturdy seventy-nine-year-old

English woman, remained hopeful that her husband's journey records might yet appear in one of the far-north settlements.

Lydia didn't know much else. She had been told that Lady Franklin preferred to keep to herself or to the company of her niece. Gazing out now across the water to Sitka, Lydia tried to focus on the small log settlement.

"That's the Indian village to the left."

One of the ship's officers was at her left shoulder. She couldn't recall his name but gave him a brief smile. "Are the Indians happily settled there?"

"I suppose they might be," the man replied. "They call that area the Ranche. The Russians gave it that name after a term they picked up in one of their California colonies."

Lydia let her gaze travel to the rows of long log houses. They were quite large, and she supposed several families could live within one structure. A high wooden stockade ran up from the beach to the first of three blockhouses. Aunt Zerelda had told her many stories about the Tlingit Indians of the area. Her aunt had a strong affection for these people, although she admitted that their ways often confused her.

"Many of the town's buildings are in

disrepair," the officer told her. "When most of the Russians left, taking their businesses with them, the town suffered greatly. However, there are still numerous stores and saloons." He smiled. "Always there must be saloons."

Lydia nodded. Zerelda had told her of at least two breweries that made liquor for the area people. It seemed importing liquor to Alaska was not legal, but creating it there apparently was acceptable. Zerelda hated it because the Tlingits seemed to have little physical tolerance for the stuff, yet found it much desired.

"I understand you have family here."

Lydia gave the man a brief nod. "My aunt has lived here since before the purchase. She is a nurse."

"Did she come to help with the military hospital?"

"No. She was hired by a German family. It seems the wife was taken with bouts of illness, and the husband wanted her to have a learned companion who could aid her when sickness kept her bedfast."

A young sailor approached them. "Beggin' your pardon, Captain said to tell you the launch is ready."

"I suppose this is farewell," Lydia's companion declared. "We will be here for a short time, so perhaps I will see you again."

Lydia realized the man seemed more than a little interested in her response to his suggestion. She felt her stomach roil and pitch as the ship shifted in the water. "Perhaps." She offered nothing more.

Collecting her things, Lydia refused the officer's help and made her way to where the launch awaited passengers. Lady Franklin and Miss Cracroft were already settled when Lydia took her place on board. She allowed the young man there to take her carpetbag, while she held tightly to her violin.

"The rest of your things will be brought ashore later today."

Lydia nodded. "I'll send someone for them."

If the larger ship had proven difficult for Lydia's composure, the smaller vessel was even worse. The constant motion made her nauseated, and she feared she might be sick once again.

She straightened and again dabbed the handkerchief to her face, hoping the boat would soon dock. Lady Franklin whispered something to her niece and it was only a moment before the woman reached toward Lydia.

"My aunt suggests a bit of peppermint

will help."

Lydia took the offering and put it in her mouth, anxious to try anything that might settle her stomach. Almost immediately the candy seemed to help. She drew a deep breath and eased back against the seat, hugging the violin case close for comfort. The journey was nearly over. Soon she would see Zerelda, and all would be well.

Forcing her mind to focus on the happiness she hoped to find in Sitka, Lydia gazed up at the mountains. The snowy peaks were majestic, washed in sunshine that seemed to drift down the mountainside, illuminating thick forests of spruce and fir. It was every bit as lovely as Zerelda had described.

Tiny green islets dotted the water around the harbor as they approached the small wharf. Some of the islands actually appeared to have people living on them. Lydia wondered what it might be like to live isolated from everyone else, and then realized that in many ways, that was exactly what life in Sitka would be like for her.

Lydia couldn't help but wonder where Zerelda lived. Her aunt had described the property and her cabin on Baranof Island, but Lydia had no idea how to find her. She could only hope that someone would know Zerelda and be able to point the way.

The men tied off the small launch, then went to work helping the women onto the dock. Lydia felt a wave of nausea wash over her again. She would be so glad to be off the water. Apparently she wasn't well suited to ocean travel. Not that she planned to depart Sitka any time soon. She was determined to stay even if she hated the isolation and primitive ways.

"Careful, ma'am, the dockboards are uneven," a grizzled seaman announced, handing Lydia her bag. She nodded, fighting to get even footing.

"You'll probably not have your land legs yet . . . I mean limbs." The man flushed red and turned away.

Lydia was glad that he went off to help Lady Franklin. She didn't want to stand around waiting. With a cautious step forward, Lydia marveled at how weak she felt. Her legs acted like rubber sticks, not fully willing to support her weight. She longed to sit down, but there was nothing available until the end of the wharf.

People bustled around the docks. Most were men either coming off small fishing boats or preparing to head out. Some threw her an appreciative glance but remained focused on their work. Lydia tried to keep her eye on the rough-hewn bench at the end of the wharf. If she could just make it there, she could rest.

She forced herself to watch the men work at their various tasks in order to keep her mind off of being sick. She marveled at the way young men jumped on and off the tethered fishing boats. Ahead on the dock, there were several freighters loading supplies. They seemed to have little trouble at all with the massive crates. Their arms bulged muscle, yet their expressions remained relaxed, as if they carried nothing more than a baby.

Taking another step, dizziness blurred Lydia's vision. She struggled with her bag a moment, then put it down, lest she drop her violin. Reaching to take hold of something to steady herself, Lydia realized there was nothing. She closed her eyes, hoping the world would right itself.

"Are you all right?"

Lydia opened her eyes again. She saw a tall, blond-haired man at her side, but when she tried to answer him words would not come. Blackness overtook her as warm arms wrapped around her shoulders.

Kjell Lindquist stared in dumbfounded silence at the woman in his arms. He had come to the docks to check on the new saw blade he was expecting, and now . . . this. He shifted the young woman's weight and lifted her. Looking around, Kjell couldn't help but wonder what he should do. His wagon was at the edge of the road. Maybe he could take her to the hospital.

"Looks like you've hauled in a good catch," Briney Roberts called from his boat, the *Merry Maid*.

"She just fell into my arms out of no-where."

Briney laughed. "Well, weren't you just saying the other day that if the good Lord had a wife for you, He'd have to drop her into your arms?"

Kjell nearly let go of the woman. He *had* said just that. Pushing aside the thought, he decided it was just coincidence and not providence. The young woman moaned, and Kjell couldn't help but look at her. Her skin was so pale, yet she was quite lovely. She reminded him of a fine china doll.

Looking at the stranger with a mix of amazement and concern, Kjell felt strangely at peace holding her. There was something about the dark-haired beauty that intrigued him. The woman started to stir. What would he say to her? How could he help her?

Black lashes fluttered open to reveal dark brown eyes. At first, the woman said nothing; she was clearly stunned. Kjell smiled, hoping to assuage any fears she might have.

"Hello," he said softly. "I believe you fainted."

"I suppose I did." She put her hand to her head. "I don't travel well on the water."

Kjell gave a chuckle. "You aren't alone. Many folks have a hard time." He thought she might ask him to put her down, but when she didn't, he started walking toward his carriage. "My name is Kjell. Kjell Lindquist."

"Chell? What kind of name is that?"

"It's Swedish. Doesn't look a thing like it sounds."

She closed her eyes and reopened them as if trying to focus. Kjell thought she might faint again, but instead she said, "My name is Lydia Gray."

"I have my wagon here. Can I drive you someplace?" he offered.

"I don't know. I don't know where I'm going."

He grinned. "Well, I'm bettin' you'd rather it be someplace other than the dock."

She nodded. "My aunt lives here, but I don't know where."

"What's her name? I know just about everyone. Sitka isn't that big, you know." He reached the wagon and stepped up with

Lydia held tightly in his arms. *She hardly weighs anything,* he thought, depositing her on the seat. He sat down beside her. "So do you know your aunt's name?"

"Of course I do. It's Zerelda Rockford."

"Oh, Zee. Of course I know her. Wonderful woman — great friend to everyone she meets. Everyone loves her. She lives down a ways on the Saberhagen property."

Nodding, the small woman smiled. "Yes, that's her. She worked for Mr. Saberhagen and his wife. You call her Zee? How unusual."

"She started it. Some of the Tlingit children had trouble saying her name, so she shortened it to Zee."

Lydia suddenly turned and pointed. "My bag! My violin." She started to climb down from the wagon, but Kjell stopped her.

"I'll get them. Sorry, I didn't see them." He bounded out of the wagon and back down toward the dock, where a heavy carpetbag and violin case awaited retrieval.

When everything was secured, Kjell took up the reins and urged the matched draft horses forward. "Get along now, boys." They headed south along Sitka's main road, pulling the load in their effortless manner. They seemed to instinctively know where their master wanted them to go, which allowed

Kjell time to consider the woman at his side. What in the world had brought her to Alaska? She hardly looked prepared for life in the small island community — she wasn't even wearing sturdy boots.

"I want to thank you for helping me back there. I've not felt well since leaving San Francisco." She straightened a little but remained pale. "I had thought maybe Zerelda would be there to meet me, but I realized too late that my last letter to her likely hadn't preceded me."

"It's probably on the same ship that brought you," Kjell said. "Zee won't care, though. She'll be so happy to see you it won't matter."

"And how can you be so sure?" Lydia asked. "You don't know anything about me."

"Don't be so sure about that. I've heard Zee talk quite a bit about her one and only niece. She thinks of you as a sort of daughter." Kjell could see that Lydia was not bearing well with the bouncing wagon. "Why don't you stop trying to impress me with your ladylike posture and lean against me? You're sick, and there's no reason to be ashamed of it."

To Kjell's surprise, she didn't fight him on the idea. Nodding, she slouched against

93

him. "I am sorry."

"You don't need to be. Truth be told, I'm the sorry one. Sorry that the roads aren't better and that the wagon springs are so bad."

Lydia looked up at him and shook her head. "What will your wife think when word gets back to her that you were seen like . . . like this?"

"I'm not married, so I don't anticipate a problem," he said with a wink. "I hope there won't be any jealous husbands hunting me down."

The woman blushed and lowered her gaze. "No, I'm a widow."

"I'm sorry," he murmured, not knowing what else to say.

"Don't be," Lydia replied without even pausing for breath.

This truly served to confuse Kjell. There was a bitter hatred edging the woman's words. She must have lived a pretty awful life if she could say such a thing. Maybe someday she would tell him more about it.

"I bought supplies in San Francisco. I'm afraid there is quite a bit. I wasn't at all sure what would be useful to Zerelda. Might I hire your services, Mr. Lindquist, to bring them to Zerelda's place once they are unloaded from the *Newbern*?

"I'd be happy to help, but there's no need to offer me pay. Folks up here help each other without it. We have to help one another, you know."

"My aunt has often said as much." She closed her eyes and sighed.

The wheels sank into a deep hole, bouncing the wagon hard. Lydia sprang up as if she intended to jump. She didn't reach for Kjell, but he put out his arm to keep her in place.

"Sorry. We do the best we can," he told her.

Lydia nodded and remained rigid in her seat. She stole a glance at him, and Kjell couldn't help but return her gaze. *My, but she sure is pretty,* he thought. *Like a spring blossom.* He had to admit he wasn't in the least bit sorry that he'd been the one to catch her.

With no reserve strength, Lydia let herself lean on Kjell once again. It went totally against her better judgment, but she couldn't help herself. Men had caused her nothing but pain and misery — always betraying her trust. Still, despite her misgivings, she felt at ease with this man.

How strange. I've never felt comfortable with any man, and now this total stranger leaves me without concern. It's almost as if I've known him a lifetime.

Paying little attention to the surroundings, Lydia felt her stomach lurch. She was going to be sick again. "Oh, please stop."

Kjell reined back on the horses just as Lydia leaned over the side of the wagon. Her abdominal muscles churned violently, bringing up what little was left in her stomach. To her embarrassment, she felt Kjell's arms slip around her — steadying her as she continued to be sick. She waited for the misery to end and then drew a deep breath.

"I'm afraid there's no ladylike way to do this. I'm sorry," she said in a tone that came out more whimper than anything.

"Don't be on my account," Kjell said, pulling her gently back toward him. "Lots of folks get seasick. I had a friend who didn't stop feeling the rocking of the waves for weeks."

"I hope that won't be my case," she said, shaking her head weakly. "I don't think I could live that long in this state."

"I'll pray it passes much quicker for you," Kjell stated softly.

She didn't argue with him. If there was even a remote possibility that God truly cared, she would welcome any help in overcoming this sickness.

"Do you feel good enough for us to go on?" he asked. "Your aunt's place is just up the hillside over there."

Lydia nodded and tried to see the cabin she would soon call home. It looked quite small. What if it was too small? What if Zerelda had no desire for her to stay there?

"Are there other places to rent?" Lydia asked. "I mean, if my aunt can't have me."

He chuckled. "You'd be hard-pressed to get away from Zerelda once she sees you. Besides, there aren't any places available."

"It's just that I hate to impose myself upon her. She might not have the room."

"My guess is she'll make the space if she doesn't have it," Kjell replied. "But don't worry about it. If she won't have you, there are dozens of men in town who would seek your hand in marriage before the sun goes down. Zerelda gets asked at least ten times a day, I'm sure."

"That may be. However, they would ask in vain where I'm concerned. I don't intend to ever marry again."

Kjell surprised her by shaking his head. "That husband of yours must have really hurt you."

Lydia met his gaze. "You have no idea."

CHAPTER 7

Kjell helped Lydia to the cabin door and knocked. "Zee? You in there?"

A slender woman opened the door. "Kjell, what brings you here?" Her mouth dropped open at the sight of the woman at his side. "Liddie? Is that you?"

"It's me," she replied in a weak voice.

"She's not in good shape. Been sick all the way up." As if on cue, Lydia's strength gave out, and Kjell caught her as she started to sink. He lifted her into his arms again. "I think she'd better lie down."

"I'm so sorry to be a bother," Lydia interjected while Zerelda and Kjell took over.

"Bah, you aren't a bother. Here, Kjell, bring her right in," the woman declared. "I got the letter you sent about your father and husband dying. I knew you wanted to come north but didn't figure to see you so soon. I thought you'd still be laying plans for the trip."

Lydia studied her aunt. She was different than she remembered. At forty-five, Zerelda Rockford was a most unconventional woman. She had given her hair a blunt cut at the shoulder, and it gave her face an angular appearance.

"Here, she can have this room," Zerelda said, opening the door.

Kjell followed her in and deposited Lydia on the bed. "Is there anything I can do to help you out? You need wood brought in, Zee?"

"That would be good. You can build up the fire, too. The day has a chill, and we need to keep Liddie warm."

"I'm really not helpless," Lydia said when her aunt began unbuttoning her suit jacket.

"You look pretty bad off. Your eyes are sunken. I'd say your fluids are depleted, and you probably haven't had a decent bit of food in a while," Zerelda said. She smiled down at her niece. "You look just as you did as a girl. I can't believe so much time has passed."

"A lifetime of nightmares," Lydia whispered. "And now this. I haven't been able to keep food down since we set sail. It was all just too much."

"Well, it's behind you now. I'll take good care of you, and soon you'll be up and running. You bring that violin of yours?"

Lydia was so exhausted that she'd not even given it much consideration. "I did. Can we ask Kjell to bring it in?"

"Of course."

"There were times the violin was all that got me through the bad times. Floyd was so . . ." Her words trailed into silence.

Zerelda stroked her hair. "I know, and I'm so sorry. Had I any say in the matter, I would have convinced Zachary to send you to me rather than to sell you off in marriage." She shook her head. "But despite the man's poor judgment, I can't believe he's gone."

"My father thought he was doing the best for the family, I'm sure. He wrote me a letter of apology before he died. I'm not entirely sure I forgive him, but I am happy to say he left me enough money to comfortably live out my years."

Zerelda helped Lydia from her jacket and then unfastened the button on her skirt. "Doesn't do a body any good to withhold forgiveness. The devil is the only one who stands to gain anything from that."

"Then the devil gained a great deal in the Gray household. You've never met more vindictive people, and forgiveness isn't a word in their vocabulary."

"Your letters truly painted an ugly picture." Zerelda went to the foot of the bed. "Take hold of the bed frame."

Lydia did as she was instructed while Zerelda pulled her skirt off. Lydia barely had the strength to hold on to the iron post. The coolness that swept over her body made Lydia realize her condition. Lying there in her petticoats, chemise, and corset, she felt almost naked. What if that man Kjell returned?

As if reading her niece's mind, Zerelda went to the door and closed it before retrieving a nightgown from the trunk at the foot of the bed. "This should be a great deal more comfortable." Without asking Lydia's permission, Zerelda unhooked her corset. Lydia tried to sit up, but dizziness washed over her anew.

"The room won't stop spinning."

"Sometimes it's like that," Zerelda said. "Some folks get what they call motion sick."

She maneuvered the rest of Lydia's clothes from her body, then placed the nightgown over her head. Lydia found she barely had the strength to put her arms through. She fell back against the pillow and sighed.

"Goodness, but you're skin and bones. I'll

get some soup going for you as soon as I have you tucked into bed."

"I can't eat," Lydia said, feeling sick at the thought.

"You'll be able to take a little soup. I have a special recipe that helps with the nausea. Then I'll give you some tea to help you sleep. You'll see," Zerelda said, straightening. "You'll soon be right as rain."

Lydia reached out. "I'm sorry I wasn't able to get you the information about my arrival. Everything happened so fast."

"Don't fret about it. We can discuss it later."

"But I've imposed myself upon you, and I never even gave you a chance to approve my coming."

Zerelda laughed. "You are such a silly goose. Of course I approve your coming here. I wouldn't have had it any other way. My employer is leaving for Germany at the end of the summer. His wife passed on a few months back. I think I told you about that."

Lydia nodded.

"Well, I was seriously wondering what the Lord had for me next, but now I guess I know." She offered Lydia a sweet smile. "I'm so glad you've come, Lydia. You are going to be a blessing to me."

"I demand you tell us where Lydia has gone," a red-faced Mitchell Gray declared.

Dwight Robinson merely shrugged. "I presume that if Mrs. Gray wanted you to know her whereabouts, she would have left a forwarding address."

"So she has moved?" Marston eyed the lawyer closely. It was clear by his expression that he hadn't meant to reveal even this much. The man quickly recovered, however.

"Well, she isn't living at the mansion anymore, so don't you imagine she has?" Robinson replied.

"And is she still in the city?" Mitchell asked. "Look, we have a business to run. There's a guard there who tells us we are no longer needed. This is our family's business, and we have a right to it."

"Not according to the will." Robinson looked at both of them before momentarily settling his gaze on Marston. "Sirs, I have no authority to share any information with you. Mrs. Gray has given me no instruction to share her whereabouts."

"But what of the legal business that involves her?" Mitchell again pressed for answers.

Marston leaned back in his seat and held his temper in check. So Lydia had finally learned to stand up for herself. He almost smiled at the thought. He rather liked this new temperament. It made her more of a challenge.

"I assure you both I am quite capable of handling Mrs. Gray's legal affairs. She has given me her full permission to see to her best interests."

"Then you have her permission to share with us her current address," Marston said with a smile.

Robinson shook his head and returned Marston's stiff smile. "My dear sir, I think without saying anything more, we both know that giving you access to her whereabouts is not at all in keeping with her best interests."

Marston narrowed his eyes. "You are playing a dangerous game, Robinson. We have strong allies."

"You may have had at one time, but only because your father bullied everyone. Times are changing. The politics, the atmosphere of the city — it's all transforming for the better. New laws will make it more difficult for people like you to harass and harm others."

Mitchell slammed his fist on the arm of

the chair. "That's slander, I daresay."

"Mrs. Gray endured a great deal at your father's hand. As I understand it, there was much that was questionable in his actions."

"No one cares about such things, and well you know it. She's a woman," Marston declared. "She was a wife, nothing more than my father's property. When she refused to be obedient as she had pledged in her marriage contract, my father was forced to be heavy-handed at times."

"All that to say, you would do well to remember that your father wasn't the only one who knew how to utilize information," Robinson replied. "If I were you, I would refrain from bringing too much attention to myself. Society may accept such matters, but I do not. I see nothing acceptable in beating women and children. A man must surely be a weakling if he has to take such actions."

"I don't recall asking for your opinion," Marston said. He had received enough beatings at the hand of his father to completely agree with Robinson, but he wasn't about to let him know.

"Very well." Robinson glanced down at his papers. "At this point in time, Mrs. Gray is quite willing to make arrangements with the Gray family. However, should I feel that it is in her best interest to do otherwise, say should she seem under threat of harm, then I would not hesitate to dissuade her from her generous suggestions."

Marston was no longer able to contain his rage. "Of all the underhanded threats . . . And you suggest that we are the ones who bully. You have not yet won this, Mr. Robinson. The will is still under consideration."

"But I don't believe it will be for long. I am confident it will be resolved within days."

"Has someone given you information to suggest such a thing?" Marston asked.

"As a matter of fact, they have." Robinson fixed Marston with a stern look. "I believe your lawyer will be receiving word of a meeting, even now."

This wasn't good news. Marston knew that if the judge had resolved the matter this quickly, it most likely would not go in favor of his family. He said nothing, however. There was no sense in letting Robinson see his distress.

"There's no reason to remain," Marston suddenly declared.

Mitchell looked at his brother in surprise. "But we haven't yet learned of Lydia's whereabouts."

"Nor will we. Not here, at least." Marston

headed for the door. "I will say this, however." He turned and gave Robinson what he knew to be his most disturbing glare. "You and Mrs. Gray would do well to remember that we will not take bad news without a challenge. You haven't won yet, and if I have anything to say about it, you won't win — ever."

Zerelda pulled on gloves and gave Lydia a smile. "It's a good day to work in the garden." She worried about Lydia. Her complexion was still quite pale, and while she was finally able to keep food down, she was still so thin. "We have a beautiful sunny day, and in Sitka, you don't get too many of those. You have to take advantage of them when you can."

Lydia nodded. "I'm glad it's turned out nice."

"You don't seem happy. Is there anything you want to talk about?"

The younger woman looked toward the dining room window with such longing that Zerelda had to look, as well. What was going through her mind? She acted as though there were prison bars keeping her in.

"This is really the first day I've felt strong enough to be up," Lydia said. "But I still feel so very weak. Will I ever recover?"

"Of course you will. I hate being sick. I always wonder if I'll ever get any better." She pulled on a thin leather apron to cover her serviceable brown skirt and calico blouse. "Take heart, you will soon be back up on your feet. You'll be out there hiking with me in the mountains."

"I hope so." Lydia's voice was wistful.

"Look, why don't you sit out on the porch for a time? We can bundle you up so you don't catch a chill. I think the fresh air and change of scenery will do you good."

Lydia seemed to perk up at this. "Do you truly think it would be all right?"

Zerelda laughed. "I'm the nurse here. Of course it will be all right. What I say goes."

She helped Lydia to stand, then walked her slowly to the front door. To her surprise she found Kjell on the other side, just about to knock.

"That's timely," she told him. "I was just taking Lydia outside to enjoy a sit on the porch. Why don't you help her to the rocking chair while I get some blankets?"

Kjell smiled and took hold of Lydia's arm. She pulled back momentarily, then relaxed. He didn't frown or otherwise acknowledge her action, which led Zerelda to believe he understood and knew more about her niece's feelings toward men than most would. Kjell had always been the kind of man to notice things, however. Zerelda had come to truly appreciate the man's kindness.

Bringing the blankets, Zerelda couldn't help but laugh at the way Kjell fussed over Lydia. "She's not broken, Kjell. Just a bit weathered."

This actually made Lydia smile. "I'm a great deal weathered."

"You look no worse for it," Kjell said. "In fact, I was just going to comment that your color seems much better than when I saw you two days ago."

Lydia said nothing, as if embarrassed at the compliment. Zerelda took that opportunity to tuck blankets around her niece and question Kjell about the events of the past couple of days.

"What's the news?" she asked.

Kjell leaned back against the porch support. "Not a whole lot. The *Newbern* has finally unloaded all the supplies. That's why I've come. There's a load of goods for you out there." He pointed and Zerelda noticed the wagon for the first time. "There's more at the dock."

"Mercy, did you bring all of that up here?"

Lydia nodded. "I didn't know what you might need. I thought maybe I should bring a lot of food and such. I didn't know what you'd already have, so I just purchased a little of everything."

"Must have cost a fortune to ship," Zerelda said, shaking her head. "But we'll make use of it — don't you worry."

"Where'd ya like it, Zee?" Kjell asked in his singsong cadence. Sometimes his Swedish ancestry made itself very clear in his comments. Swedes had a way of almost bouncing their words up and down when they spoke. Zerelda had always enjoyed that about them.

"There ought to be room in the storage shed. We'll put the food in the cache, then store anything else down below."

"I'll take care of it."

Zerelda noticed that Lydia was watching him cautiously. She decided to put off the gardening for a few moments and talk to her niece. "You know, he's a very good man. He's not like what you're used to. Not all men are that way, you know."

"What way?" Lydia asked, her voice barely audible.

"Like your husband. Like his sons."

"How can you be sure?" Lydia looked at Zerelda, her gaze searching for answers.

"Some men are lost souls who care nothing about the Lord or their fellow man. But some are given to listening to God — to putting others first. Kjell is the latter kind. I've never known him to raise his voice. I've seen him offer the best he has to those in need. He doesn't deserve your suspicion."

"I wasn't truly offering it. I suppose that's just the way I tend to be. I'm sorry. Should I apologize to him?"

"Kjell probably never even gave it a second thought. I think, however, it would suit you well to spend some time just talking to him. Get to know him. Restore your opinion of men in general. They aren't all like those you've known."

"I hope not. But please understand," Lydia said, turning back to Zerelda, "I didn't come here seeking romance or a husband. I want only to live out my days in peace. There was never any peace in Floyd Gray's home." She grew thoughtful. "I remember the joy and contentment I had when I was a little girl. That's really all I want now."

"I hope you'll find it here, sweetheart." Zerelda patted her hand. "Sunday, if you're well enough, I'll introduce you to my friends at the church. I think you'll like them very much."

Lydia shook her head. "I'm not much interested in church. Floyd was a firm

111

believer in being seen at church every Sunday. It promoted his social standing with the community to be known for his attendance and supposed benevolence. Sitting there week after week and seeing the mockery he made of such institutions left me with little desire to participate. Especially since I don't believe God cares about me anyway."

Zerelda could hardly comprehend the gravity of her niece's words. Never in their correspondence had Lydia made such a declaration. "You really believe that God doesn't care about you?"

"I know He doesn't. He's let so much bad happen to me that I want nothing to do with church and religious nonsense."

"Oh, Liddie, I am sorry. You've been wronged, no doubt about it."

Her niece shrugged. "Maybe, but I've definitely learned my lesson over the years. If I want peace, I have to make it myself."

"And if you want love?" Zerelda asked, watching her intently.

Lydia shook her head sadly. "I gave up on having that a long time ago."

"I'm sorry for all the work I've put on you," Lydia apologized when Kjell came to sit on the porch rail opposite her. "I was overzealous in my purchases."

"There's nothing there that can't be used. You picked wisely. A lot of that will be consumed through the winter. Although I will say, had you bought even one more thing, there wouldn't have been room to store it. Zerelda was ready to ask her former employer, Mr. Saberhagen, if we could use the main house."

Lydia glanced the short distance up the hill to where a two-story log structure stood. That house seemed to have been given more care than Zerelda's smaller cabin.

"Mr. Saberhagen wouldn't have minded, but I think *I* would have," Kjell said with a grin. "That trek up and down the hill would have been hard on the horses pulling such a load."

"I'm glad you didn't have to resort to that," Lydia replied. She shifted uneasily and pulled her blanket closer. She braved a glance at the blond-haired man and asked, "Have you always lived here?"

"For the most part. I was actually born here. My mother's people were Russian and my father was Swedish. He came here to work in the otter fur trade. My mother's parents befriended him, and in doing so, introduced their only daughter to romance."

Lydia considered how it must have been,

113

growing up in such an isolated place. "This was, no doubt, a very different kind of life. So far away from civilization and big cities."

"Well, you have to remember, Sitka was much larger at one point. There was a great deal going on here, and commerce flowed freely. The Russians used this as their capital in Alaska. People were always coming and going. It was a very busy town."

She considered his comment for a moment, trying her best to imagine such a thing. "And what happened to change it? Everything seems . . . well . . . run down. The buildings look old and tired. Zerelda said that many of the businesses are gone."

"That's true enough," Kjell said, nodding. "When America purchased the area from Russia, there was a great exodus. For the most part, Russians wanted to return to their own land. Some stayed, of course. Many of the businesses were sold off or closed down. Some folks took their wares with them back to Russia, while others sold them outright to ships coming into the harbor."

His voice sounded sad, and Lydia couldn't help but wonder what had happened to his own people. "And what of your parents?" she finally asked.

Kjell met her gaze, his blue eyes seeming

to see through to her soul. "They're gone now. My father and grandfather were taken at sea. We never found their bodies. My mother died of a broken heart just a year later."

Lydia was sorry for having brought up the subject. She looked away and sighed. "I think I greatly prefer the quiet here to the noise of the city. I've never known anything like this, but I find it has a healing effect."

"Yes," Kjell agreed. "I find it that way, too."

"Is that why you never left?"

"I think so. After my mother's death, my wife, Raisa, wanted to return to Russia. Her family was there, and she longed for her friends and the familiar comforts."

Lydia stiffened. "I thought you said earlier that you weren't married."

"She's dead. Fell ill and never recovered. She's buried next to my mother," Kjell said with a hint of a shrug. "It's been nearly eight years past."

"I'm sorry." Lydia looked at her hands and tried to think of some way to change the uncomfortable topic. She didn't have long to worry, however.

"You two look hungry," Zerelda said, coming from around the side of the cabin. "Can you stay for lunch, Kjell?"

115

He pushed off the rail. "No, actually I've left the business idle too long. I need to get back to work. We're putting in a new saw blade, and I want to make sure it goes well."

"Then stop by for supper sometime. You know you don't have to give me any warning — just come on by. Liddie and I will have plenty of food — thanks to her generosity and foresight."

Lydia felt her cheeks grow hot with embarrassment, but she wasn't really sure why. She supposed it was just her general discomfort with being the center of attention.

"I'll do that, Zerelda. A fella shouldn't pass up too many opportunities to take a meal with such beautiful women."

"Oh, go on with you," Zerelda said, laughing, "or I'll change my mind."

"Yes, ma'am," he said, bounding down the steps. "Good day to ya, ladies. *Gud vare med dig.*"

"And with you, Kjell," Zerelda called out.

"What did he say?" Lydia asked. She watched Kjell direct the horse down the road to town.

"It's Swedish. He said, 'God be with you.'"

Lydia frowned. Yet another reference to God — that illusive judge who sat on high and did nothing to deliver His children from

116

pain and sorrow. Why would she ever want Him to be with her when He seemed to regard her with such indifference?

CHAPTER 8

Kjell couldn't keep his mind on his work. The sawmill business had picked up enough that he needed to implement new equipment and even hire some extra help, but today that still wasn't enough to hold his attention.

He looked at his ledgers, but it was Lydia Gray he found looking back at him. Her image was firmly etched in his memory. Her dark brown eyes betrayed pain and misery that he couldn't possibly know. Kjell wanted to offer her comfort, but Lydia seemed to have found her own ways to cope. She wanted no one to get too close. She even seemed to hold Zerelda at arm's length.

"Kjell, can we talk?"

A short, squat man stood in the doorway to Kjell's tiny office. He held his hat in his hand and wore a frown on his face that suggested this was not a visit of pleasantries.

"Of course." Kjell got to his feet and

motioned the man in. "What's wrong, Arnie?"

The man fingered the edge of his hat nervously before looking up to meet Kjell's face. "I'm not happy about the increase in price."

Shaking his head, Kjell tried to remember what increase the man might be referencing. "I'm not sure I understand."

"Your men told me that the lumber I ordered would be an extra twenty-five dollars. That may not seem like much to you, but I'm just getting my business started. It doesn't seem fair that you should change the price now."

"But I didn't," Kjell protested. "What are you talking about?"

The man seemed to relax a bit when he saw that Kjell was siding with him. "Your men, the Sidorov brothers. They came to deliver part of the lumber and told me the price had been miscalculated. They said I would owe an extra fifty dollars, but only twenty-five if I paid in cash instead of on account."

"That's ridiculous. I didn't send them to tell you that. Hold on," Kjell said, getting up from his desk. "I'll call them in here, and they can explain themselves."

He walked out to where his foreman,

Joshua Broadstreet, worked at adjusting the new saw blade. "Josh, I need to talk to you for a minute."

The younger man looked up. "What is it, boss?"

"Where are the Sidorovs?" Kjell surveyed the shop but saw nothing of the Russian brothers.

"Delivering another load to the military." Josh straightened and wiped his hands on a nearby rag. "Why?"

"What do you know about them asking Mr. Seymour for an additional fifty dollars?"

Josh frowned. "Nothing. I didn't know they had."

Kjell looked back over his shoulders. "Don't say anything to them, but when they get back, tell them to come see me."

"Sure, boss."

"And, Josh?" The younger man waited expectantly. Kjell smiled. "You don't need to call me *boss,* remember?"

"Sorry. Force of habit. When I was working in the railroad shops in Seattle, it was required."

Kjell chuckled as he made his way back to the office. He liked the young man, who'd only come to work for him the month before. Josh showed great skill when it came to anything mechanical, and Kjell knew he'd be an asset for the sawmill. He sobered as he rejoined Arnie.

"The brothers aren't here right now, but that isn't important. Just know this. I haven't raised the price on you. Things stay as they are."

The older man nodded with relief. "Thank you, Kjell. The Sidorovs told me they would settle up with me tomorrow when they brought the last of the load, but I didn't want to wait until then."

"You were wise to come to me. I'll deal with them. I'm not sure what the misunderstanding was on their part, but I'll get to the bottom of it."

He shook hands with Arnie and returned to his seat. "If you have any more problems, just come directly to me."

The man nodded. "Thank you, Kjell."

Kjell waited for several minutes until he was sure Arnie had gone before he summoned Aakashook and Keegaa'n, the two Tlingit boys who worked for him.

"Boys, I have a question for you. You helped Anatolli and Ioann load the wood on the wagon yesterday, didn't you?"

The boys nodded. Kjell could see they were worried that they had somehow done something wrong. He sought to ease their concerns. "You aren't in trouble. I just wondered if you knew anything about the price of the wood being increased."

"No," Aakashook said, looking to his brother. "Can't know nothing more." This was his routine way of explaining that he didn't know anything else about a matter.

Kjell nodded. The boys' English had improved considerably since coming to work for Kjell. They actually spoke Russian quite fluently, but Kjell knew their mother wanted them to speak better English, so he spoke it almost exclusively with them. Now, however, he wanted them comfortable, so he switched to Russian.

"Did the Sidorovs say anything at all about the delivery?"

The boys exchanged a look, and Kjell could see they were still uneasy. "You can tell me if something is wrong."

Keegaa'n, the elder of the two at thirteen, spoke up. "They are mean to us, Kjell. They hit us and if we talk bad about them, they will hit us again."

Kjell frowned. "They have no right. When did this happen?"

Aakashook had to join in. "They do it all the time. All the time they tell us they will hurt us if we don't do all the work they give us."

122

"Well, I don't intend to see that go on anymore. You should have talked to me about it. You will in the future, yes?"

The boys said they would.

"Good. Now it's nearly time for them to lock the gate. Go on home before you get in trouble." Kjell despised that the Tlingits in Sitka were confined each evening. The law held that the native people were not to be allowed to roam about the town after six o'clock. It was said this was for their safety more than anything, but Kjell knew the whites saw the Indians as a nuisance and had found a way to eliminate their presence, at least for part of the day. Night after night, soldiers rounded up the Indians like wild dogs. The natives would flee ahead of the soldiers, some trying to hide out, but generally they were caught. At six in the morning, the stockade gates were opened and the people of color were allowed to once again meld into the white Sitka society.

Though Kjell was bothered by the injustice of it, the boys didn't seem to give it any thought. It was all they knew. They hurried off, playfully punching at each other's arm. Each one tried to be the first to reach the large open door. Kjell followed slowly after them, watching the siblings race across the yard and down the road. They were good boys who had come to him at the insistence of their grandfather. The man had owed Kjell a debt and would not rest until some form of payment had been established. Kjell knew the man couldn't afford to buy the wood and would have just given it to him, but the old man's pride would not allow for it. Instead, he offered to let the boys come every afternoon to work at his mill. Their mother especially liked this idea because she saw the benefit in their learning better English.

Kjell heard the wagon coming down the road and realized the Sidorovs were returning. He wondered what they would say when confronted with the question of the money. And then there was the issue of their hitting the boys. Kjell wasn't entirely sure how to approach the subject. He certainly didn't want the Sidorovs to somehow make the boys pay for their admission.

Two strong draft horses plodded up the drive and came to a stop when Anatolli pulled back hard on the reins. Ioann jumped from the wagon and began to unhitch the horses.

"I need to talk to you about something," Kjell said, looking from one broad-shouldered brother to the other. "Josh will take care of the horses. Why don't you step into my office." He turned and called for Josh and waited until the younger man was in sight before joining the brothers.

"I need to talk to them — will you see to the horses?"

"Sure thing, b— . . . Kjell." He grinned. "See? I'm getting better already."

Kjell gave a chuckle, but it was half-hearted. He hated confrontation with any-one, but even more so with employees. He entered his office.

"I had a talk today with Mr. Seymour. It seems you told him the price of his lumber was to go up by fifty dollars. If he would pay you in cash, it was to be half that amount. Now, which one of you wants to tell me what this is all about?" he asked, crossing his arms and taking a stand behind his desk.

The two men were noticeably unhappy. Anatolli's jaw clenched tight, and Ioann crossed his arms in a defiant manner.

"The man speaks lies," Ioann said, narrowing his eyes.

"Does he?" Kjell countered. "And what purpose would that serve? Perhaps I should go speak with some of the other customers and see if they've had similar problems."

Anatolli shook his head and reached out to take hold of his brother's arm. "We must not lie. It is true. But please understand. We did not do this bad for our own pleasure."

Kjell looked from one man to the other. "I'm listening."

"It's our mother." Anatolli glanced at Ioann for support.

"*Da,* our mother is very sick. We get word that she may die," Ioann said. His entire countenance changed before Kjell's eyes. His expression took on one of a chastised pup. "We need money for the journey home."

"Why not just tell me about it? Instead, you go steal from my customers?"

"We did not think a little here and there would be missed," Anatolli said, shrugging.

"Twenty-five dollars is hardly a little amount. Who else have you done this to?"

"I can't remember," Ioann replied.

"That many, eh?" Kjell shook his head and sat down at the desk. "You will return the money immediately, or I will turn this situation over to the army."

Anatolli jumped forward. "But please, we cannot do that. We have already purchased the tickets to Russia. We cannot get back our money. Please do not take us to the soldiers, or we might never see our mother again."

Kjell considered his words for a moment.

The man was probably right. If he made this a matter of public knowledge, it would be months before they could go home. Against his better judgment, he nodded.

"Very well." Both men smiled and nodded as if to assure him he'd made the right decision. "But I want a list of the people you overcharged. I need to make everything right with these folks."

"We will work on it together. Maybe we will have the names come to us," Anatolli suggested.

Kjell decided to say nothing more for the moment. He could scarcely believe there had been so many other people involved that the brothers couldn't simply give him a handful of names. He would have to take the account books home and go over each entry and then seek out each man. Who knew how much this would cost him in the long run? But money was nothing to a man's reputation. In this part of the world, a reputation was everything, and Kjell wasn't about to have his ruined by the likes of the Sidorov brothers.

"Get out of here. Come back in the morning with my list."

"And you will not turn us over . . . to the soldiers?" Ioann asked in a hesitant manner.

127

"No, but neither will I keep you in my employ. I cannot stand thieves." Kjell stood. "Leave me now before I change my mind."

The two men hurried from the room much as the Tlingit boys had done earlier. With a heavy sigh, Kjell picked up the ledger and slammed it shut. It was going to be a long night.

He thought for a moment of Zerelda's offer of supper. Maybe he should take her up on it. After all, he would get to see Lydia again. The book weighed heavy in his arm, however. He wouldn't be good company, given the problem at hand. No, it would be best if he kept to himself.

By the end of the week, Lydia felt considerably stronger. She had managed to recover completely from her seasickness and finally felt able to converse with Zerelda about the things that had happened in Kansas City.

Lingering over supper one night, Lydia shared her heart. "I feel safe here. For the first time in my life, I feel truly safe."

Her aunt frowned. "I'm so sorry. A young woman shouldn't have to come to the wilds of a barely settled land to experience such a thing. I'm truly angry with my brother for putting you in such circumstances, but I know that holding a grudge against the dead is hardly reasonable. He obviously didn't think of the pain he was causing you."

"No, I suppose he didn't," Lydia agreed. "My poor mother worried herself into the grave over the situation. I'm certain it was this and not the pneumonia that killed her."

"May your parents both be at rest now."

Lydia said nothing. She wasn't sure she really cared if her father had found peace or not. She still felt a hardness inside when she remembered pleading with him to annul the contract so she wouldn't have to marry Floyd Gray.

"Well," she said, putting thoughts of her parents aside, "there won't be any rest when it comes to the Grays trying to get back at me for taking their fortune. I've made arrangements with my lawyer to see their physical properties returned, but I'm sure they will remain unhappy. They had expected to get everything. They won't like that I've kept a part of what they deem to be theirs."

"This will make them dangerous," Zerelda said. "Men who feel they have been cheated seldom rest until the dispute is made right by their standards."

"That's why I left."

"I'm glad you did. I worried so about you. Many was the night I spent on my knees in prayer for your deliverance."

"Surely even you can see that it didn't work, Aunt Zerelda. You can't expect me to put any stock in your prayers when they so obviously failed."

"But they didn't. You were delivered," Zerelda said, looking surprised. "Can't you see that for yourself?"

"You can't tell me that Floyd's death was some divine intervention by God on my behalf." Lydia shook her head. "Why not simply make Floyd a kind man who truly loved me? Why not change the hearts of Floyd's children and give me a good life in their company?"

"We can't always know why God answers our prayers in one way instead of another."

Lydia got to her feet. "Or doesn't answer them at all. Honestly, Zerelda, I cannot see things your way when it comes to God. If you'll excuse me now, I'd like to go outside and play my violin."

Zerelda looked as if she wanted to say something more, but she remained silent. Lydia went to her violin case and opened it. She lovingly took up the bow and tightened the horsehair. Next she ran it across the rosin and, when satisfied, picked up the violin and tucked it under her arm.

Outside, the world seemed at peace. The

sun wouldn't yet set for hours, given the long summer days. Lydia walked a little ways down the path and stood overlooking the harbor below. The tiny islands looked like shadowy mounds against the gray-blue water. Several fishing boats made their way across the inlet, and in the far distance, a ship sat anchored in the stillness.

Lydia tested the strings of the violin, listening for the perfect pitch she desired. When this was accomplished, she raised the violin and rested it against her shoulder. Since she'd been a young girl, this very action had given her spirit a sense of calming. Drawing the bow across the strings, Lydia sighed. Her soul took flight on the wings of the melody, the haunting strains drifting down the valley to fill up all the hushed nooks with song.

Closing her eyes, Lydia lost herself in the moment. Here, nothing could harm her. Here, there was true peace and comfort for her weary and damaged heart.

CHAPTER 9

July 1870

On the twenty-seventh of July, the *George S. Wright* sailed into Sitka Sound with the mail. Lydia was anxious for word from Mr. Robinson. She hoped that the wills had been settled and that she could put the ordeal behind her. Especially now. Now that she was certain she carried Floyd's child.

Having a baby was the last thing Lydia had expected or planned for. She was still rather dumbfounded by the idea, but there was also a bit of pleasure and happiness at the thought that she would have a child of her own — a child Floyd and the rest of the Grays couldn't harm and influence.

She hadn't yet told Zerelda, but her aunt was a nurse and Lydia presumed she'd already suspected. Lydia figured to talk to her that night at dinner. After all, they would have to plan for the future. The baby would come sometime around Christmas, and Lydia wanted to be completely prepared.

"This what you're waiting for?" the postmaster asked. He extended a thick envelope to Lydia.

"Thank you, Mr. Fuller. I believe it is." She didn't wait to open it. Zerelda was next door at the bakery visiting with a friend, so Lydia found a place to sit not far away and began to read.

My dear Mrs. Gray,

I hope this missive finds you in good health. As I am certain you are wondering about the resolution of your husband's and father's estates, I will get right to the heart of the subject.

Lydia read on to see that the court had ruled in her favor. Marston and Mitchell were appealing the ruling, of course, but Robinson was unconcerned. He did, however, wish to know if Lydia still desired him to settle everything in the same way she had dictated upon her departure.

This gave Lydia pause to reconsider. Before, she hadn't known about the baby. This babe, after all, was entitled to the wealth as much as any of his half siblings. She shook her head, still finding it hard to imagine that she was actually carrying Floyd's baby in her womb. Because of her previous miscarriages, Lydia had feared she would be unable to have a baby of her own. Finding herself pregnant was somewhat like having the last laugh.

She continued reading, seeing that Robinson would await her final decision before proceeding. Perhaps it was time to give the entire matter another look. She had the money her father had left her in trust. She also had his estate and investments. And then there was the business her father and Floyd had built together. The casket business was producing an incredible profit, as Lydia could see by the statements issued from Robinson's office. Should she take that potential inheritance from her son or daughter?

Frowning, Lydia considered her options. To continue ties with the business would mean having to deal with Marston and Mitchell in some capacity. Or would it? She drew a deep breath and glanced out at the activity going on around her. What if she completely removed Marston and Mitchell from the business? Robinson was telling her that at this point everything belonged to her. What if she simply had Robinson dismiss them from any business dealings with the manufacturing company?

That would make them hate her more than they already did, but what of it? She honestly didn't care about their opinion. What she cared about was offering a fair and just life for her child.

"You seem deep in thought. I hope the news isn't bad," Zerelda said as she joined Lydia. She carried a basket that was now heaped with goods from the bakery and held them up like some kind of prize bestowed upon her. "We will certainly eat well for lunch. We have fresh bread and some wonderful pastries."

Lydia nodded and tucked the letter back into the envelope. She said nothing but picked up the pace to follow Zerelda. Clouds were moving in, and in all likelihood it would be raining soon. Sitka often received more rain in a few days than Lydia had seen Kansas City welcome in weeks.

"So is the letter good news or bad? I presume it's from your lawyer, since you said no one else knows of your being here."

"It is from Mr. Robinson. He says the courts have ruled in my favor."

"That's wonderful news," Zerelda said, smiling. "You surely have nothing to fear anymore."

"I wouldn't say that. Mr. Robinson also

says that Marston and Mitchell have appealed the decision. He wants to know how I want to handle things, as he hasn't yet moved on the distribution of properties that I left for him to see to."

"But why? Didn't you tell him exactly what you wanted to do?" Zerelda shook her head. "Won't the delay just cause further animosity between you and your dead husband's children?"

Lydia blurted out the news she'd been longing to share with Zerelda. "I'm going to have a baby."

"Well, I must admit I had wondered. I thought maybe you were already going through the change, since you hadn't had your monthly cycles since coming here. And while I've seen it happen before, you're much too young."

"It honestly didn't dawn on me until of late. I realized I'd missed my cycles for some time. I was almost too scared to believe it might be true."

Zerelda stopped and looked at her niece. "Then you are happy about this child?"

Lydia drew a deep breath. "I am." She turned to meet her aunt's intense brown eyes. "I've always wanted a child of my own. As you know, it's not my first time to carry a baby."

"Are you feeling movement?"

Lydia nodded and grinned. "Like butterfly wings fluttering inside me."

Zerelda shook her head in wonder. "I suppose that is something I shall never know, except through you. Are you feeling well?"

"I am. Now that I've recovered from my trip here, I honestly can say I've never felt better. I believe Sitka agrees with me."

"Good. Then this is a blessing. Children are a gift from God, you know. The Bible says so, and I believe it to be true."

Lydia didn't want the moment spoiled with reminders of God. She shrugged. "Well, I'm thinking there is much to be done before the babe arrives."

"And when will that be?"

"I can't be sure, but I think sometime around Christmas."

Zerelda started walking again and Lydia could see that her aunt was thinking over the logistics of the baby's arrival. No doubt Zerelda was focused on the medical aspects. There was a military hospital in Sitka with medical doctors, but given that Zerelda was a nurse, Lydia had figured to have her assist with the delivery.

"We have time to make things quite nice," Zerelda finally said. "We might want to consider adding on to the cabin, however.

With Mr. Saberhagen selling the property before he leaves for Germany, we might have to move altogether."

"Would you ladies care for a ride home?"

Lydia looked over her shoulder to find Kjell reining back on his black draft horses. He grinned down at them. "It would be a tight fit, but I think we can squeeze three on the bench."

"That would be just fine," Zerelda said, not giving Lydia a chance to comment one way or another. She handed up her basket to Kjell, then climbed into the wagon as effortlessly as a younger woman. Lydia so admired her aunt. Many women of her age were already old — worn from the duties of life. But not Zerelda.

Kjell reached down to Lydia as she carefully positioned her foot for the climb. She allowed him to take hold of her and nearly gasped as he hoisted her as effortlessly as a sack of flour. He unhanded her and took his seat between her and Zerelda.

"I'd say I'm getting the better end of this deal," he said, snapping the reins lightly. The horses stepped into action, and the wagon lurched forward. "I get to ride with a beautiful lady on each side. Not many men around here can boast that."

"Just for that," Zerelda said with a grin, "I

138

think I'll invite you to lunch with us. Would that be acceptable to you, Liddie?"

Lydia nodded. "I believe the ride home alone deserves some reward." The fact of the matter was, she enjoyed Kjell's company. He was gradually putting her at ease with his calming charm and sensitive understanding. Zerelda had been right when it came to him. Kjell Lindquist was unlike any other man Lydia had ever known.

"I'm sure you've heard by now that Dr. and Mrs. Ensign are planning to throw another ball," Kjell declared. "When they found out Lydia had missed the first one because of her illness after arriving, they were adamant that they should have another to welcome her to Sitka."

"I hadn't heard," Zerelda replied, looking past Kjell to Lydia.

"Neither had I."

"Good, since I am the first to share such happenings, I will expect you both to attend with me."

Zerelda laughed. "I'm much too old for a ball, and Lydia is —" She fell silent as Lydia's eyes widened.

Kjell didn't seem to even notice. "Nonsense, Zee. You're one of the only eligible women available. You have to come. The date is set for two weeks from today."

A light rain began to fall as they approached the turn for the Saberhagen property. "Looks like your timing is perfect," Zerelda said as Kjell hurried the horses to the cabin. "Come along inside and we can further discuss this party."

Zerelda hopped down from the wagon and reached back up for her basket. "You two get a move on before the rain comes down in earnest."

Kjell moved from the seat, leaving Lydia feeling strangely alone for the moment. She had liked the warmth of his body next to hers. Much more than she wanted to admit.

Lydia moved to the edge of the wagon and started to step down when Kjell surprised her and took hold of her waist and lowered her to the ground. "I see Zee's food has put a bit of flesh on your bones," he commented as they sought the shelter of the porch.

Lydia stiffened. "Are you calling me fleshy?"

He laughed. "You came here skin and bones. You needed a little thickening up, and I'm glad to see you're doing so much better."

She felt her face grow hot. If only he knew the real reason for her extra weight. Lydia wondered what Kjell would say if she told him of the baby. She looked at him a moment longer, then smiled. "Aunt Zerelda is a good cook. I must say, she's teaching me a great deal."

"That doesn't surprise me." Kjell ushered her through the open door. "Hmm, smells like stew."

Zerelda nodded. "I put it on when we walked to town this morning. I figured it would be just about ready when we returned." She pulled on an apron and motioned to Lydia. "Would you set the table? Kjell, how about bringing in some wood?"

"You betcha, Zee." He bounded back out the door before Lydia had a chance to even reply.

"Kjell said I'm getting fat," Lydia commented as she went to the cupboard for the bowls.

"He what?" Zerelda sounded shocked, and Lydia couldn't help but laugh.

"He said it in a nice way. Said it was good to see me getting some flesh on my bones."

"Did you mention the baby?"

Lydia cradled the bowls and shook her head. "I wasn't sure what to say. I'm still not. I mean, I realize everyone will know soon; I can hardly expect to keep it hidden for much longer."

"Well, you are a widow — there's no shame in expecting your husband's child."

141

Zerelda's matter-of-fact statement was followed with a softening in her tone. "If you're worried about what people will think, you needn't. You've done nothing wrong."

"I know, but I can't help but wonder how this will change my life."

Zerelda brought the stew to the table. "That remains to be seen. It will change . . . but it would have anyway."

Lydia heard Kjell's boot steps on the porch just outside the door. "Please don't say anything. I'm not ready to talk about it with . . . him."

"Here you go, Zee. And you were right. It's really coming down now." Kjell made his way to the fireplace with an armload of wood. "You want more than this? I have a feeling the night's going to turn chilly."

"This will be fine. I can get more if we need it. Now come on and eat." Zerelda returned to the table with a loaf of bread and a crock of butter.

Kjell and Lydia took their places at the table and waited for Zerelda to do likewise before Kjell offered a blessing. Lydia was uncomfortable with the prayer. She didn't bother to bow her head, but instead looked directly at Kjell as he spoke of his gratitude for the hands that had prepared the meal and for the food itself. He talked as casually to God as he did to her or Zerelda. When he concluded the prayer with *amen,* Lydia looked away and cleared her throat. She quickly busied herself by cutting the bread while Zerelda ladled soup into the bowls.

"So what's the news, Kjell?"

He grinned and took the bowl Zerelda offered. "Well, there's going to be a census taken in October. Seems the government wants to know exactly how many folks are still here."

Zerelda leaned over and placed a bowl in front of Lydia. "And what will they do with that count?"

"Hard to say. Usually they use a census for the purpose of voting and such, but we don't have any voting rights up here. We're not even a territory yet. I suppose they might also want to judge whether they have enough military in place to keep the law. Maybe consider various taxes to pay for our keep."

Lydia quietly ate while her aunt and Kjell further discussed the census. She thought of her move to Sitka and how she would be counted among the citizens there. Her unborn child would not yet be numbered.

She thought again of Mr. Robinson's letter. Should she reply and tell him to hold off on doing anything more until after the birth of the baby? Marston had once commented that Gray money should be for Gray heirs, and now she carried just such a child.

There was a part of her that wanted nothing related to the Grays, however. What if she allowed Robinson to simply give it all back? She could walk away from the entire matter and never give those people another thought. Maybe that was the answer. Maybe real peace could be found in such an action.

"So what do you think, Lydia?"

She startled and looked up, realizing she hadn't heard a word of the conversation between Kjell and her aunt. "About . . . what?"

Kjell chuckled and gave her a wink. "Zee was just suggesting we might be able to convince you to give us a little concert one of these nights. Maybe have a few other folks in to enjoy the music, as well."

Lydia tried to imagine being the focus of the evening. "I . . . well . . . I don't know that I would be comfortable. I mean . . . my music has always been for my . . . for my . . ." She fell silent. How could she explain to them that she had sought a lifetime of solace and companionship in an object of wood and strings?

"I'm sure that, like my guitar playing, it's

always been a rather private thing, ja?" Kjell asked.

She met his eyes and nodded. She found understanding there along with a gentleness that she could not begin to comprehend. This man had a way about him — a way of seeing through her pain and suffering. It frightened and intrigued her.

CHAPTER 10

September 1870

Evie Gray Gadston sat next to her sister as they awaited the arrival of Dwight Robinson. Lydia's lawyer had called the meeting, much to Marston and Mitchell's displeasure. Evie had already heard from her bellowing brothers that things were not going in their favor, and she couldn't help but wonder what the future held.

Shifting uncomfortably in her new walking suit, Evie tried not to draw any attention to herself. It was best, she had learned over the years, to simply fade into the background if at all possible. She pretended to pick lint from her upper skirt of mousseline de laine. The patterns of gray and black against the underskirt of dark plum made the outfit look rich and sophisticated. Even Jeannette had commented on the fashion more than once — a sure sign that the style had met her approval.

"Why does he keep us waiting?" Jeannette whined. "The chill in here is unbearable. Why didn't his clerk offer us some refreshment?"

"Oh, do be quiet, Jeannette," Mitchell said, glaring her way. "I don't even know why it was necessary to have you two here. Things would have gone much better had you simply stayed home."

"I have an interest in the outcome as well as you — perhaps even more so. My husband stands to lose a great deal if this isn't resolved soon and in our favor."

Evie heard the door open and turned to see Dwight Robinson enter. She silently issued a word of thanksgiving; she was sorely tired of her family's company.

"I am sorry to have kept you waiting. I had a last-minute message from the court and thought it important to bring the information with me." He went to stand behind his desk. "If you'll be seated, I will share this information with you."

Evie could see that her brothers were less than interested in doing as instructed but nevertheless took their seats. Marston seemed particularly agitated by the comment about new information. He clenched his jaw and narrowed his eyes in anticipation of what the man would say.

"As you know," Robinson began, "the courts have rejected your appeal. The will is to be processed as it stands."

"Our lawyer has already told us this," Mitchell said. "He is, however, exploring other possibilities."

"I have spoken to Mr. Sterling. In fact, he will join us shortly. However, I wanted to see you first. I believe it will be in your best interest to hear me out."

"Pray continue," Marston replied, his irritation evident.

"Mr. Sterling agrees with me that your options are basically in the hands of Mrs. Gray."

Mitchell pounded his fist against the arm of his chair. "That's outrageous! We won't stand for this."

"It's robbery. Our inheritance is being stolen from us," Jeannette declared. She looked to her sister for some sort of support, but Evie remained silent.

"If you will allow me to continue," Robinson said, pulling on his glasses, "I have more to share with you."

The room fell silent and all gazes turned to the lawyer. Evie watched as he carefully unfolded a single sheet of paper. "I have a letter here from Mrs. Gray."

"Where is she, by the way?" Mitchell

questioned. "Shouldn't she be in atten-dance?"

"Mrs. Gray is not needed here, as I am to act on her behalf. I thought we had estab-lished that before." He peered down his nose over the rim of his glasses, awaiting further comment.

"It seems that if this business is to be resolved today, as you suggested in your missive last week, then it would behoove her to be here," Mitchell said.

"Nevertheless, she is not to join us. Should I continue?"

"Of course, you fool." Marston was clearly as angry as Mitchell, but Evie knew he would hold his tongue until he found a bet-ter angle of attack. He was like that — crafty and capable when it came to manipulating anything for his own pleasure or benefit.

"I received this letter a couple of weeks ago."

Mitchell looked indignant. "And you're only now sharing it with us? Why the delay?"

"There seemed no reason to rush the mat-ter, and there were other issues that needed to be dealt with. As you know, Mrs. Gray had already agreed to let you take posses-sion of the house and the belongings there within. Of course, we were forced to delay until the court decisions were handed down, but now that this has been established, I believe you will agree that it is time to see this case through to conclusion."

Marston crossed his arms. "Very well. Continue."

Robinson focused once again on the paper. "Mrs. Gray has decided to settle most generously with you."

This comment did not surprise Evie. Lydia had never been a vindictive person. She had often made some effort on behalf of Evie or Jeannette, even knowing her actions would not bode well for her own comfort.

"The property and belongings are yours to share equally amongst you. The stocks and bonds held by your father prior to his marriage to Lydia Rockford are also to be returned to you to be shared."

"And what of the businesses?" Mitchell questioned.

"The Gray furniture business and that of the Rockfords were merged to create the Rockford and Gray's Casket Company. Then there are the smaller business concerns of your father, such as the freighting company and the two mortuaries." Robinson drew a deep breath and paused to consult his paper once again.

Mitchell's impatience got the better of

him. "Get on with it, man."

"Mrs. Gray has agreed to return the freight business interests and mortuaries to the Gray family. Rockford and Gray's Casket Company, however, will remain in her control, via operational managers that she will appoint through my counsel."

"Never!" Mitchell jumped to his feet. "I will not stand for this."

Robinson looked at him for a moment, then glanced back to the paper. "Where did I leave off?"

"Did you not hear me? This is unacceptable," Mitchell declared. He leaned forward on Robinson's desk and was nearly nose to nose with the man. "Rockford and Gray's Casket Company will not be given over to that woman."

"I'm afraid you have no further say in the settlement," Robinson declared. He took off his glasses and relaxed back against his chair. For a moment, he studied Marston and Mitchell.

Evie couldn't help but wonder what the lawyer was thinking. It was obvious Lydia had been most generous with her family. There would be thousands of dollars to share between the children of Floyd Gray, but still it was not enough for her greedy siblings.

"I believe now would be a good time to bring in my associate," Robinson said, getting to his feet. He walked to the closed office door and opened it. "Mr. Sterling, would you join us, please?"

Nash Sterling entered the office, looking for all the world like a man afraid of his own shadow. Evie felt sorry for him as her brothers turned accusing eyes on the man. Sterling nodded in greeting but said nothing. He took a seat as far from the others as possible and seemed to cower there as Mr. Robinson rejoined them.

"Mr. Sterling and I have been in communication regarding the settlement. He has supervised the drawing up of the paperwork and is here to advise you at this time for the signing of said papers."

"I won't sign anything," Mitchell declared. He stalked back to his seat and plopped down like a spoiled child who hadn't been allowed pudding with his supper.

"Gentlemen, ladies, I have to say that Mrs. Gray has been quite considerate of your family. Should you reject this offer, I will advise her to pull any further offers from the table."

Marston uncrossed his arms. "And if we agree to this, how soon will the transfer take place? She told us last April that she was yielding the house and its possession, yet you put a stop to that before we could do anything about it."

"The transfer would take place immediately. That is why Mr. Sterling is here. I felt it would behoove all of us to settle this amicably and quickly."

Marston nodded. "Very well."

Mitchell looked to Marston in stunned silence.

"Does this mean there will be funds immediately?" Jeannette questioned.

"If a sale of the house and goods takes place immediately, there will be," Robinson replied. "Your brothers will, no doubt, advise you in such matters."

"We will," Marston said. "Now let me consider the papers you've drawn up."

"I can't believe you agreed to any of that," Mitchell said. He sat nursing a brandy in Marston's office.

Marston shook his head. "There was nothing else to be done. Do you suppose I've sat idle while Sterling handled all of this? I had other lawyers researching and exploring our possibilities. The fact of the matter is that unless we can somehow force Lydia to do otherwise, we are at her mercy."

It was ironic, really. For years, she had

153

been forced to yield to their desires, and now she held the cards. He stirred sugar into his coffee and pondered.

The key to the entire situation was to locate Lydia. Robinson was still unwilling to explain where she had gone. He obviously didn't want the Grays to have any contact with her. He was smart in that decision, and Marston had to give the man credit. Robinson no doubt knew that Marston and his brother would do whatever it took to regain their father's entire fortune.

"Will you not even discuss the matter?" Mitchell asked.

Marston looked at him, then took a long sip of the steaming coffee. The liquid burned slightly, but Marston almost welcomed the pain. "I'm considering what is to be done. You would do well to stop blabbering and do likewise."

"But you simply agreed to the offering. You didn't fight back in any way." The accusation in Mitchell's tone was clear.

"And what would you have had me do? Reject the offer and delay our benefits for that much longer? To me, it seemed reasonable to take what we could get at this point and go after the rest at another time. Lydia hasn't heard the last of us, to be sure, but now we are free to sell the house and other properties. We can cash in the stocks, or at least reinvest them in our own names, and get Jeannette and her husband off of our backs."

"And then what?"

Marston smiled. "Then we continue with our plans. I'm still not so sure that our original idea to get Lydia to marry me is such a bad one. She will need persuading, of course, but there are ways to entice her."

"That will be much harder now that she's financially independent. She doesn't need our kindness to see her through."

Marston put the cup down and nodded. "It will be more difficult, but that doesn't mean it will prove to be impossible. What we need is a solid plan."

"You both look exceptionally beautiful," Kjell said as Lydia and Zerelda entered the main room of the cabin.

"I certainly didn't come to Sitka with a thought to attending a ball every month, but Zerelda assured me that this simple gown would once again suffice," Lydia told him. "Even though I wore it last month at Mrs. Ensign's ball."

"You look perfect," Kjell replied. "That color suits you."

Lydia touched the bodice of the burnished

copper–colored dress. "I thought here in the wilds of the north country, such fashion worries would be happily absent."

"You sound as though you don't enjoy such things. Most women like to show off their pretty dresses at a good party."

Zerelda laughed and pulled on a shawl. "Lydia has become quite the wallflower, I'm afraid. She prefers quiet nights at the fire's side with a book and a cup of warm milk."

"Sounds perfect to me," Kjell admitted. The only thing he would have changed about the scene was to insert himself alongside Lydia during one of those private evenings at home. He couldn't deny his attraction to her. He longed to know her better.

Lydia said very little on the way to the residence, and once there, Kjell found her quickly whisked away to dance with a bevy of officers from the fort. Zerelda, too, became an instant focus of attention, and before he realized it, Kjell was standing alone.

He watched Lydia waltzing with first one man and then another. She smiled and made conversation with each person, but Kjell could sense she was not truly enjoying herself. He still wondered about her past and the pain that had been inflicted upon her. Lydia never talked about anything to do with her dead husband, but Zerelda had indicated the situation had been horrific.

The music stopped, and Lydia and her partner stopped directly to his right. Kjell had thought to claim Lydia for the next dance, but to his surprise, she approached him first.

"I hope you won't think me forward, but I wonder if you might escort me outside for a bit of air." She reached for her wrap hanging by the front door.

He smiled. "I'd be happy to." Extending his arm, he felt her place her small hand in the crook of his elbow.

"You aren't leaving us, are you?" one of the officers questioned when Kjell led Lydia to the door.

"We'll return, never fear. The lady would like a bit of air." Kjell's explanation seemed to assuage the man's concerns. He stepped aside and let them pass into the coolness of the night.

Lydia shivered as they stepped onto the porch, and Kjell realized she was still holding her woolen shawl. "Here, let me help you." He took hold of the wrap and secured it around her shoulders. In doing so, he allowed his arm to linger around her for just a moment.

"Will it snow soon?" she asked.

"In the mountains, perhaps, but not down here — not yet. We get more rain than snow. It actually stays pretty mild throughout the winter. Some years are worse than others, of course, but for the most part, we make out all right."

Lydia nodded. "I remember Zerelda saying something to that effect. I suppose I had forgotten. It snowed back in Kansas City most winters. It wasn't always deep or long lasting, but we generally had some."

"Is it a large city?" Kjell asked, hoping she would feel free to discuss the past with him.

Lydia considered his question for a moment. "It is. Much too large to suit me after living here. I thought I might miss it, but I don't. Here I find myself feeling a . . . a sense of coming home." She gave a small laugh. "There's a peace here that I've never experienced. Sitka somehow fills an emptiness inside me. I suppose that sounds silly."

"Not at all," Kjell assured her.

"So now I've answered a question. Will you do the same for me?" she asked.

"Certainly." He grinned. "What would you like to know?"

"Kjell. What does that mean — what kind of name is it?"

"It's Swedish. It's from the word *kettil,*

meaning caldron or kettle. Why do you ask?"

"I suppose because it's so foreign to me." Lydia gave him a smile. "But now I have answered two of your questions, so you must take another of mine."

He leaned back against the house and shrugged. "You can ask me anything. I don't mind at all. My life is pretty much what you see."

Lydia was silent for several minutes, and Kjell thought she'd changed her mind. When she did speak, he was surprised by her request.

"Tell me about your wife."

"Raisa? Well, she was from a Russian family who had moved here from the old country to run a flour mill. I met her first when she was fourteen. I was twenty at the time and didn't give her much attention. A couple of years passed, however, and I started to notice her plenty." He laughed. "She was like no other girl I'd ever known. She had a natural happiness that seemed to make life easier for everyone around her. That's not to say she didn't have moments of sadness. When her parents returned to Russia, she was devastated. I didn't want to leave Sitka. My mother had just died, and I wasn't yet ready to say good-bye to all I'd known here. I suppose now, looking back, it

159

was selfish of me. Probably the most selfish decision I've ever made."

"If that's the worst choice you've made, you've fared better than most," Lydia said, her voice barely audible. "I've known selfish men, and that hardly measures up."

"It hurt her just the same. She knew her place was with me, but she longed for her family. They were all very close. By the time I was ready to consider the possibility of leaving, Raisa took ill. The doctors never knew exactly what the problem was, but she wasted away before my very eyes. Within a month of getting sick, she was gone."

"I'm sorry. It sounds as if you loved her very much."

Kjell nodded. "I did. She was a good woman with a sweet spirit. Much like you."

Lydia turned away from him. "My spirit is not so sweet. I have a great deal of bitterness inside me. I'm not enough of a liar to deny that."

Kjell came to where she stood and turned her to face him. "You've been through a great deal. I don't know much about it, but I can see it in your eyes. If you ever want to talk to me about it, I'll listen."

The soft glow from the house windows shed just enough light on Lydia's face for him to see her surprise. "I don't suppose

I'm used to a man even caring about such things, much less offering to listen to me."

He reached up to gently touch her face. He felt a moment of victory when she didn't pull away. "I care."

Lydia held his gaze for a moment and said nothing. It almost seemed that she was assessing him, to somehow prove to herself he spoke the truth. She drew her lower lip in and bit down on it before backing away.

"I suppose we should get back," she said. "Zerelda will worry about me."

Kjell nodded. He wished she would remain with him on the porch but didn't try to change her mind. Instead, he did the only thing he could to keep her in his company a bit longer. "Will you give me the next dance?"

She paused at the door and nodded. "I will."

CHAPTER 11

Gerald Lytle looked at the substantial amount of cash offered him and drew a deep breath. Marston Gray knew the man needed the money. Needed it desperately to offset gambling debts he'd incurred just the week before.

"You don't plan any harm to come to her?" Lytle asked, clearly considering what Marston wanted.

"Of course not, you fool. I'm a gentleman, not a killer. I merely wish to thank her for her generosity to my family and apologize for the way she was treated. I tried approaching Robinson, but he seems to think we are all associated with our father's actions against Lydia."

"She was terribly mistreated," Gerald agreed.

Marston said nothing but nodded as if in agreement. "Rest assured, I only desire to communicate my appreciation and to know that she is truly all right. She might not feel that correspondence from me is necessary, but for my own peace of mind, it is."

"Perhaps you could pen the letter and I could mail it for you," Gerald suggested. "That way you could accomplish your desires, and I wouldn't betray any confidences."

Marston shook his head. "No. I think it would be best to do it just as I've described. I want access to the files — to her correspondence with Mr. Robinson. I want assurance that she's not being cheated in any way."

The man frowned. "But Mr. Robinson's reputation is irrefutable."

"Men are still fallible — even Mr. Robinson." Marston held the money higher. "So, do we have a deal or not?" He started to put the money back in his pocket, but Lytle reached out to stop him.

"Very well. I'll leave the back door to the office open tonight. If you want to review the correspondence, I'll see to it that it's placed in the center of Mr. Robinson's desk. Write down the information if you need to, but remove nothing." He took the money and stared at it for a moment. "Nothing is to be otherwise disturbed."

Marston nodded and drew out a cigar.

"I'll make sure my man understands."

"What do you mean? Won't you be the one to review the materials?"

A thin smile edged Marston's lips. He clipped the end of the cigar and shook his head. "That would hardly be prudent. Should I be found by some overly observant policeman, it would be hard to explain my presence. However, if my man is caught, he can plead guilty to petty thievery, and no one will be the wiser."

Lytle swallowed hard. "I see."

The man slipped away as Marston lit his cigar. He was satisfied with the turn of events; now he would simply have to get the right man for the job.

Sitka's size made it impossible to keep secrets. Kjell had learned this early on, and today proved to be no exception. Twice now he'd heard talk that the Sidorov brothers had never left the area. He wondered if this could possibly be true, but he felt he had no time to devote to investigation. He had settled his differences with his customers over the summer, and everything had returned to normal. If the Sidorovs were still in the area, Kjell wasn't exactly sure what he would do. To charge them now seemed futile, and since they were no longer a threat to him or his business, Kjell couldn't see holding a grudge.

"What chores are you seeing to on this dismal day?"

Kjell looked up to find Zerelda Rockford standing directly in front of him. He hadn't been watching where he was going and nearly walked right into her. "Sorry, Zee. I didn't mean to be so caught up in my own thoughts. How are you?"

"I'm doing well. And you?"

This question caused Kjell to think of yet another rumor he'd heard. He wanted to know the truth of the matter and had never known Zee to be uncomfortable with his questions. "I wonder if we can talk?" he asked.

"I have time. Where would you like to go?" Zerelda shifted a basket of goods from one arm to the other. "I wouldn't mind a cup of coffee."

"Sounds good. I'll buy." Kjell took her basket and pointed the way to the Russian Teahouse.

The small yellow house held a charm all its own. Several tables were set up in what must have once been the main living area. Kjell knew the Putshukoff family who owned the place. They kept the business on the ground floor and lived upstairs.

Mrs. Putshukoff greeted them with her usual enthusiasm. "Kjell, Zerelda, it's good to see you. Come and sit. I have fresh *rasstegai.*"

Kjell grinned and gave his stomach a rub. "With minced meat?"

"Of course," the stocky woman replied with a beaming smile.

Once they were seated and served some of the minced pies to go along with their coffee, Kjell cleared his throat. "I hope this doesn't seem out of place, Zee. I don't want to overstep my bounds, but . . . well, you know me."

She nodded. "I do, and I've never known you to walk around a subject as wide as you're taking this one."

He chuckled. "Well, it has to do with Lydia."

Her eyes fairly danced with amusement. "Now, why am I not surprised? What is it you want to know?"

"I've heard rumors," he began. "Being I don't much care for such things, I figured to speak directly with someone who would know the truth."

Zerelda sipped her coffee, making no attempt to comment or acknowledge his statement. Kjell shifted nervously and toyed with the handle of his mug. "Fact of the matter is, I care about you two and feel that I need to keep an eye out for you."

This made Zerelda smile. "Goodness, man, just get to the heart of your question."

Kjell nodded and leaned forward. "I've heard talk that Lydia is . . . that she's . . ." He couldn't bring himself to say it.

"With child?" Zee whispered.

He sighed and felt a weight taken off his shoulders. "Yes."

"It's true. Lydia is carrying her dead husband's child. Should be born around Christmas."

Kjell frowned. "Is she . . . well?"

"Certainly. I've seen to that. She's as healthy as you or me. She keeps to herself now more than ever, but it doesn't stop the bevy of fellows who come to call. I've chased off more potential suitors for the both of us than I can count."

"Those men ought to respect your situation and leave you be."

Zee laughed and lifted the pastry to her lips. "Maybe you ought to be stakin' your claim before she's swept up by someone else."

He felt his face grow hot at this comment, and Kjell wondered how to respond. He did want to "stake his claim," as Zee put it, but how to go about it was an entirely different matter.

"Tell me about her life, Zee."

"I should let her be the one to do the telling," the woman said, looking past Kjell out the window.

He glanced over his shoulder but could see nothing that should draw her attention. It had started raining again, so Lincoln Street was fairly deserted.

"I suppose it can't hurt to give you a bit of insight," Zee finally said, leaning back in her chair. "Lydia had an arranged marriage to a cruel man at a very young age. I believe the agreement was struck when she was just fifteen. I thought it an awful arrangement with him being so much older than Lydia, but my brother thought my objections nonsense. He pointed out that many women were married before they reached twenty, and often to older widowers. Still, I thought it most objectionable.

"Lydia was married when she was sixteen and after that, knew nothing but heartache and misery. Her husband was only interested in money and power, as I heard it from Lydia. He had four children — the two boys were grown by the time Lydia married into the family — and they treated her just as poorly as he did. There were two

168

younger girls: a twelve-year-old and the youngest, who was only four at the time."

"No wonder Lydia is so bitter," Kjell said thoughtfully.

"You don't know the half of it, and I won't be the one to tell it. Suffice it to say, most of Lydia's adult life has been a living hell. She holds God responsible, although she says she wants nothing to do with Him." Zee shook her head sadly. "The truth is, she'd love to have a real understanding of Him — to feel close and safe, but she's been disappointed so many times in the past, she isn't willing to risk it."

"So she probably wouldn't want to risk marriage again, either?" He looked to Zee to see if she was shocked by the comment. She wasn't.

"I think the right man could show her that things could be different," Zee answered. "I'd like to believe you are that man, Kjell. You have infinite patience, and you're kind. Your gentle nature and generosity of spirit are exactly what she needs. However, you belong to the Lord, and Lydia does not. You can't be unequally yoked with her. She needs to overcome her separation from God before she can be with you. Otherwise, it will only prove misery for both of you."

Kjell hadn't thought about spiritual matters where Lydia was concerned. "But she's going to have a baby. She needs a husband. The baby needs a father."

"Those things would be nice," Zee replied, "but unless she learns to leave the past behind her, Lydia could do you and herself more harm than good. Only God can help her get over her past."

He considered this for a moment. "But maybe I could help her to see the truth. Maybe that's why I've come to care about her. The Lord might well have put me in this frame of mind for just such a purpose."

Zee reached out and patted his hand. "Kjell, anything is possible. I won't be one to limit the Lord. Just be careful. I can see now you've already lost your heart — don't lose your values, as well."

"She's pregnant!" Mitchell declared in disbelief. "A woman of such loose moral character has no right to —"

"Oh, do be quiet," Marston said, shaking his head. "Don't you see that the child is due in December? That means she's carrying our father's baby."

Mitchell sat down rather hard, as if the shock were too much to bear. "Why didn't she say something before she left?"

"Most likely she didn't know or didn't

want us to know." Marston studied the notes his man had furnished. "She wanted to depart for Sitka to be with her aunt and probably paid it no mind." Of course, there was the possibility she *had* known that she was pregnant — and wanted to leave before anyone else found out. But why? What else was she hiding?

"Will you go to Alaska and bring her back?"

"Yes." Marston's attitude was matter-of-fact.

Mitchell sat up in the chair. "She won't want to return, will she?"

"Probably not," Marston said, taking a seat behind his desk. "But she will come."

"I suppose this also explains her desire to keep the business."

"Why do you say that?"

Mitchell shrugged. "She wants it for the child. After all, he or she will be a Gray heir."

"I hadn't considered that, but you may be right." Marston leaned back in the chair and pressed his fingertips together. "But that can also work to our advantage. We can point out to her that this child will need family to support him or her with education and training."

"Lydia will never want any of us around

her child," Mitchell said, shaking his head. "She hates us all. She'll refuse to come."

"Then maybe she needn't come at all."

Mitchell's eyes narrowed. "What are you saying?"

"Just this: Perhaps I will go to Alaska and approach the subject from a concerned stepson's perspective. I will gently woo her with compliments and appreciation for her generosity, proclaim myself a changed man because of her sweetness, then propose that she is in desperate need of my help. After all, a widowed woman alone in the world, struggling to raise a child, will face many difficulties."

"But this is a rich widow."

"It doesn't matter, Mitchell. Good grief, man, you're married — have you not yet come to understand the emotional needs of your wife? Money means little to a woman when she is frightened and insecure about her future. Now that a child is involved, I would imagine her fears are even greater."

"But what if she doesn't even want the child? We haven't yet considered that possibility."

Marston thought about it for a moment. Everything he knew about Lydia Rockford Gray told him that would not be the case. If anything, she would keep the baby as a trophy, of sorts. A mark of her victory over her abusive husband and the family that had done her such harm.

"If she doesn't want the child, I will offer to take it and raise it as my own. Honestly, Mitchell, there are more possibilities than obstacles here. If she doesn't want to co-operate, she can die, for all I care."

Mitchell's mouth dropped open, but no words were uttered. Marston couldn't help but laugh. "Don't look so shocked. We've talked about her demise before this. The notes here say she has already made provision for the child. She's asked Robinson to make up a will that leaves all of her worldly goods to the child, in care of his or her great aunt, Zerelda Rockford. She intends to keep the child, but even if she didn't, it's not the child or Lydia I care about. It's the business and the money she's robbed from us. That's all that truly matters at this point, and resolution of this problem is all I shall concern myself with."

Lydia accompanied her aunt to the Indian settlement to take some of the extra supplies she'd brought to Alaska. Zerelda assured her they wouldn't need so much, and there was great poverty amongst the Indians.

"They're proud, but exceedingly poor. We will trade with them, and that way they can support themselves," Zerelda told Lydia. "I think it's important that folks feel useful and know the value of working. We do no good to any man by giving him everything."

"I agree. I saw the damage done by that with many of our wealthy neighbors. Their sons had no reason to worry about where their money would come from, and therefore they did nothing to better themselves."

Zerelda nodded sadly. "We cannot continue to provide for their needs, then fault them for lacking ambition to improve their situation."

They had borrowed a small one-horse cart from a friend, as well as a very gentle old gelding. The wagon, though rickety, was solid enough. The seat was barely adequate for one person, but neither Lydia nor Zerelda were all that big, so they squeezed in together just fine.

Riding along in silence for several minutes, Lydia couldn't help but think back on the things Kjell had told her on the night of the last dance. She couldn't help but wonder what her aunt might have to say on the topic. "Zerelda, do you ever question God?"

Zerelda chuckled. "I suppose I used to do it more than I do now. He never saw fit to consult me, so I started to figure He didn't owe me any answers."

"But doesn't He want us to understand?"

Her aunt looked at her. "Understand what?"

"Life. Death. The reason things happen as they do. If I could better understand why I had to go through all the pain and ugliness of my past, I might feel more inclined to trust God. If He would just give me that much."

"And you think knowing why my brother made the choice he did in giving you to Floyd Gray would honestly help you to trust God?"

Lydia knew it sounded silly, and in all truth, maybe she was just fooling herself. "I don't know. It just seems better when I understand *why* something is happening. When I was a little girl and my doll fell in the river, I was heartbroken and insisted my father go in after her. Mama explained that he couldn't do that because he couldn't swim and would die. That helped me to understand, and in knowing why a thing couldn't be done, I was better able to accept what had happened."

Zerelda nodded. "It sometimes helps to know the whys, but not always. If you knew why God had allowed you to marry a heartless man and miscarry the very babies you longed to mother, it wouldn't take away the past."

"No, but it might give that past meaning. Right now it feels as if it was all for nothing."

"But what of the child you carry?"

Lydia put her hand to her waist. "What do you mean?"

"You wouldn't have this baby if not for Floyd."

"If Floyd had lived, I most certainly wouldn't have this child. He would have beaten me like all the other times."

"So maybe God has a special purpose for this child and interceded on his behalf and yours."

She considered her aunt's words for a moment. "Then what of the others? Were they not also precious? Did they have no special purpose? Is God so uncaring that He saves one child and deserts another?"

Zerelda pulled back on the reins. "Child, I know you're hurting. I know you want to fill that empty space inside you with answers. But answers aren't what will make you feel better. Only God can do that. Only making it right with Him will fill that longing."

Lydia sat quietly pondering her questions

when they passed without trouble through the stockade gate. The Ranche was bustling with activity. The gate wouldn't be locked until six o'clock, hours away, so the people moved freely in and out of the settlement, and business carried on as usual. Lydia felt uncomfortable at the sight of the market-place, where deer carcasses, wild ducks, and drying halibut hung. The smell was pungent, and Lydia feared her nausea would return.

All along the road, native women sat by their wares, ready to do business. Zerelda stopped the wagon before one such woman whose chubby toddler sat at her side, happily chewing a piece of leather hide.

Zerelda got down and squatted beside the woman. Lydia watched as they talked for several minutes. The woman nodded enthusiastically and showed Zerelda several baskets. Her aunt motioned, and Lydia climbed down to join them.

"She has some lovely basket work. One of the larger ones would serve well for a baby bed. At least to begin with."

Lydia examined the workmanship and was notably impressed. The basket was as lovely as anything she'd ever seen.

"Daax'oon sitkum," the woman told Zerelda.

"It's a good buy. Figures roughly two dollars." Zerelda got up and went to the cart, where she took up a heavy wool blanket and several other items. She spoke again to the woman and spread out the items on the ground. The woman considered each article. After a while, she and Zerelda seemed to come to an agreement.

Zerelda turned to Lydia. "I've also arranged to have some fish for our supper."

The woman went to a stack of fresh fish. She chose two large ones and wrapped them in newspaper. When she returned, Zerelda took up the bundle and nodded. Lydia placed the basket in the wagon and waited while Zerelda concluded her business. This experience was followed with several additional trades with other women until finally all the goods in the wagon were exchanged.

As they prepared to turn the cart for home, one of the Tlingit women rushed out to greet them. She jabbered excitedly about something, but Lydia couldn't understand a single word. Zerelda stopped the cart.

"There's been a new birth. We're invited to come see the baby."

Lydia followed Zerelda inside the darkened house. They were led past several box-like partitions, used to divide the various family areas. Several families lived together in one long house, Zerelda told her. They were all of one clan.

Against one wall, Lydia could see that someone had adorned the wood with playing cards and handbills. The pieces seemed to hold a place of respect just as the fine oil painting of Charlotte Gray had back in Kansas City.

Zerelda and Lydia were ushered to the farthest side of the room and presented with a young woman, really no more than a girl, breastfeeding her infant. Lydia's aunt immediately squatted down and began to converse. The girl seemed quite happy to see Zerelda. Apparently they were friends.

Lydia couldn't help but wonder at the girl's age. She didn't look much older than thirteen or fourteen. She was so tiny and clearly very happy with her baby. The girl spoke rapidly and with such animation that Lydia couldn't help but smile. The entire atmosphere was like a party. Lydia felt her own baby kick, as if to join in the celebration.

Once Zerelda and Lydia were bid farewell and headed for home, Lydia couldn't help but request an explanation of the situation. "That girl seemed much too young to be a mother."

"They marry young here. When a girl

begins her monthly cycles, it becomes public knowledge. She is isolated for several months in a small building away from the main house. Chastity is highly valued here, so during her time of isolation, she will see no one but the older women and small children. She is taught that she is no longer a child but a woman ready for marriage. With everyone in the village knowing this, suitors will approach her parents to declare interest or the family will simply begin the finalization of contracts already agreed upon."

"How awful. And I thought to escape that kind of thing up here," Lydia said, remembering her own marriage contract.

"At least in their village, it isn't considered the oddity that it is in our world. Still, many of the girls die during childbirth. Their bodies struggle with the changes and the new responsibility of growing a life."

"She seemed happy. Do you think she'll be all right?"

Zerelda smiled. "She told me that the baby is her mother come back to life. The girl's mother died just before her marriage, and when she found herself pregnant almost immediately, the shaman told her that this was a sign of her mother's reincarnation."

"And she believed it?" Lydia asked,

amazed at such a thought.

"She did indeed. She is happy that this child has come to her, because it is the return of her mother. She believes her mother will help her now, and she will be strong and brave because of this."

"It seems such a hard life, especially for the women," Lydia said, shaking her head. It was difficult to imagine the little girl mothering a child.

"They manage," Zerelda replied. "They have for hundreds of years, and they will go on despite our presence. The family will help her, and she will be fine."

"I hope I shall manage half so well," Lydia murmured, putting her hand to her growing abdomen. The idea of giving birth frightened her more than she liked to admit.

CHAPTER 12

October 1870

It wasn't long before Lydia's condition, both physical and financial, was the talk of the town. Frankly, Lydia would have just as soon been unknown and left alone, but instead, she had become quite popular. People showed up at all hours of the day, especially would-be suitors. They came pleading their affection and desire for marriage. Some suggested the arrangement for convenience to both, while others were more creative. One man begged Lydia to marry him and let the baby be his, as he had suffered mumps as a young man and could not have a child of his own.

Kjell said such proposals were to be expected and Zerelda agreed. They lived in much too isolated a place for Lydia's presence and situation to go unnoticed. Women were a premium commodity in this part of the world; white women were even more scarce.

"It's hard to imagine they would want to marry me when they don't even know me. I'm a stranger to most of them."

"Yes, but you are a rich stranger," Zerelda mused. "And more important, you are the right gender — a woman."

"A woman great with child," Lydia said, looking at her expanded belly.

"But you won't be that way forever," Zerelda said, laughing. "Men have learned to overlook such things when the other benefits outweigh the concerns. Besides, you're quite pretty."

Lydia had never considered herself such. Floyd had often commented on how much more beautiful his first wife had been and Lydia had always lived in the sad shadow of Charlotte Gray. Charlotte had been beautiful in her youth, with blond hair and blue eyes. Her voluptuous figure gave her a womanly silhouette, whereas Lydia had always been tall and waiflike. Floyd had often complained that she was too skinny. Well, that certainly wasn't a problem now.

"Oh look," Zerelda said, gazing out the window. "Kjell has come to visit, and he's brought his guitar." She started toward the door. "It would be so wonderful to have the two of you play together."

"We shall see," Lydia said, not wanting to promise anything. "I'll put on a pot of coffee." She moved to the kitchen and checked the fire in the stove. Lately her emotions were rattled by his presence. Zerelda had convinced her that Kjell deserved to be accused or merited on his own actions rather than those of Floyd, but Lydia still found it difficult to put aside the mistrust she felt for any man.

"Are you hungry, Kjell?" Zerelda asked as she greeted him. "We could heat up some food."

Kjell shrugged out of his coat and shook his head. "I ate already, but thanks."

"I can't tell you how pleased I was to see that you'd brought your guitar. I told Lydia I would love to hear the two of you play together."

Kjell looked past Zerelda to where Lydia was watching him. He smiled. "That's up to Lydia. She's no doubt the better musician, and my poor attempts would be disruptive."

"You've played for us on many occasions," Lydia said, turning back to measure coffee into the pot. "You are quite accomplished, so don't pretend otherwise."

Laughing, Kjell picked up his guitar as Zerelda went to hang up his coat. He placed the guitar near the fireplace, then paused to warm his hands. "The air has a bite to it tonight."

"Well, it is October," Zerelda commented. "I was just telling Lydia that her extra wool blankets were going to come in handy this winter. I think it's going to be unusually cold."

"Could be. Say, I heard today that Mr. Saberhagen has arranged for the property to be sold."

Zerelda nodded. "It's true. He has decided against returning to Sitka. He's offered to let us stay here until the place is sold, however, so I'm happy about that. Given that winter is soon to be upon us, I don't anticipate much interest in the property until spring."

"I don't want to sound negative here," Kjell said, coming to join the women in the kitchen, "but it could be the army might want the property. Houses are at a premium, and there are two on this land, as well as storage buildings."

"Yes, but we're far enough away from town that it would be a chore to live out here."

"Oh, Zee, nothing is that far away from town. Not here." He gave her a grin and leaned back against the wall. "You should

185

also know that the census will take place on the twenty-fourth of this month. There will be three men assisting Lieutenant Lyle."

"Just three?" Zerelda asked. "Seems they would need more."

"Well, they don't plan to count the Tlingit at the Ranche."

"And why not?"

Lydia saw Kjell shake his head. "The government doesn't deem them necessary to count. They don't matter."

Remembering her time in the Ranche with Zerelda, Lydia couldn't help but speak up. "They are a burden to the government — at least that's how others see it. You have lived among these people for a long time, but as an outsider newly arrived, I can see perhaps what they feel."

Zerelda and Kjell looked at her oddly, and Lydia felt compelled to continue. "It is my belief that the officials consider them uneducated and incapable of being a benefit to the country or any part of society. They don't speak English well, they have few job skills that interest the whites, and they seem overly susceptible to disease and problems with alcohol."

"It's sad that an entire people could be judged so worthless. They have, after all, done just fine without our interference,"

Kjell replied.

Lydia thought he sounded annoyed with her and so she spoke again. "I do not believe that the attitude is a good one. It is not my heart. I agree with Zerelda that it is cruel to force them to be locked up like common criminals. I would much rather see them released to live free — wherever they saw fit to live."

"Unfortunately," Zerelda interrupted, "I believe that enough time has passed that we have crippled them. We have made them dependent on the white culture in some ways, while in others, we have taken away their customs and traditions."

"It's only going to get worse," Kjell said. "When the government encourages a larger population here in Alaska, the Tlingit will be pushed farther out. There will be new rules and regulations and maybe even a new location for them to live. It will all depend on whether this area is found to be valuable to the whites."

"Well," Zerelda sighed, "enough of this sadness. We can't change things tonight." She smiled. "Let's have some music, Kjell. While Lydia pours the coffee, why don't you show me what you can do with that guitar."

Kjell nodded and offered his arm rather

187

formally to Zerelda. She laughed and accepted his elbow, letting him escort her to the chairs by the fireplace. Kjell took up the instrument and tuned it before he began picking out a melodious strain. Lydia liked it when he played for them. The music comforted her, and she felt herself relax. She couldn't imagine Floyd or any of his sons spending time in such respite. Floyd had found music a waste of time and had threatened to take Lydia's violin on more occasions than she could count. Several times, he had made good on his threats, leaving her heartbroken and inconsolable.

She stiffened. *Things are different now,* she reminded herself. *Floyd can't hurt me anymore.* She touched her hand to where the baby grew. Her husband had caused the death of their other children, but not this one. Had God truly interceded, as Zerelda suggested? Could Lydia dare to believe that God cared about her and the baby? And if she did accept this, then what did that say about the past and the other children she had lost? She was so confused.

Glancing up, Lydia found Kjell watching her, even as he played. Unable to turn away from him, Lydia wondered what kind of husband Kjell would make.

He was definitely cut from a different

cloth. Lydia had never seen him lose his patience, and even when he shared about problems at the mill, he remained calm and considerate. Floyd would have ranted and raved about any difficulty. Many had been the time that he, Marston, and Mitchell had argued vehemently about what was to be done regarding a problem at the factory.

Kjell continued to watch her as if he knew exactly what she was thinking. Lydia looked away.

"So will you join us, Liddie?" Zerelda asked. "Maybe play along?"

Lydia felt the baby move as if to encourage her response. "I will try." She went to the violin case and opened it slowly. She very much enjoyed Kjell's abilities and hated to let go of the moment too soon. Taking the violin and bow in hand, she made her preparations, all the while waiting for him to conclude. When he did, she couldn't help but comment, "That was beautiful. I've never heard that tune before. What is it called?"

Kjell shrugged. "It's just something I made up. I haven't named it, but you can if you want."

She shook her head. "I wouldn't dream of it. You gave it life — you should name it."

"I'll think on it," he told her with a wink.

"Now what shall we play together?"

Lydia named a couple of possibilities and Kjell smiled. "Why don't you start in, and I'll follow as best I can."

She lifted the violin and drew the bow. Music filled the air of the small cabin. Lydia focused on the notes of a song she hadn't played in years. The gentle refrain swelled to a crescendo, then eased back again. Kjell joined in, gently filling in the background as he accompanied her. She hesitated a moment in her nervousness, then quickly recovered as Kjell continued. It wasn't long before Lydia completely lost herself in the moment. How wonderful it was to make music with someone. How incredible it was to feel that, for even a few moments of time, her soul had touched that of another human being.

When the final notes sounded, Zerelda clapped heartily. "I've never heard anything more beautiful. You two play . . . well, it's as if you've always played together. I am completely amazed."

"I have to say, I'm just as taken," Kjell said, looking at Lydia.

His gaze seemed to burn through her, and Lydia flushed but found she couldn't look away. And it was in that moment that Lydia knew she was losing her heart to Kjell. How strange it felt . . . almost like slipping on the ice. There was a sense of exhilaration at free falling, but in the back of her mind, Lydia knew the impact would hurt.

"I'm afraid I need to rest," Lydia declared, quickly putting the violin away.

"Are you all right?" Kjell asked, coming to her side.

"Yes. I'm fine. I just want to rest." She hurried from the room without giving him another look — frightened that if she stayed, she might lose control and tell him how she felt.

Zerelda came to Lydia nearly an hour later and found her sitting up in bed, a book in her hand. She thought her niece looked confused and offered to listen.

"Sometimes it helps to talk a thing through."

Lydia shrugged. "I don't know where I'd even begin."

"Maybe start by telling me what caused you to flee our company this evening," Zerelda suggested. She sat down on the side of the bed and smiled. "Or you could start with Kjell showing up."

"I don't know what to think of him," Lydia admitted. She looked at Zerelda. "Why did you never marry?"

Zerelda hadn't anticipated this change of topic, but if it helped Lydia to relate her concerns, it was just as good a place to start as any other.

"I was in love once. It was before the War Between the States. He was a wonderful young man — a minister, in fact. I thought . . . well, I thought the entire world turned around him." She smiled sadly. "I was twenty-three, and he was twenty-nine."

"What happened?"

"He didn't return my love." Pain washed over her anew.

"How did you know?"

The interest evident in Lydia's tone encouraged Zerelda to bear the sorrow once again. "I asked him. Actually, I told him of my feelings, and while he was kind, he told me he couldn't return my love. He left the area shortly after that. The gold rush in California had become well known, and he felt God was calling him west."

"But didn't he say why he couldn't love you?"

Zerelda shook her head. There had never been any explanation beyond his gentle apology. He had almost seemed embarrassed that he had somehow allowed it to happen — as if he could have stopped Zerelda from losing her heart in the first place.

Lydia's voice softened. "Did you ever hear from him again?"

"No. I heard about him from one of his relatives. He left the ministry and was taken with gold fever. He never made it rich, but that's all I ever knew of him."

"Were you angry at God?"

She smiled at Lydia. It was the second time Lydia had asked a similar question. "No. How could I blame God for the fact that the man didn't feel the same way I did?"

Her niece seemed to consider this for a moment. "Well, my mother always said that God knows everything and has all power. Since you loved God even then, why couldn't He have returned that love through this man?"

"Sort of a situation where, because I did something for God, He should do something for me?" Zerelda asked.

Lydia nodded. "Exactly. You had shown your loyalty and love to God, so why couldn't He reward you with a love of your own?"

"I suppose He could have done anything He wanted," Zerelda replied. "But that really isn't how it works with Him. He has already given us the best and most precious love He could. He sent His Son to die an awful death for our sins. How could I hold up my puny attempts at love and faithfulness and demand He bless me for my efforts?"

"But if He is the loving God you and Mother always declared Him to be, why not expect that?"

"Let me say this," Zerelda began. "I do expect good things from God. I believe He wants to bless me and does all of the time. However, I also trust that there was a good reason for not marrying my young man. I can honestly say I wouldn't have done well traipsing around the gold fields. I would never have been happy, especially to see him give up the ministry. Added to that, I never would have become a nurse — that was heavily influenced by the war."

"So we are to just look at life and its sorrows and disappointments as blessings in disguise?"

"Well, if we can, why not?"

Lydia frowned. "I just don't understand. If God truly loves us, why doesn't He just keep us from the painful things to begin with? Why not just . . . well, force other people to . . ." She seemed at a loss for words.

Zerelda gave a chuckle. "Force other people to do what we want? That would take away their free will, then, wouldn't it?"

"But what if they are evil people? Why do they deserve free will or God's blessings? Surely God doesn't love the evil man as much as He loves the good man."

She heard the desperate need in Lydia's voice and wished she could explain. "Suppose you have twins growing inside you. You give birth, and they grow up. One child is truly good, and one is bad. The good child obeys you and works hard to earn your approval, while the bad one grieves you and disappoints. Would you love one more than the other?"

"Well, it would certainly be easier to love the good child," Lydia said thoughtfully. "He would be more pleasant to be around, and you would want to reward his actions."

"True, but would you cease to love the child who did wrong — who showed no concern for you or your desires?"

Lydia seemed to consider this for several moments, until finally she spoke. "I cannot say. I can't imagine turning away from any babe I give life to, but neither can I see myself happy with the actions of a selfish, willful child."

"And so it is with God. He isn't happy with the evil man or his actions, but neither can He completely turn His back on the man. He wants all to be saved and none to perish to eternal damnation."

"So He even wanted Floyd to be saved? Marston and Mitchell, too? Despite all the suffering they have caused over the years, God would simply open the gates of heaven and welcome them in should they decide to ask Him?"

Zerelda did not miss the accusing tone of her voice. "My dear girl, who can know the mind of God? It's more than we can fathom. However, if you again think of the situation in regard to your own child or children, then I think understanding begins to dawn. Just consider it in that manner for a time."

"I'm sorry, Zerelda. I don't mean to be so unpleasant when it comes to something you hold so dear. A year ago, I wouldn't have even engaged in such a conversation," she admitted. "But you are helping me to see that maybe I have been wrong about other things in my life, so maybe . . . maybe I'm wrong about God, as well."

Her confession gave Zerelda's heart hope. She squeezed Lydia's hand. "I only want you to know about love — real love. It's there for you, my darling."

"I'd like to believe so," Lydia said with a deep sigh. "I'd really like to believe that."

"Then do. Let go of the past and allow

yourself to fall in love again," Zerelda encouraged.

Lydia looked at her blankly. "I can't fall in love again. I've never fallen in love to begin with."

Zerelda smiled. "Then let this be the first — and hopefully last — time. Kjell is a good man, and I believe he cares a great deal about you."

CHAPTER 13

Lydia heard a wagon approaching far down the drive and figured Kjell was bringing Zerelda home from town. Earlier that day, her aunt had felt consumed by the need to go and check on some of the families in the Ranche. She said oftentimes God prompted her to go just when her help was needed the most. Lydia considered such beliefs with skepticism. No one had been prompted to come to her aid when she had been in trouble. No divine intervention had kept her safe from harm. She supposed that was the very thing she could not reconcile in considering a relationship with God: Where had He been all those years? Why did He seem to care for one person, yet let another suffer?

She forced the thought from her mind and went to the door. Taking the last of the rugs outside, she set about beating them on the far side of the porch. It had been raining off an on all day, but for the moment, there was little more than a mist against the growing twilight of the early evening. A single bay gelding appeared around the bend, and Lydia recognized the horse and closed carriage owned by the postmaster. Perhaps Zerelda had gotten a ride from Mr. Fuller.

The rug nearly slipped over the rail, causing Lydia to return her attention to her task. There would be time for visiting soon enough. She knew her aunt would invite Mr. Fuller inside for coffee or tea. On days like this, it was more than a neighborly thing to do — it was necessary in order to let folks warm up and dry off.

At the sound of footsteps on the porch, Lydia turned and smiled. "The coffee is on and . . ." Her words faded into silence. She stared at the man before her as if he were some kind of ghost from the past.

"Hello, Lydia. I can see that you are rather shocked to find me here, but coffee sounds wonderful."

Marston Gray stood not six feet away, looking for all the world as if he were accustomed to visiting her on a daily basis. He smiled and then his expression grew concerned. Lydia couldn't form words. She stared, eyes fixed and unblinking. This couldn't be happening. How had he found her?

"Perhaps you should sit down, what with your condition and all."

Lydia still held the wire beater she'd been using on the rug. She gripped it so tightly, she thought it might break in her hand. Backing up a few steps, she felt her hips come in contact with the rug and rail.

Marston stepped forward, but Lydia held up the beater and shook her head. Still she couldn't find her voice. To see him there, after so many months of peace and healing, was enough to make her ill. Lydia longed to run for help, but there was no one close at hand. Town was miles away, and who knew when Zerelda would return.

Watching her closely, Marston held up his hands. "I didn't come here to cause you harm or worry. I heard about the baby and thought you would want to be near to family."

This was Lydia's undoing. "I . . . I am . . . near family." Her words were stilted and sounded foreign in her ears.

"I know. You have an aunt here, correct?"

"How did you find me?" In the back of her mind Lydia was already wondering if she would have to move again. Would Zerelda be willing to relocate with her? What would become of them if they had to constantly be on the run from the Gray family?

"Your lawyer, of course." He smiled. "We were worried about you. You disappeared without a word to anyone, and it had been months since we knew if you were dead or alive."

Lydia couldn't believe Mr. Robinson had betrayed her. The man had been her advocate and champion. Why would he suddenly turn on her now? Little by little, Lydia's senses returned. As the shock wore off, the anger and fear built. She couldn't show him that she was afraid. The Gray brothers fed on the terror of others. Of course, her stunned reaction might already have done her more harm than good, but Lydia was determined to take charge of the situation.

"As you can see . . . I'm fine. You needn't have made the trip."

"There was more than one reason to come, Lydia. Why didn't you tell us about the baby? That child you carry is our concern, as well."

"My baby has nothing to do with any of you."

"That is my brother or sister you speak of."

Lydia shook her head. "This child is mine alone."

Marston narrowed his gaze slightly. "Are you saying this baby isn't my father's?"

"I'm saying your father is dead, and this baby belongs to me. I left Kansas City hoping to never deal with any of you again, and that is still my intent."

"Lydia," he said softly, "you are distressed. I truly apologize for that. I didn't mean to upset you. We were quite excited to hear about the baby. I know how much my father had hoped to have more children."

"Your father was the reason I miscarried before. If he wanted children so much, he shouldn't have beaten me."

Marston shook his head. "No, he shouldn't have. The man was cruel."

"You and your brother are just as cruel, so don't think to convince me otherwise." Lydia felt the baby move wildly and could only pray that her anger would not cause the unborn too much distress. She felt her breath come in pants, like a wild animal after a run.

"Lydia, we were unkind to you. We wanted to please our father, and strength and severity were the only things that impressed the man. I'm not sure why we cared so much about what he thought, but it is no longer a concern. We want you to come home. Come back to Kansas City, where we can help you.

We haven't even sold the house. You can live there and raise the child."

"You can't possibly be serious." She'd had enough. The entire situation was madness. "Just go. You should never have come here."

He stepped forward again. "Lydia, be reasonable. I haven't come here in anger or with thoughts of causing you harm. Your kindness to our family caused me to see the error of my ways."

"Stay away from me," Lydia said, pushing past him. "I don't believe a word you say."

Marston reached out and took hold of her wrist. "Please hear me out."

Lydia froze. She looked at her wrist, remembering all the times Floyd had done the same thing. How many times had she hidden bruises with lace-edged sleeves so that no one could see the marks?

"Let me go."

"Not until you calm down and hear me out."

Marston's tone took on an edge that drew Lydia's attention back to his face. He smiled with his lips, but she could see the anger in his eyes. It was unmistakable.

"You said what you came to say. My answer is no. I will not return to Kansas City. Sitka is my home now."

"But there isn't even proper medical care

here," he protested. "Think of the child. What if you were to die giving birth?"

"Then my aunt would raise the baby."

"But what of the rest of us? This child is our brother or sister. Lydia, you aren't thinking clearly. You need a doctor to attend you. The stress of this situation has obviously taken its toll."

Lydia shook her head. "I am perfectly healthy. My aunt is a nurse and she has attended me most faithfully." She straightened and pulled back just a bit. "Now release me."

"Please don't be like this, Lydia. I don't want to have to take matters out of your hands."

"Ah, so now you show your true colors. I wondered when the force and ugliness would start."

Marston's jaw clenched. His grip tightened on her wrist. "No one wants to force you into anything. Especially me, but for your own good and the good of this child, I will do what is necessary. Lydia, I would even marry you to make you feel more at ease."

This took her completely by surprise. She felt her eyes widen and her mouth drop open. "Marriage? Are you mad?"

"Why should such a suggestion be considered madness?" he asked. "There will, no doubt, be those people who scoff at this child belonging to my father. After all, you could bear him no children during the marriage. They might well believe this child is the product of an illicit affair. Your reputation would be ruined."

"Not in Sitka, it won't be. People here not only do not care who fathered this baby, they are unimpressed with the Gray name and reputation. I have no concern for my social standing."

"But what of the baby? Would you ruin his or her reputation, as well?"

Lydia had taken all that she could stomach. "Let me go."

"Please don't —"

"Let me go!" she yelled. "Release me now!" Her voice rose even as she brought the beater up to hit Marston. He easily blocked the strike and wrenched the piece from her hand.

"I think the lady would like you to unhand her," Kjell said from behind Lydia.

His coming to her rescue was enough of a surprise that Marston loosened his hold. It was just enough for Lydia to break free and throw herself into the arms of Kjell.

"Please make him go away," she begged.

"Did he hurt you?"

She nodded, then shook her head. "Not really. He grabbed my wrist too tightly, but otherwise, he's simply been a bother."

Kjell's blue eyes seemed to darken. He kept his arm around Lydia in a protective manner. "I believe you should go now."

Marston shook his head. "We've not yet been introduced." He watched Kjell closely as he approached. "Lydia was married to my father. I'm Marston Gray."

"I've heard tell of you," Kjell replied.

Lydia lowered her gaze to keep from showing her surprise and rubbed her wrist. She had no idea what Kjell had or hadn't heard about the man, but he apparently knew enough to be cautious.

"I'm sorry to say that I was once a harsh man. But now I am much changed. I'm afraid, however, that Lydia has been quite disturbed since our father's death. Her coming here was just one of the ways she showed her distress. She's been missing for months, and we were gravely concerned — especially given her condition. We are hoping to bring her home, where she can give birth in the safety and care of her family."

"She's got the care of family right here. Her aunt is a loving woman who also happens to be a nurse. Lydia has constant care, so you needn't concern yourself further."

"But perhaps she's in need of better help than a place like this can offer."

Lydia shot Marston a glare. "He's trying to suggest I'm not in my right mind. It's a wonder, after twelve years of marriage to his monstrous father and life with such hateful people, that I am. However, I'm not crazy, and I'm not going back to Kansas City. I want him to go, Kjell, and I want him to go now."

She left the security of Kjell's embrace and strode to the door of the cabin, where she paused. "You should never have come here, Marston. You say you aren't the same man; well, I'm definitely not the same woman. You will find that your bullying and force will get you nowhere with me. I'm not afraid anymore."

"You need to go now."

Marston eyed the man who had come to Lydia's rescue. "I don't believe I caught your name. Did Lydia call you Chill?"

"My name is unimportant. I am a friend of Lydia and her aunt, and you are not. I would suggest you give up whatever game you're about and leave Sitka on the next available ship."

This man clearly cared a great deal about Lydia. Marston hadn't missed the way he'd held her after she'd thrown herself at him. No doubt her morals were in question. Perhaps that alone would allow him to take the child from her. If Marston knew anything for certain, it was that Lydia would follow wherever the child went.

"I am truly sorry to have upset Lydia. I came to apologize and offer my assistance. I certainly meant no harm."

"Then prove it by leaving."

"But of course." Marston made his way down the porch steps and crossed in the rain to the waiting carriage. They hadn't seen the last of him, but for now, it was enough. Lydia knew he was here and knew he desired her return to Kansas City. He would find a place to stay and then see what he could arrange. Of course, this backwoods character was going to be trouble.

Climbing into the carriage, Marston settled in. He fumed at the way he'd been treated. He'd shown nothing but concern for Lydia, yet she'd refused to allow that he could have changed.

"Of course I haven't changed," he murmured, flicking the reins. The horse turned to make his way back to town.

Once he'd returned, Marston sought the advice of Mr. Fuller. "I thank you for the loan of your carriage. Now I wonder if you might direct me to a place where I could stay."

"There isn't much. The ship will be in harbor for several days. That will be your best bet for now."

"I had already planned to return to the ship tonight but hoped to stay on land after that. I need to be here for several weeks, possibly."

Fuller considered this for a moment. "There is a priest who lives with his daughter. They sometimes take in visitors. I could ask for you."

Marston nodded. "If you would be so kind. I'll return in the morning and see what you've learned."

Fuller seemed agreeable, and Marston took the opportunity to walk back to the docks. He waited for the launch, ignoring the persistent rain. His mind was taken up with what he should do next. Seeing Lydia so great with child had taken him by surprise. Of course, he'd known of her pregnancy, but seeing it was different. She had actually grown more beautiful, if that were possible. Marston had always thought her attractive, although he would never have admitted as much.

He looked back toward the town. Such a hideous place. Logs and mud and poverty were everywhere. Russian-made buildings were evident here and there, with their yellow walls and red roofs. The traditional dome and spire of the Russian Orthodox church drew Marston's attention for a moment. Funny that it remained, even after the bulk of the congregation had returned to their homeland.

Frowning, Marston considered what might be done. He would have to act quickly to get Lydia out of Sitka before the baby was born. That would be the easiest way. Of course, if the baby were to come early, that could complicate the situation.

"Ready to return to the ship, mister?"

Marston turned to the sailor and nodded. "Yes." He gave one more glance back at the town. There were plenty of seedy characters milling the streets, especially here at the docks. Perhaps they would be of use to him. The key to any successful transaction was to have people who were willing to do your bidding.

A smile came to Marston's face. He was good at enticing men who were down on their luck to do whatever he wanted — be it steal or scare or kill. Surely there was someone in this town who held as much anger toward this Chill person as Marston felt. Maybe someone hated the man enough to even eliminate the problem altogether.

CHAPTER 14

"Zee, that was the best berry pie I've ever had," Kjell said after his second helping. "You certainly know your way to a man's heart."

"It wasn't my doing," Zerelda replied. "Liddie baked that pie."

Kjell smiled at the exhausted Lydia. "A masterpiece, I tell you. Thank you for going to all the trouble."

"It wasn't that hard," Lydia told him. "We had the berries preserved from summer."

"I appreciate the effort, nevertheless. It's always such a pleasure to come here and enjoy the company and the food. I'm getting very spoiled."

Zerelda laughed. "Well, we wouldn't want that. What say you sing for your supper? I'd like to hear some tunes while we see to the dishes."

"Sure thing, Zee. I think I can manage that." He got up and reached over to offer

Lydia a hand. "You look tired tonight."

"I am," she admitted.

Kjell noted the dark circles under her eyes and the worried expression on her face. "You aren't fretting over that Gray fellow, are you?"

"That would be putting it mildly," Zerelda answered before Lydia could speak. "She's so restless and fearful, she won't even go to town with me."

Kjell looked deep into Lydia's dark brown eyes. "You don't have to worry about him."

"That's easy for you to say — you are a strong, capable man," Lydia replied. Zerelda had already begun taking care of the dishes, and Lydia leaned over toward Kjell. "Don't give it another thought. I'm fine, really."

But Kjell knew the truth. It was written on her face and evident in her step. Lydia wasn't the same woman. It was as if she carried a heavy weight on her shoulders, and Kjell longed to take that burden from her. He wanted nothing more than to convince her that he would care for her, protect her.

"Did Lydia tell you she had another proposal today?" Zerelda called from the kitchen.

Kjell looked to Lydia with raised brows. "How many is that this week?"

"Five," she barely whispered.

"Shall I make it an even six?" he teased.

Lydia straightened. "Make it whatever you want. It won't change a thing. I didn't come here looking to marry again."

"Well, that certainly won't stop the men from asking," Zerelda stated as she crossed to the front door. "You two get settled in. I'll be right back. There are some things I want to fetch from the cache."

"You want help, Zee?"

She shot him a wink. "No, I think I can manage just fine."

Kjell felt his cheeks redden, realizing she was purposefully giving him time alone with Lydia. He shook his head and went to where he'd left his guitar. Tuning the strings, he looked up to find Lydia watching him.

"Marston's still in town, isn't he?" she asked.

"Yes."

"I knew he probably was but had hoped you'd answer otherwise."

Putting the guitar aside, Kjell came to her chair and knelt down beside her. "Liddie," he paused and smiled. "I hope you don't mind me calling you that. Zee does it so often that it just sounds fitting."

"I don't mind," she replied, gazing into his eyes.

"Good. Look, I don't want you becoming upset by that man. It can't be good for the baby."

"The baby is the reason he's still here," Lydia countered. "And that worries me most of all. I don't know what he's planning, but I know it won't be good."

"I won't let him hurt you or the baby."

Lydia turned away from him and focused on the blazing hearth. "You don't know the Grays. They always get what they want. They scheme and bully to get their way. I still don't understand why Mr. Robinson would give them information about where I had gone, but now that they've found me, I don't expect they will ever leave me alone. I suppose I shall have to move again."

Kjell put his hand on Lydia's arm. "I hope you won't do that. I'd like you to stay."

"You've been nothing but good to me since I arrived and collapsed in your arms." Lydia smiled ever so slightly but didn't turn back to face him. "Zerelda told me that you're probably the best man she's ever known — that you are a man of your word."

"Zee would say something like that."

"I just don't want to be a burden to you or anyone else." Lydia glanced at him and then lowered her head. "I just don't want you feeling sorry for me."

He couldn't suppress the laughter that erupted. Lydia's head snapped up in surprise, and Kjell leaned forward and took her face in his hands. "I feel a great many things for you, Lydia Gray, but sorry isn't one of them."

Kjell bent down and lightly kissed Lydia on the lips. It was a quick and gentle kiss that he followed with a smile. "I guess I should get back to the guitar." He got up, noting that Lydia hadn't moved at all — she appeared a bit stunned. Kjell, however, had wanted to kiss her for a long while now and wasn't the least bit sorry for his actions.

Then Lydia gave her head a quick shake. "You can't just kiss me and pretend nothing happened," she said.

"I'm not pretending anything." Kjell took up the guitar. "I —"

"Kjell! Come quick!"

It was Zerelda, and her voice sounded panicked. Kjell quickly handed the guitar over to Lydia and raced out the door. "What is it, Zee?"

"Joshua is here — there's a fire in town." She spun around to face him. "It's your sawmill."

Captain Dimpfel and his firemen soldiers did an admirable job of containing the fire.

Even though the engine house was on the farthest side of town, they responded with great haste. Everyone feared fire in a town made of wood, and Sitka was no exception. Keeping this in mind, the firemen worked fervently and managed to pump enough water onto the blaze so that by midnight, the fire was out.

Kjell surveyed the smoky remains. The main work area was still standing, but his office and living quarters had been the first to go.

"Might have been a spark from a stove fire," one of the soldiers suggested.

"I didn't have a fire going," Kjell said, shaking his head. "I left about five-thirty and knew I'd be out most of the evening, so I didn't need the stove."

"That's right," Joshua said as he and Captain Dimpfel joined the conversation. "I was just telling the captain here that I left right after you did. The boys were the only ones remaining. They were trying to finish up that stripping you gave them to do and get back to the Ranche before curfew."

"Do you suppose the boys might have started the fire?" the captain asked.

Kjell shook his head. "I can't figure why they would."

Joshua kicked at the damp ground. "Well,

they could have. I didn't want to say anything, but I did catch them smoking the
other day. Could have been they were doing
it again and got careless."

Frowning, Kjell walked to the corner of
the building. He couldn't imagine the boys
smoking, much less setting fire to the place.
Besides, they would have had no reason to
be in his office or living quarters.

He blew out a long held breath just as
Joshua approached. "We can still produce
lumber," he told Kjell. "We'll have some
cleanup to do, but at least the main supply
of logs was untouched."

"I suppose we should find the boys and
ask them if they know what happened,"
Kjell said, shaking his head. "I just can't
figure them starting it."

"I don't think they ever would have done
it on purpose," Joshua said, "but if they got
spooked and threw a cigarette down in the
sawdust, it could have smoldered there for a
time and they might never have known what
happened. Captain Dimpfel said he'd send
some of his men to find the boys in the
morning and have them brought to the
engine house for questioning."

"I suppose that's the best way to find out
if they know anything." Kjell wanted to go
into his office and home and see if anything

was salvageable, but Captain Dimpfel had suggested he wait until morning when the light would reveal more.

"You're welcome to stay the night with me," Joshua offered. "There's not much room, but it beats staying in the saw room."

"Thanks, I appreciate that. I suppose I'll take you up on the offer and see what's to be done in the morning." He cast a final glance back at the main entrance to the mill and frowned. Something just didn't sit right with him. Was this a careless accident? Or were darker forces at work? Could Marston Gray have had something to do with the fire?

"I can't understand why anyone would do something like this," Zerelda said. She had decided to come to town the next morning and see the remains of the fire. To her surprise, Lydia had wanted to come with her.

Kjell shook his head. "I don't understand a lot of things."

"If it involves Marston Gray, there doesn't have to be any reasoning behind it," Lydia said bitterly.

"Now, you don't know that he had anything to do with this," Zerelda countered. Lydia had been talking about the possibility of the man setting the fire since they'd first heard about the blaze the night before.

"It seems too coincidental not to consider him," Lydia replied. "After all, Kjell made him very angry by standing up for me."

Zerelda decided to change the subject. "Where are you staying, Kjell?"

"I stayed last night with Joshua, but I figured I'd rig up something temporary here at the mill for tonight."

"Nonsense," Zerelda said. "Come stay with us."

"Now, Zee, you know there isn't room in that tiny cabin for all of us." He smiled at Lydia. "Besides, Liddie here would probably suffer irreparable damage to her reputation if I were to take up residence there."

"I think my reputation could stand the strain," Lydia said, still staring at the charred remains. "Besides, what of Zerelda? Her reputation could be just as damaged."

"Not Zee," Kjell said with a smile.

Zerelda laughed. "Folks got used to my antics a long time ago. Look, why don't we talk to the man handling the sale of Mr. Saberhagen's property? Maybe he would let you stay in the main house."

"Better yet," Lydia said, excitement edging her tone, "why don't I buy the property? Then Zee and I could move there, and you could live in the cabin."

"You don't need to buy a piece of property just because of the fire. I'll have a room built before you know it."

"But I've actually been considering this for some time," Lydia said, looking to Zerelda. "Ever since you mentioned the property going up for sale, I couldn't keep from wondering if I should buy it. I'm sure I can afford it, and like you said, with it being nearly winter and all, there will likely be few other offers."

Zerelda nodded. "It would be nice to have a bigger place eventually. The main house is good for a young family: There are two good-sized bedrooms upstairs, as well as a smaller bedroom plus a bathroom, and there's a large living area on the main level. Much of the furniture has been left behind — quality pieces. Mr. Saberhagen spared no expense for his wife."

"Good. Then it's settled. Kjell, I know you have your plate full, but would you be willing to talk to the agent on my behalf?" Lydia asked.

Zerelda didn't miss the look in Kjell's eyes. There wasn't anything he wouldn't do for her niece. Of this, she was certain. The man was crazy in love with Lydia, and Zerelda was just as certain Lydia cared for him.

Once they both figured it all out, she had no doubts she'd be welcoming Kjell into the family.

"Sure, I'll talk to him, Liddie. If you really want me to," Kjell replied.

"Good morning, all," Captain Dimpfel announced. "I'm glad to find you here, Kjell."

"Do you have news about the fire?" Zerelda asked.

He shook his head. "Not exactly. I sent my men into the Ranche this morning to look for the two Tlingit boys Kjell employed. No one has seen anything of them since yesterday. Of course, I think the family could be lying."

"I know that family well," Zerelda said. "I don't believe they would lie about it, but just in case, I'll go have a talk with their mother."

She looked at Lydia. "Why don't I take you home first?"

"I'll get her home, Zee," Kjell said. "You go ahead. I truly appreciate the help you're giving. I doubt the family would be so willing to talk to me."

"If you find them, Miss Rockford, please see to it that they come in immediately for questioning."

"I will, Captain. You needn't fear on that

222

account."

Lydia allowed Kjell to help her onto the wagon. It was extremely difficult with her long skirts and heavy abdomen. She thought it might have taken more effort to climb up onto the wagon seat than if she'd merely tried to walk the few miles home.

"Are you all right?" Kjell asked once she'd settled beside him.

"I found that positively exhausting," she said with a laugh.

Kjell smiled. "I'll have you home in a quick minute."

"Shouldn't you stop by the land office first and see about the property?"

"No, that can wait. I don't want you sitting out in the cold, and I sure don't want you having to get down from here more than once today."

He guided the horses in the direction of Zerelda's cabin. Lydia tried to focus on the scenery around her but found herself wishing she could offer Kjell some comfort regarding the fire. He seemed, however, to be taking it all fairly well.

"Kjell, how is it that you can be so . . . well, you don't seem upset about the fire."

"Oh, I'm plenty upset about it," he admitted. "I lost some things that were pretty special to me, but in the end, they were only things. I'm worried about the boys. I hope if they did cause the fire that they will just admit it. I'll forgive them, of course — I wouldn't hold an accident like that against anyone."

"But if it wasn't an accident . . . If some-one . . ." She thought again of Marston. He could have done this to exact revenge for Kjell's confrontation.

"Are you all right?" Kjell asked. He moved to touch her arm with his gloved hand. "Liddie?"

"What if Marston did this to you?" She found she was unable to say anything more. Had she brought this misery upon Kjell? Was this all her fault?

"Liddie, stop it. I can almost hear your thoughts."

She looked up at this and found him smiling. She shook her head. "This isn't funny."

"I didn't say it was, but it doesn't have anything to do with you. If Gray did this, then he did it because I stood up to him — told him to leave. Not for any other reason." Kjell urged the horses to pick up speed for the hill. "We'll get to the bottom of what happened, but you need not concern your-self with it. I won't have this fire be the cause of bringing on the baby too soon."

The cold penetrated Lydia's woolen skirts and coat, and by the time they pulled up in front of the cabin, her limbs felt half frozen. Kjell didn't seem to mind that she moved ever so slow. He was good to assist her and seemed to enjoy lingering at her side as they moved up the porch steps.

"Why don't I come in and get the fire built up? You look like you need to unthaw."

Lydia nodded. "I would like that very much." She decided against ridding herself of her coat and went to take her favorite chair at the fireside. The rocking chair was nearly identical to the one she'd left behind in Kansas City.

She watched Kjell set the logs on the dying embers. He worked with the kindling and soon brought the fire back to life. Once the logs were sufficiently blazing, he held out his hands to warm them.

Without thinking, Lydia looked up at him and asked, "Why did you kiss me last night?"

Kjell didn't turn to acknowledge her but kept staring straight into the fire. "Seemed like the right thing to do. You appeared to be misunderstanding my feelings toward you, and I guess I didn't want there to be any doubt about where I stood."

Lydia considered this for a moment. She

wasn't about to pretend she didn't understand, but at the same time, she wasn't entirely sure she wanted to hear Kjell make any declarations of love or affection.

"I'll get some wood in here, and then I'd better head back to the mill," Kjell said after several minutes of silence.

She thought about stopping him but decided against it. She waited until he'd gone outside to get to her feet and move closer to the fire. What should she say to him? What could she say? She wasn't sure of her feelings. Furthermore, there was the baby to consider. She had to do whatever was in the best interest of the child.

The sound of wood being chopped rang out. Lydia moved to the kitchen window, where she could see Kjell hard at work. He had taken off his coat, revealing the outline of muscles against the material of his shirt. With each swing of the ax, he displayed his strength and agility. Lydia found she could not look away. It was only the sound of a wagon approaching that drew her focus from the tall man.

Fear edged up her spine. What if Marston had come to pay her another call? She went to the door and cracked it open to look out. It was Zerelda.

"What did you find out, Zee?" Kjell called

out. He was approaching the cart even as Lydia moved down the porch steps.

"No one has seen the boys, and I believe them. Their mother is frantic, and their grandfather has everyone in the clan looking for them."

"I hope they haven't come to harm," Lydia said. She could see the frown on Kjell's face and longed to ease his worry.

"Mr. Fuller had this for you, Liddie," Zerelda announced, approaching with a letter. "He apologized for not getting it to you sooner. It came in on the last ship."

Lydia took the missive, which was from Mr. Robinson. She stiffened. Her anger toward him for sharing information with Marston kindled anew. While Zerelda continued to speak with Kjell, Lydia went back into the house to read the missive.

Dear Mrs. Gray,

I write this letter with grave concern and to offer a warning for your well-being. My clerk, Mr. Lytle, was recently attacked. On his deathbed, he told me of something most grievous. It seems your stepsons coerced him into allowing them to see my records regarding your whereabouts and other correspondences.

I have no way of knowing what, if

anything, the Grays plan to do with this information, but suffice it to say they now know of your location. I would be on the watch for them or their representative.

The letter continued with his most sincere apologies and concerns for what problems this might cause Lydia. She sighed in relief. Mr. Robinson had not betrayed her trust. She felt sadness that Mr. Lytle should have suffered such a vicious attack, but she could not bring herself to think in a forgiving manner for what he had done in giving Marston and Mitchell her information.

She read through the letter again, noting the date had been nearly a month earlier. So they had known about her all this time. Known where she was and that she carried their father's baby. No doubt they had plotted and planned how to come to her — how to force her return.

But why? Why should they care so much where I live or what I do? Why do they need me to return to Kansas City?

CHAPTER 15

November 1870

Sad news of the Tlingit boys' death came a few days later. The bodies of the brothers had been found by a local fisherman, who stated it looked as if the boys had both been beaten and strangled. Kjell didn't take the news well. Now he was certain that the boys were innocent in setting the fire. But they had probably witnessed the real culprit.

"I'm heading over to Swan Lake to help cut ice," Joshua announced. "You'll let me know if there's any work to be had here, won't you?"

Kjell nodded. "If the weather stays decent, we'll go cut some trees at the beginning of next week."

"Good. I'd much rather log than deal with the ice." Joshua paused by the door. He seemed hesitant to speak. "Kjell, there's something you ought to know. I saw the Sidorovs earlier today. I think they're staying at the Double-Decker."

Kjell looked at the man for a moment. The place he spoke of was known to house anywhere from one hundred to two hundred destitute Russians at any given time. The people there were good about hiding their own, if the need arose.

"You're sure?"

Joshua nodded. "I just wondered if maybe they had something to do with the fire — maybe even with the deaths of the boys. You know they treated them poorly. If they had snuck in here to set the place on the fire and the boys saw them, it wouldn't have gone well."

"No, I'm sure you're right." Kjell hadn't considered the Sidorovs as suspects, however. He had treated them fairly, and they really had no reason to turn against him.

"Well, I just thought you should know, boss."

Kjell didn't bother to correct the younger man for his choice of title. "Thanks, Joshua."

"I see no real reason to pay you in full," Marston told the Sidorov brothers. "You didn't accomplish the job I paid you to do."

Anatolli leaned in, nose to nose with Marston. "You refuse to pay us?"

Marston could see that the man hoped to intimidate him, but he was unconcerned. The Sidorovs had come recommended to him as two men who often spoke of their hatred for Kjell Lindquist. That was the only reason they were useful to Marston.

He narrowed his eyes. "Don't think to try and scare me; it won't work. Don't forget: I know what you did to those boys."

The younger man backed up a pace, while his brother came to stand beside him. "We did the job," Ioann stated. "It is no fault of ours that the firemen were able to control it. As for the boys — they were nothing. No one cares that they are gone, because they were only Tlingit."

He eyed Marston as if sizing him up. Marston considered that the two men were larger than he was and could definitely take him in a fight. However, he had something they didn't: a quick mind. The brothers were more brawn than brains, and Marston intended to use that to his advantage.

"I am not a man who is easily intimidated," Marston said, crossing his arms against his chest. "And I have no intention of going back on my agreement with you. However, I don't like to pay for sloppy work. There may be jobs for you in the future with me — jobs that will pay you far more money than you can imagine — but only if you can actually prove your capabilities."

His statement about money caught their attention, just as Marston had known it would. The brothers exchanged a conspiratorial look, and Anatolli shrugged. "We did as we were instructed. We could have set a better fire had the boys not interfered. We didn't know they were still around — they surprised us, and we had to do what we could to get rid of them before someone found out what we were doing."

Marston nodded. "Perhaps I have been too hard on you. You make a good point." He pulled out some cash and handed it over to Anatolli. "I will give you this now, but you will need to prove yourselves to me."

"What must we do?" Ioann asked.

Smiling, Marston knew he had regained their cooperation. "I will be in touch. In a few days, I will explain everything, but for now I have to make a few plans."

He waited until the Sidorov brothers had gone their way before pulling on his coat and heading to the Russian Teahouse, where he'd made a habit of taking his midday meals. Marston was more than a little aware of the people surrounding him. He had made it his business to carefully watch the transactions of the people in this little town. Observation and attention to detail had benefited him on more than one occasion, and he had no reason to believe his time in Sitka would prove to be any different.

On the brief space of boardwalk just ahead of him, Marston spied Lydia's aunt. He had introduced himself to the woman once before and knew she had no liking of him. Still, Marston had not yet had the opportunity to speak to her at any great length. Perhaps he could enlist her help for the right incentive.

"Good day to you, Miss Rockford," he said, coming alongside the older woman.

Zerelda peered at the man for a moment before recognition dawned. "What do you want?"

He laughed. "You are one to get right to the heart of a matter. I like that. I wonder if you might join me. I was just going to take lunch."

"I have no desire to share the company of someone who would cause my niece harm."

"But that is where you are wrong, Miss Rockford." He smiled at the plain-looking woman. No doubt she was unused to the attention and favors of men — at least men of means and attractive appearance. Maybe he could woo her. "I really have been misunderstood in this entire situation. I would like the chance to explain."

"Go ahead."

"It's cold out here. Won't you reconsider?"

Zerelda shook her head. "If you have something to say, say it here."

Marston wanted to slap the woman. "Very well. You should know that I only came here with the greatest concerns for Lydia and the baby. The Grays have always looked out for their own, and the child she carries is my brother or sister."

"I suppose the abuse she endured for twelve years was your father's way of showing that concern and care. I cannot accept that anything has ever been done by your family in Lydia's best interest."

"You can think what you will, but there is something Lydia and you should know. My brother and I will not allow this child to be raised in such an uncivilized part of the world. The child's welfare and education must be considered. Of course, should the baby be a girl, the education won't be such a concern, but should it be a boy, then his upbringing will need to be overseen by men."

Zerelda shifted the basket she carried to her left arm. "I believe I've heard enough to know that you hold no real consideration for Lydia. Therefore, I have no desire to listen to anything more."

Marston stepped closer. "I want you to understand one thing, Miss Rockford. I am a powerful man with many friends. I won't stand by and allow Lydia to ruin the life of my father's child."

"Are you threatening to take the baby from her?" Zerelda asked. "Because if you are, you should know that Lydia has a great many friends here, none of whom will allow you to bully and impose your will upon her."

"I'm not threatening anyone. I have the ability to work through the legal systems of this land. I have judges and lawyers who owe me many favors. It shouldn't be that hard to convince them that Lydia is not of sound mind. After all, she came here in a delicate condition — risking not only her life, but that of the baby." He noted Zerelda's obvious discomfort. She knew his words held merit. Lydia's stories over the years were bound to have given her an understanding of the power the Gray men possessed and the force of their will.

"It's just something you should keep in mind. Perhaps help Lydia to understand, as well."

"I won't trouble that poor child with idle threats." Zerelda squared her shoulders and looked him dead in the eye. "Just as you are used to accomplishing things through your acquaintances, so too am I. I first have God on my side, which is enough to see me through anything. But second, I have a good many friends in positions of authority on this island. I doubt they would give it a second thought should I suggest to them that you need to be removed from this place in order to offer my niece greater protection."

Marston was taken aback by her bold statement. This was not a woman who was easily coerced. "Very well, Miss Rockford. I had hoped to reason with you, but I see you are just as stubborn as your niece. Such thinking will only bode ill for you both."

Zerelda laughed, further unnerving him. "Mr. Gray, your threats only serve to prove to me that my niece has shared nothing but the truth in regard to you and your family. I'm glad she chose to come live with me, and you should know that I will defend and protect her, no matter the cost. And I am not the only one to feel that way. Alaskans are a different kind of people, and you would do well to learn that now."

She stalked off down the road without another glance. Marston wanted to demand that she return. In truth, he wanted to kill her for her insolent manner. The rage rushed through him, energizing him. He would make them all pay.

"I come bearing good news," Kjell said, greeting Lydia at the cabin door.

"Marston has gone?"

"No, it's not as good as that. The property sale is going through, and you are welcome to move into the main house anytime you like. Your letter from the bank was good enough to hold the place until the full exchange of funds can be arranged."

Lydia smiled. "That is good news — the best, in fact. Come on in. Zerelda should be back soon, and she will be so excited to hear the details."

"I'm sorry that I couldn't tell you what you really longed to hear." He eyed her sympathetically. "I wish there was some way to make the man leave, but he can't be forced."

"I know." Lydia smoothed the calico blouse down over her bulging stomach and drew as deep a breath as she could. Zerelda had told her that it wouldn't be long before the child would drop lower and ease the pressure on her lungs. Lydia hoped it would be soon.

"I'm glad you've decided to stay," Kjell

said, following her. He helped her into her rocking chair and added, "I know it pleases Zee, as well."

"It seems the reasonable thing to do, at least for the time," Lydia said, placing her hand atop her expanded waist. "Besides, I've come to love it here. I find it both peaceful and restorative. It seems Sitka has a way of wiping away my memories of the past. I never thought anything could do that."

He smiled and pulled up a chair. "I'm glad you feel that way."

Lydia felt her cheeks warm as she studied his handsome face. She had come to accept her feelings for him, although she had never spoken of them — not even to Zerelda. She'd never known the sensation of being in love before. It came to her as something of a shock at first, but now — now that she was more used to the idea — it came as a fulfillment of all she had missed in life. The emptiness she had once known was gradually being replaced with a fullness of spirit and heart that Lydia had only hoped to experience.

"You keep staring at me like that and I'm probably going to kiss you again."

She laughed. "What a punishment that would be!" She saw his grin double in size.

"Kjell, I never thought I would be happy, but I am. You have been so good to me — such a dear friend."

"I'd like to be more than a friend," he said, his voice low and husky.

Lydia felt her heart skip a beat. She swallowed hard. She knew he would most certainly propose to her. Did she want that? Could she accept such a proposal? For a moment her own fears overwhelmed her and she looked away.

Kjell leaned forward to take hold of her face. He gently turned her back to face him. "You must know how I feel about you."

Lydia surprised them both by getting to her feet quickly. She was so awkward these days, but she found it impossible to remain seated. "I do know," she began. "I suppose I've at least suspected for some time. My own feelings have taken me by surprise, I must admit. I never came here expecting to . . ." She paused and looked back at him. Dare she say the words?

"You didn't come here expecting to what?" he asked, coming to take hold of her arms.

Lydia found her courage. "I didn't expect to fall in love."

He gently touched her cheek. "And is that what happened?"

She nodded, unable to speak. Her heart raced at his touch, and despite the baby's bulk between them, she couldn't help but put her hand up to mimic his action. She felt the warmth of his skin and trailed her fingers along his jaw.

He pulled her close and kissed her with great passion. Lydia clung to him for fear the moment might end too soon. She heard him sigh as if the kiss were the culmination of a long, arduous journey.

"Marry me, Lydia. Let me take care of you — love you." He trailed kisses along her jaw.

The words sobered her momentarily. "Kjell." She pulled back just a bit. "I'm going to have a baby very soon."

He laughed. "I hadn't noticed."

She couldn't help but smile. "It's just that . . . well, this child is important to me. I cannot put it aside, even for your love."

This made him frown. "Lydia, what kind of man do you think I am?"

"I know so little of men, except the very worst of them. I know you are different, Kjell, but I still have my fears. This baby will need a father who can love him or her with all of his heart. Can you give this child that pledge?"

He put his hand to her stomach. "I can

and I do. I want nothing more than to share this child with you. I would never have considered asking you to marry me if I felt otherwise. I love children — I wanted to have them with Raisa, and now I desire only to have them with you."

Lydia felt the truth of his statement deep in her heart. "I had a horrible marriage, you know. My husband was not kind — in fact, he was cruel. He . . . he hurt me . . . often."

Pulling her into his arms, Kjell wrapped her in a warm embrace. "I'm not that man. I will never do those things to you."

"But what if . . . what if I . . ." She couldn't find the words to explain. How could she explain that intimacy terrified her? How could she hope for him to understand that she had never been shown the slightest bit of consideration as a wife?

"Lydia, what is it you're trying to tell me? Just say what you want me to know."

She lowered her chin, unable to meet his gaze. "What if I can't be a good wife to you? What if I'm not pleasing?"

He took her face in his hands, forcing her to look up. "I think I understand," he whispered. "Please know that I will be understanding of your needs. I would never betray your trust in me." His expression was so very tender. "Lydia, do you love me?"

She nodded. "I do."

"And I love you. I have from almost the first minute you fainted into my arms." He smiled and stroked her cheeks with his thumbs. "I had just told a friend of mine that if God wanted to give me a wife, He would have to put one in my arms. And then there you were."

"You believe God brought us together?" she asked curiously. Zerelda had often spoken of God ordering things in such a way to bring about His will.

"I do believe it," he replied. "Lydia, I know your heart is fearful of trusting — both God and me — but I want you to know that while I might make mistakes and disappoint, God never will."

"I'd like to believe that," Lydia said, "but it's just so hard. After all, God was never there for me in all those troubled years of my youth. I tried to pray and believe, but He was sadly absent."

Kjell shook his head. "He was never absent, Lydia. Neither was He pleased with what was happening. But whether you realized it or not, He never left you to face it on your own. He was there for you then, just as He is here for you now. He wants to be your comfort and salvation, and He's the only one who can truly heal you from all

242

the hurts and wounds given you over the years."

Something in Lydia's soul craved the truth he spoke — longed for the hope he offered. Could she trust God — love Him as Zerelda promised He loved her?

She felt like a child taking a leap from a hayloft. "I want to try," she whispered. "I want very much to know Him."

Kjell's eyes dampened with tears, surprising Lydia. "All you have to do is ask. Believe in Jesus and trust that He will save you, and He will."

Lydia considered his explanation for a moment. For much of her life, she had blamed God for her troubles. Could she really let go of the past and press on with a new heart, a new hope? She felt a warmth spread over her — a wonderful warmth that felt like nothing she'd ever known before. Her heart seemed to leap for joy. It was the right thing; it was the true thing. Looking up at Kjell, Lydia let her own tears come. "I believe, Kjell. I do believe."

CHAPTER 16

"Oh, but this is wonderful news!" Zerelda fairly danced a jig. Her pleasure at the announcement that Lydia had made peace with God and accepted Kjell's proposal was clearly evident.

Kjell grinned. "I thought you might approve." He put his arm around Lydia. "Not only that, but Liddie's bid for the property was acceptable to the agent."

"And does that meet well with you?" Zerelda asked, looking back and forth from Lydia to Kjell.

"Why wouldn't it?" he questioned.

Lydia looked at her aunt curiously. "Yes, why wouldn't it be acceptable?"

"Well, Kjell is a man, and he might find that it hurts his pride to have his wife provide the money to buy their home." She fixed her gaze on Kjell. "If that is something that bothers you, you should work it out now."

He shook his head. "It doesn't bother me. God has always provided for me in one manner or another. I have nothing that hasn't been given me through Him. I'm not at all concerned about this transaction. I know Lydia has a great deal of wealth. It doesn't interest me, except that she is happy and has what she needs for the baby."

Lydia smiled. Floyd would never have agreed to such a thing. He might have taken her money and then conducted his own purchases, but he would never have allowed her to make any decision about their future.

It touched her deeply that Kjell was so different from the other men she'd known. If he could be different, then other men could, as well. The world wouldn't necessarily have to be filled with cruel tyrants who only wanted to use and hurt women.

"When will you marry?"

"The sooner, the better," Lydia said, surprising herself as well as the others.

Kjell laughed out loud and gave her shoulders a squeeze. "I'm such a great catch, she's afraid I'll get away."

Zerelda nodded with a smile. "And well she should be. You are the best man in Sitka."

"Yes, but I have eyes for no one but Liddie. She needn't worry about me slipping away."

"My honest concern is to marry before the baby arrives. I'd like for him or her to have the Lindquist name," Lydia declared.

"And so he shall," Kjell replied. "We'll marry tomorrow, if we can. The Russian priest can probably do the job, since we really have no other men of the cloth in Sitka. Then we can all move into the main house before the weather turns bad."

"Oh, it would probably be best for the two of you to move into the main house on your own," Zerelda countered. "A couple needs time to themselves, and I have lived quite contentedly in this cabin for many years."

"I know you have," Kjell told her, "but I have other reasons for wanting you close. I don't want Liddie alone — especially with Gray still in town. I don't want you alone, either, for that matter. The threat he presents is real, and I don't want something happening to you."

"Do you think he will dare come here again?" Lydia asked. He'd done nothing to again impose himself at the cabin.

"I think he's capable of about anything. I'm not going to risk him showing up while I'm working one day when you're alone. Together, you and Zee are capable of holding off a small army."

"Mainly because of Zerelda," Lydia said with a smile. "She's a fierce foe to be encountered."

Zerelda laughed. "Well, I have shot my share of beasts in the past. None were two-legged, but it could happen, I suppose. I usually find that men are willing to reason with the end of my shotgun."

Kjell nodded. "So that is why I want us all under one roof. At least until Gray leaves. Would you be willing to do that, Zee?"

The serious expression on Zerelda's face left little doubt in Lydia's mind that she fully understood the gravity of the situation. "I will do whatever you think best, Kjell. Especially if it means keeping Liddie safe."

Lydia slept very little that night. She thought of how things would be after tomorrow. She was about to marry again, and she had more than a little fear of what that would mean. Was she making the right decision?

She turned over slowly and tried to soothe her aching back with extra pillows. The thought of praying came to mind, but Lydia still felt awkward about trying it.

"I don't really know what to say," she whispered. "I know that I desire safety for myself and the child. Oh, and for Kjell and Zerelda, too." She thought for a moment. "I want to know you better, Lord. I know that my faith is weak right now, but Zerelda tells me that in time it will grow."

Thoughts of Marston gave her a shiver. "I wish you'd make him go away. I wish you would send him back to Kansas City and make him realize that he cannot force me to return with him. He frightens me, Lord. I can't help it." She rubbed her hand over her bulky stomach. "I fear for my child."

For a moment, Lydia paused. Praying was so very foreign to her. Was God really listening? Did He really hear the prayers of unimportant people? She frowned and closed her eyes. She wanted to feel as sure of her faith as Zerelda and Kjell did, but how did that happen? Was there something more she needed to do?

Lydia awoke the next morning feeling a sense of anticipation. For a moment, she didn't know what it was all about, but then Kjell's proposal came back to her. They were to marry today! She drew a deep breath and cautiously maneuvered out of bed. She studied her wardrobe and knew there was little choice to be had. She had a simple navy-colored skirt, as well as a brown one, both of which had been styled to accommodate her pregnancy. There were also several full-cut pleated blouses that Zerelda had made for her.

"Not exactly like the grand wedding gown I wore when I married Floyd," she mused. "But then, that marriage didn't turn out well, so apparently the finery didn't help."

Choosing her best white blouse to accompany the navy skirt, Lydia dressed and then styled her hair. She arranged the straight brown mass into a simple bun at the back of her neck. There was no full-length mirror to study her reflection, and Lydia could only hope that her efforts would suffice. Kjell would think her beautiful no matter what, and that thrilled her heart as nothing else could. Floyd had never thought her pretty, but Kjell looked at her in such a way that she had no doubt of his appreciation and approval.

"There you are," Zerelda said as Lydia exited her bedroom. "I thought maybe you'd changed your mind. My, but don't you look lovely."

"I was just thinking how very different this wedding would be to the one I had at sixteen. No expensive wedding gown or masses of hothouse flowers. But also, no pretense. No force."

Zerelda nodded and came to take hold of Lydia's hands. "Only a man who loves you dearly. I'm blessed to see this happening, Liddie. I can't imagine a more perfect union."

"I hope so. I'm still frightened." She paused and thought about her struggle to pray. "I tried to pray about it last night, but it's all so new to me. I wish I had your faith, but I don't know God very well."

"It will come in time. Just trust Him, and He will reveal himself to you. Read the Word. I know Kjell takes time each morning to read the Bible, and I'm sure if you asked him, he would read it to you. Then maybe you could even discuss the meaning of the verses and what God wants to teach you through the Scriptures."

"I'd like that, I think. I want to learn. I really want that with all my heart. I've thought a lot about the things you've told me about God. It's hard to just let go of the past, but I'm trying. I'm trying hard to find a way to forgive, but it won't be easy."

"Just remember, forgiveness is a way of setting yourself free of the bondage put on you by others. There is liberty to be had in it."

They heard the wagon outside and smiled at each other. "That would be Kjell," Zerelda said, leaning forward to kiss Lydia on the cheek. "Let's see if he has managed to arrange everything."

Half an hour later, Lydia stood before the Russian Orthodox priest with Kjell at her side. The man's daughter and Zerelda stood as witnesses to the marriage, along with two elderly men who boarded at the priest's home.

The ceremony was over quickly, and when Lydia turned to receive Kjell's kiss, she thought she might faint from the excitement of the moment. Kjell pulled her close and kissed her firmly. It wasn't lengthy, but it left Lydia weak in the knees, just as his other kisses had.

"Congratulations," Zerelda said, kissing Kjell on the cheek. "You are truly a member of my family now."

"And happy to be so, Zee. I can't imagine a better family."

With the ceremony and legalities concluded, Kjell paid the priest and motioned to the door. "Let's go. I have another surprise."

Lydia allowed Zerelda to help her into her coat, then followed Kjell into the hallway. She stopped, however, causing Zerelda to bump into her. Kjell and Marston Gray stood not a foot apart from each other.

"And to what do I owe the pleasure of this visit?" Marston asked. "I didn't realize you knew I was staying here."

"We didn't," Kjell answered. He glanced back at Lydia and Zerelda. "We didn't come here today to see you."

"No? Then what was the occasion?"

Lydia stepped forward. "Our marriage. Kjell and I have married. So you see, you can go back to Kansas City, assured that my child will have a father. There is no reason for you to any longer be concerned."

"You married?" Marston sounded genuinely stunned. He looked at Kjell a moment longer before turning his full attention on Lydia. "You married him?"

"I did."

Marston's anger was undeniable. Lydia watched him clench and unclench his jaw several times before speaking again. "This changes nothing. That baby is still a Gray."

Kjell took hold of Lydia's arm. "This baby is a Lindquist."

Lydia smiled up at her husband and drew strength from his reassuring expression. Marston could no longer hurt her. Not with Kjell at her side.

"We will see about that," Marston replied. "There are laws about such things, and I will pursue them."

"Do what you will, Mr. Gray, but please do it as far from Sitka as possible," Zerelda said, pushing past him. "The army is in charge here, and I happen to know that none of the authorities think overly much of you and your bullying. You would do best to invest in a ticket on the first ship home."

Kjell followed Zerelda with Lydia at his side. He said nothing, and Lydia refused to even look at Marston. An angry Gray man had a way of making everyone around him just as miserable, and that frightened her.

"So what's your surprise?" Zerelda asked.

"I arranged with Mrs. DuPont to serve us a little wedding luncheon," Kjell said, smiling. He seemed to have put the incident with Marston behind him already. "She's waiting for us just down the street."

Lydia was grateful that they wouldn't have to climb back into the wagon just yet. The jarring ride had been a most uncomfortable affair, and she vowed to herself not to make another trip into town until after Christmas and the birth of her child. She clung to Kjell's arm and allowed him to lead the way, all the while begging God to send Marston Gray as far away from her as possible.

Kjell felt a sense of great accomplishment as he helped Lydia down from the wagon.

Their new house awaited them, and while he still had his own things to bring up from town, he already felt this to be home.

"I have a surprise for you two," Zerelda announced. "I know I took matters into my own hands, but I'm hoping you won't mind."

Kjell eyed her curiously. "What have you been up to, Zee?"

"Only this." She went up the porch steps and knocked. The door opened to reveal Joshua and several others — all good friends of Kjell's.

"We moved your things in from town. Lydia's stuff is here, too," Joshua announced.

"And for this one night, you will have the place to yourself," Zerelda added. "I'm going to town to stay with my friend since you don't want me staying alone at the cabin. A newly married couple should at least have some privacy."

Lydia blushed crimson, and Kjell nearly laughed. He held back, however, fearful that Lydia might take it the wrong way. In her condition, privacy was not going to be that important, but he wouldn't have traded the gift for anything. He looked forward to having Lydia to himself.

"Zee, this was a most thoughtful gift."

"I thought you might see it my way. Now come along, boys."

Kjell's friends followed her down the path. Joshua broke into a round of song, but Kjell couldn't quite make out the tune. He turned instead to Lydia. "Welcome home, wife."

She smiled. "Welcome home, husband."

They went inside, and Kjell couldn't help but marvel at Zerelda's efficiency. There was even a fire burning in the hearth. On the stove, a pot of stew simmered with an enticing aroma alongside a pot of coffee.

"Looks like she thought of everything."

"Zerelda is like that," Lydia said, putting her hand to her back. "I knew she'd put a stew together this morning, but I didn't give it any thought." She yawned and added, "She must have had the fellows bring it over with my things."

"Here, come sit down. You need to rest." Kjell guided Lydia to her rocking chair. Apparently Zerelda had thought it fitting to part with this, as well.

"I'm sorry there won't be any . . . well . . . real wedding night for you." Lydia flushed and looked away.

Kjell laughed softly and knelt on the floor. "Who says there won't be?"

She looked back in horror, her eyes widened in fear. "But . . . the baby."

Putting his hand atop hers, he shook his head. "Liddie, I would not hurt you. I merely meant that we would be together. I can hold you and caress your soft skin — taste your sweet kisses. It will be special. And it can start right now." He began to unfasten her boots.

Patiently, he worked the hooks until he had each boot off. Next, he began to massage her feet. Lydia moaned softly and closed her eyes.

"That feels good," she murmured.

"I thought it might. I remembered you saying that your feet hurt."

She met his gaze. "You seem to remember a lot of things."

He grinned. "Just the good ones, and you are always among them."

December 1870

December came in with cold winds and snow, and still no word of who had killed the Tlingit brothers or set fire to Kjell's shop. The trajedies had been, it seemed, completely forgotten in the wake of holiday festivities. The damage done to the property had been minimal and had caused no harm to the rest of the town. This, coupled with the fact that the dead boys were Tlingit and not white, also served to lessen the interest of the authorities. Kjell was determined to figure out what had happened, however. He owed it to those boys to see justice done.

He brought a cup of coffee to his desk and checked the time. He had come home to tend his ledgers and get caught up on bookwork while Lydia took a much-needed nap. The growing burden of the child kept her from sleeping well at night.

Kjell was glad that Liddie was content to remain home instead of going into town, as Marston Gray was still present. He had hoped the man would have left by now, and his presence worried Kjell. What was the man waiting for? The only obvious answer seemed to be the baby's birth.

Would Gray truly try to take the child, as he had threatened? Kjell had talked to one of the town's two lawyers, who assured him Gray could do very little. At least not legally. This caused Kjell even more anxiety. He knew from Lydia's stories and Marston's own actions that operating within the confines of legality didn't seem to be of a concern to the man.

A knock on the door sent Kjell to answer it before Lydia woke up. He found Joshua on the other side of the door, looking worried.

"What's wrong?"

"I thought I'd better come share something I heard."

"Come on in but keep quiet," Kjell told Joshua. "Lydia's sleeping."

Joshua nodded and removed his cap. "I was cutting ice today, and a couple of the fellows there were from the Double-Decker."

Kjell went to the stove and held up the pot. "Coffee?"

Joshua nodded. Kjell poured him a cup and handed it over. "Go on."

"Well, it seems they knew about the Sidorovs and the problems they'd had with you. One of them was commenting on how if he'd been hired to burn us out, there wouldn't be a stick of wood left standing."

Kjell's eyes narrowed. "If he'd been hired . . . Is he implying the Sidorovs were hired to do the job? That they didn't just do it from their own desire for vengeance?"

"That's the way he talked, Kjell. I don't know who might have paid them to do something like that, but I figured you ought to know that you have an enemy out there somewhere. If it happened once, it could happen again."

"And what of the boys?"

"He didn't say anything about them, but

258

it all fits together. If the Sidorovs were hired to burn us out and the boys were there, they would have had reason to kill them. They were the only ones who could have identified them."

Kjell clenched his jaw and fought to contain the anger welling within him. He felt confident that Gray had been the one to hire the Sidorovs, but how could he ever prove it?

"I'd best go," Joshua said, putting down the cup. "I'm sorry to bring this kind of news."

Kjell nodded. "You were right to come."

Upstairs, the bedroom door opened, and Kjell could hear Lydia making her way downstairs. "Not a word of this to her," he told Joshua.

The young man nodded and headed for the door. Lydia was halfway down when he turned back to Kjell. "I'll see you at the mill on Monday."

"I'll be there," Kjell replied.

"Afternoon to you, Mrs. Lindquist."

"Afternoon, Joshua." She looked at her husband as the door closed. "What brought him all the way out here in the cold?"

"Nothing all that important," Kjell muttered and turned away. He didn't want Lydia to sense his concern.

"You're upset," she said, coming to touch his shoulder. "Is it bad news?"

"No!" he snapped. He pulled away and went to pour himself a cup of coffee. "Just forget about it."

It wasn't until he'd taken a long drink that he turned. He saw the fear in Lydia's eyes and immediately regretted his actions. He put the cup down and crossed the room to where she stood. To his surprise, she turned away as if to shelter herself and the baby from his blows.

"Liddie, I'm sorry."

Tears came to his eyes as she continued to hunch into the corner. Did she honestly think he would hurt her? He fought against touching her, fearing that she would fight him.

"Liddie, you don't need to be afraid of me. I'm sorry I sounded so angry. Joshua did give me some news I didn't expect, but it shouldn't cause you alarm. Please forgive me."

Lydia turned and Kjell's heart nearly broke at the sight of her tears. "Oh, sweetheart, I'm so sorry." She broke into sobs, and Kjell risked the situation to take her in his arms. She didn't push him away or fight. "I'm sorry, Lydia. I'm so very sorry."

She cried softly as he held her. Kjell felt

like six kinds of fool. Trust did not come easily for this woman, and here he'd already caused damage.

After several minutes, he gently lifted her face to his. "Lydia, you never have to be afraid of me. I might not always keep my temper, but I will never hurt you or strike you. You have to believe me. I'm not Floyd. I'm not like him."

She nodded. "I know. It just scared me."

"And knowing that breaks my heart." He smoothed back her hair and gently kissed her forehead. "I am devoted to loving you and protecting you. You have my pledge and word. I will never lay a hand to you. Please believe me."

She met his eyes and gave a little nod. "I believe you."

CHAPTER 17

Lydia awoke on December twelfth to a great deal of pain and an unfamiliar wetness making her cold. She sat up carefully, and as her head cleared of sleep, it came to her that the baby was on its way.

Kjell had already gone to work, but Zerelda would be nearby — probably downstairs working. Lydia stood as soon as the pain passed and made her way slowly to the door.

"Zerelda?"

"I'm down here, making a cake. Kjell said it had been ages since he'd had a spice cake. I don't know if you remember or not, but your grandmother prided herself on her spice cake recipe."

"Zerelda, I think the baby is coming."

There was dead silence for a moment, followed by the sound of rushing feet. Zerelda was up the stairs just as another pain hit Lydia. She took hold of her niece and steadied her while the contraction ripped through Lydia's midsection.

"How quickly are the pains coming?" Zerelda asked.

"I don't know." She panted and doubled over. Why did this have to hurt so much? She gasped for air. "I woke up . . . hurting . . . and the bed . . . was wet."

"Your water has broken. How long ago was the last pain?"

Lydia said nothing until the contraction finally started to ease. She straightened. "Just before I came out here to call for you."

Zerelda frowned. "They're coming awfully close together. Could be you've been in labor most of the night and just didn't know it. Come on, let's get you out of this wet nightgown and then I'll change the bed."

After Zerelda had seen to Lydia's comfort, she got her seated on a chair before quickly pulling the sheets from the bed and checking the down-filled mattress. "The fluid is clear — that's good. I'm glad I put the towels under the sheets," she told Lydia. "The mattress is barely damp. I'll just flip it over."

Again pain gripped her, and Lydia couldn't reply. The pressure she felt was enough to make her cry out, and in doing so she immediately had Zerelda's attention.

"There's no time. Maybe you should come to my bed." Zerelda tried to help Lydia to her feet, but the pain was too much.

Lydia moaned and doubled over. "I can't walk. I can't move. It hurts too much."

"Stay here," Zerelda instructed.

In record time she had turned the mattress and thrown down a clean sheet. Next she took up several towels and placed these atop the sheet. Then without warning, she all but carried Lydia to the bed and helped her to lie down.

"Let's see what kind of progress you've made." She quickly went to check on the baby's position. "Goodness and mercy," Zerelda declared. "The baby's head has crowned. You're just about to deliver."

Unable to keep from crying out, Lydia gripped a handful of the towels and felt the urge to push. "Can't . . . can't you . . . pull him out?"

Zerelda laughed. "So it's a boy, is it?" She shook her head. "He has to come naturally — it's best for both of you. Look, I need to get my birthing bag. It's in my room. You'll be alone for only a minute. If you have to push, go right ahead, but don't get up."

Lydia wanted to laugh. Get up? She could hardly manage to breathe against the pain, much less move. True to her word, Zerelda was back just as the next contraction hit. Lydia screamed as the pain escalated.

"Here he comes," Zerelda said, taking up her position.

The urge to push hard hit Lydia, and she found herself bearing down with a strength she hadn't known possible. She felt the baby slip from her body and marveled at the way the pain ended. Closing her eyes, Lydia felt a rush of blackness engulf her.

There was a gentle tapping on her face and the sound of something else as Lydia came to. She looked up to find Zerelda looking down at her, beaming from ear to ear.

"Can't you hear your son crying? He doesn't like it that his mama chooses his birthday to try and sleep."

"A son?" Lydia smiled wearily. "I knew it was a boy."

"What are you going to call him?"

"Dalton. It's a name Kjell and I both like."

Zerelda placed the tiny baby in Lydia's arms. "It sounds strong. Here you go, Dalton. Meet your mama."

Lydia looked into the bluest eyes she'd ever seen. The dark-haired infant gazed up at her with his tearful expression and began to cry anew. Instinct took over, and Lydia bounced him gently in her arms.

She thought of the other children she'd lost and of Floyd. This child had been conceived in violence, without any love whatsoever. His father had been a cruel and vicious man, but Kjell — his papa — would love him completely. Of this Lydia was sure.

"There, there, little one. Everything will be all right."

The baby calmed at her voice and turned his face to her breast. Zerelda laughed. "He's looking for a meal, Liddie. You'd best help him out."

Lydia remembered what Zerelda had told her of breastfeeding. She carefully eased the nightgown out of the way and directed Dalton's rooting. When he latched on, Lydia jumped in surprise. She looked up at Zerelda and found her aunt watching in amazement and awe.

"What a strange sensation," she said, shaking her head.

Zerelda smiled and leaned down to kiss Lydia on the forehead. "What a gift you've created. You did a good thing here, Liddie. You could have chosen to hate the child because of his father, but you didn't. I'm proud of you for that."

"He can't be faulted for Floyd's actions," Lydia said, still fascinated by this new life.

"I was just thinking of all the other babies I lost. I can't imagine what it would be like to have them all here now." She gently ran her fingers along the baby's head. "He's just so precious."

Kjell made his way home at ten-thirty, nervous that something was amiss. All morning, he'd been unable to keep his thoughts from Lydia and home. To ease his mind and get any work done, he would have to see for himself that all was well. Lydia would think him silly, but he'd just tell her he'd come home for lunch. Never mind that the morning was only half over.

He brought the wagon to a stop just outside the main house. With the brake set, he bounded out off the seat and hurried up the porch steps. The house was strangely quiet. There was no sign of Zee. He went into the kitchen and noted that nothing was cooking. A mixing bowl and a variety of ingredients sat on the counter. It was as if something had happened to take Zee away from her work rather abruptly.

A strange sensation came over him. What if Gray had shown up? What if something had happened?

"Zee? Liddie?" he called out. He made his

way to the large living room but found it empty.

"Zee! Lydia!" The urgency to see them heightened. Returning to the front door, he noted that their coats and boots were there waiting. They hadn't gone out, or if they had, they hadn't worn these things.

He raced up the stairs just as Zee appeared at the top. "Where's Liddie? Is she okay? Why didn't you answer me when I hollered?"

Zee grinned. "Calm down. Liddie's in bed and doing quite well. I believe she'd like to see you."

"I've been half sick with worry. All morning I had a feeling something wasn't right, and when I got home and found the place seemingly deserted . . . well . . . I guess . . ." He let the words go unsaid and drew a deep breath. "But she's all right."

"Why don't you go see for yourself? I think you'll be pleasantly surprised."

He looked at her a moment and saw the twinkle in her eyes. "The baby?"

Zerelda laughed. "Go on."

When Zee opened the door and pushed him through, he found himself staring open-mouthed at the sight of Lydia nursing an infant.

"It's a boy, Kjell," Lydia said with a weary

smile. "Oh, I'm glad you came. I prayed for you to come."

He sat down beside her on the bed and shook his head in wonder. "I couldn't stop thinking about you. Every time I tried to focus on my tasks at hand, my mind kept going back to you. I thought maybe something was wrong. I feared that . . . Well, never mind what I feared. Oh, Liddie," he sighed and leaned down to kiss her lips.

There was such joy in her expression as he pulled away, Kjell thought his heart might well burst from the happiness he felt. He examined the baby, who by now had fallen asleep. "He's so little."

"Zerelda says he's a good size. He's healthy and has all of his fingers and toes," Lydia said, laughing. "I know the latter because I counted them myself."

Kjell chuckled. "I would have loved him even if he'd been missing some of each."

"I'll go prepare something for us to eat," Zerelda suddenly announced. "Liddie never got any breakfast. She woke up in labor, and things progressed fast. I think some nourishment would be good for all of us."

After she'd gone, Kjell stretched out on the bed beside Liddie, careful to keep his boots over the side. He pulled her into his arms and held her for a long while. "I love you, Liddie. I love you so very much."

"I know you do. I can feel that love in ways that I never knew before marrying you," Lydia replied softly. "I never even knew what it was to really love another until you came into my life. I find that I care for you more and more every day . . . and sometimes it really frightens me."

Kjell lifted her face to his. "Don't be afraid. God is our Father and the keeper of our days. We needn't fear."

She nodded and stretched to press her lips to his mouth. Kjell lost himself in the moment and kissed her with a passion that he'd not expected. It seemed to surprise Lydia, as well. Shaking her head, she grinned. "You are very good at that."

He laughed. "I intend to get much better with practice."

Marston Gray had let word get around of his departure for home. He had left the company of the priest and chosen instead to take up residence in a small shack, well away from the town proper. The Sidorovs had found the place, and with Marston's money, they had purchased it. It had set him back fifty dollars, but he still had plenty of the cash he'd brought to Alaska, at least enough to see to his plans for Lydia and the child.

Writing a letter to his brother, Marston suggested that Mitchell arrange for all of Lydia's records to be removed from Mr. Robinson's office. The obvious way to hide such a theft would be by a fire — and perhaps Mr. Robinson could "accidently" die in the fire. That way, there would be no suspicion.

He continued by telling his brother he felt this was critical in order to make his plan work. If Robinson were dead, no one would know of Lydia's whereabouts or her pregnancy. He smiled to himself at the news that had reached him only three days earlier: She had given birth to a son. A Gray son.

Marston tossed back a bit of brandy before continuing to write. He informed Mitchell that plans were well underway to see things made right. Lydia might not be returning with him, but he would bring the infant.

Thinking of the future, Marston put down the pen and considered what was yet to be done. He figured to wait until the new year. This would give the child time to grow and give Lydia time to lower her guard. No doubt word had gotten back to them that Marston was gone. He'd left a letter for them with the priest, informing him that he should have it delivered once he'd set sail.

Of course, when the ship left, it went without Marston, but the priest didn't know that. And with Christmas celebrations and church services pending, the priest would be too busy to concern himself with why Marston had left in such a hurry. At least that was Marston's hope.

"You wanted to see us?" Anatolli questioned. He and Ioann stood at the door to Marston's tiny room.

"Yes, I do. Stoke the fire, and I will join you in a moment." He checked to make sure the ink on the letter was dry before folding the pages. Securing the missive in his coat pocket, Marston made his way to join the Sidorovs. It was time to share his idea and plot the future.

Christmas had been a simple but joyous affair at the Lindquist house. Kjell had given Lydia a beautiful necklace of Russian silver that had once belonged to his mother. Zerelda had made them both a new sweater, and baby Dalton was given a lovely quilt that was just his size.

Lydia felt bad that she had no gifts to exchange. Both her aunt and husband assured her, however, that the baby was blessing enough.

She understood their sentiment. Dalton was her own precious gift. The baby gave her such joy, such hope for the future, that Lydia had finally started to forget her ugly past. Now on the dawning of a new year, she felt that her life had changed for the better. Marston was gone, telling them in a letter that he wished them well. Lydia didn't believe his warm sentiments, but she was glad he was gone just the same. Life had finally eased back to one of peace and contentment.

"Happy New Year," Zerelda said, joining Lydia in the living room. "It's snowing again, I see."

"I noticed it earlier," Lydia replied. "Such beautiful flakes."

"It probably won't stay long, but it might. I thought I'd go to the Ranche and visit some of the Tlingits. Would you want me to bring you anything from town?"

"If they have fruit, I would love some. It's the one thing I really miss from my life in Missouri."

"I'll do what I can, but it will no doubt be canned or dried."

"I don't much care, so long as it's fruit." Lydia looked at the cradle and her sleeping son. "Otherwise, I think we have everything

273

we need."

"Kjell did a nice job on that bed." Zerelda gave it a gentle rock. "I've never seen anything move so smoothly. He's quite handy, that husband of yours."

Lydia smiled up at her aunt. "I think so. I think, in fact, he's very nearly perfect."

This amused Zerelda. "I think it's too soon to tell that, although I have known the man for many years."

"Well, he's perfect for me. I know now what I missed out on all of those years."

"Just don't dwell on the past," Zerelda cautioned.

Lydia shook her head. "I don't intend to. I'm happy to say that the memories fade a little more each day. Each time I take Dalton in my arms, each day I care for him, he seems to restore a part of me."

"I suppose I shall only know such feelings for myself through you." Zerelda's thoughtful words caused Lydia to frown, but she quickly admonished her niece. "Don't feel sorry for me. I'm happy with my life. I'm content in the work God has called me to do. Being single allows me to focus on others. I don't regret that calling."

"I hope not," Lydia replied. "I don't want you to ever feel alone or unloved. I know I would never have survived my marriage with Floyd had I not had your letters and love."

Zerelda gently touched Lydia's face. "You are more a daughter to me than a niece, and I find great joy in that. Even now, I feel as proud as any mother and grandmother might feel — I'm certain of it. You have been a blessing to me, and I look forward to this new year as I have no other."

Lydia nodded. "I feel the same. The bad times are behind us now. We can look to the future with great joy and hope."

CHAPTER 18

February 1871

"It's going to be a bad one," Zerelda said, noting the building storm on the horizon. "I'm going to secure the last of the shutters."

"I hope Kjell will get home before it comes," Lydia said. "I wouldn't want him to be traveling when the storm hits."

"He knows this place better than I do. He won't take foolish chances."

"Yes, but he's also trying to get that lumber order in for the army post. He may not even pay attention to what's happening with the weather."

Zerelda pulled on her coat. "I'm sure Joshua will keep him apprised. Besides, I've never known Kjell to be risky in his work." She opened the door just as the wind picked up and moaned down through the trees. "I'll be right back."

Lydia shivered. She didn't like the sound

of the coming storm. What if Kjell got hurt on the way home? She glanced at the cuckoo clock on the wall. He should have been back by now. What was keeping him?

Forcing herself to focus on something else, Lydia picked up her knitting. Zerelda had been working with her to make another blanket for Dalton. Lydia sat in the rocking chair and began to knit.

The door blew open with a great gust of wind, and Zerelda came in with it. Lydia jumped, and the fire in the hearth danced wildly until her aunt managed to close the door.

"It's turned bitterly cold out there," Zerelda said, shaking her head. "Mercy, but my hands feel like they're frozen."

"Come get warm," Lydia encouraged. "There's nothing more we can do now."

The older woman nodded and stood before the fire without bothering to take off her coat. "I hope we're not in for a hard winter. Sometimes it's like that. One year we had two feet of snow and the cold seemed to last forever."

"We had a lot of ice storms in Kansas City. Snow, too, but the ice was far worse. Nothing could remain upright when it was bad. Even the horses would lose their footing."

"I'm glad we don't have to deal with that here. We get some ice fog and pelts of ice on occasion, but usually it doesn't layer us with the stuff." She held her hands out to the fire. "I'm sure glad Kjell put the extra wood on the porch. I think I'd probably better bring a bunch of it in before it starts to rain or snow."

"Kjell can get it when he gets home."

"But it might start up before then. The way the wind is blowing, the porch won't offer much protection."

Lydia nodded. "Then I'll help. With the two of us at it, we'll get it done in half the time."

"And then we can sit and drink something hot and sample those cookies you made earlier."

They hurried to get the work done. The wind was merciless, and more than once, Lydia thought it might well knock her to the porch floor. She staggered under the load of logs, bending as much as possible to buffer herself from the icy air.

At one point, Zerelda paused and cocked her ear to one side as if she could hear something. Lydia looked at her aunt questioningly.

"I think I heard a horse."

Lydia laughed and reached for another

log. "I can hardly hear you speak. I don't know how you can hear anything, but I'm glad for it. That means Kjell will soon be here."

"Or it's just our little gelding protesting his meager stable. Come on. I think we have enough wood. I'll get some coffee on." She held the door for Lydia and followed her into the house. Securing the door, Zerelda began to peel off her coat. "Goodness, but I'll be glad to snuggle down in my covers tonight."

Lydia laughed and deposited the last of the wood by the fireplace. "Me too." She dusted her hands. "Is there something I can help with in the kitchen?"

"No, I'm fine. I'm going to stoke up the stove fire and put on a pot of coffee. You go back to your knitting. At this rate, Dalton is going to need all the blankets he can get."

Taking her place once again, Lydia began to work on the piece. She liked the added warmth of the blanket spread out over her lap. The chill of the night air gradually faded as her body thawed by the fire. Soon Kjell would be with them, and all would be well.

"I heard in town today that the Presbyterians are sending some missionaries up here," Zerelda said as she returned from the kitchen. "I'm excited to say that they hope to start a school for the native children and have a church."

"That would be wonderful," Lydia replied. "I know how you worry about the Tlingits and their children."

Zerelda took a seat opposite Lydia by the fire. "Education is so important, and few whites have the training or patience to deal with natives. They've been treated so unfairly at times. I don't blame those who run away to the other side of the island. I only hope the army will leave them alone."

"I suppose they will if the Tlingit leave the army alone."

"It doesn't work that way. For some reason seeing natives free to live on their own seems to really disturb our government. I saw it in Oregon, as well. Their preference is to have the Indians caged up like animals. They set up reservations and stockades, promising them a better life, but it's not better in the eyes of the natives."

"But aren't they dangerous? I was always hearing stories about Indian uprisings back in Kansas City. It seemed all sorts of problems were taking place on the plains and to the west."

"There is good and bad in every people," Zerelda answered, "but it has been my experience that the whites have taken it upon themselves to determine where the boundaries should be. They set the rules for how everyone should live and work, what kind of clothes and religion they should practice. They don't believe we can live in peace together."

Lydia stretched and yawned, looking again at the clock. It was nearly seven.

Zerelda could see Lydia's impatience. "He'll be here soon. If I did indeed hear someone coming, it would have to be him. He wouldn't leave the horses out in the storm, so he'll need time to care for them, as well. Don't fret so."

But a half hour later, Kjell had still not appeared. Lydia sipped the coffee Zerelda had given her and worried. "Where could he be?"

Rain was now pelting the house, and the wind had not calmed. Lydia supposed Kjell might have decided to wait until the storm passed, but what if it lasted all night?

"He'll be here when he can, Liddie. You mustn't . . ." Zerelda fell silent. "Sounds like the baby is fussing."

Dalton's cry soon reached Lydia's ears. "You do have good hearing, Zerelda." She put the coffee aside and got to her feet. "I suppose he's hungry again."

Just then something hit the porch outside.

Zerelda jumped to her feet. Lydia froze in place. Her aunt was already heading to where the Winchester hung by the door. "Might be some animal seeking shelter," Zerelda told her.

"Don't go out there. If it's an animal, you certainly don't want to have to fight it now — not with the storm," Lydia said. Dalton began to cry harder, and she headed for the stairs.

"It could be a tree branch has broken off and hit the porch. I need to at least check it out. Don't worry about me," Zerelda said. "I've taken care of myself for a long many years."

Lydia nodded. "I forget just how capable you are. But please, be careful."

She headed upstairs as Zerelda began to pull open the door. The cold wind blew in, causing Lydia to pick up her pace. Slipping into her bedroom, Lydia left the door open and quickly lit one of the lamps.

Dalton soothed as she whispered and cooed to him. "Just a minute, sweet baby. Mama is here."

A commotion from downstairs, however, drew Lydia's attention. Zerelda was shouting at someone. Lydia stepped toward the open door and strained to listen. The sound of men's voices rose, along with Zerelda's insistence that they leave or she would shoot them.

Lydia put her hand to her mouth and eased into the hall. What kind of trouble was this? A shot rang out, and Lydia heard more shouting. She wanted to go to Zerelda's aid, but her feet felt rooted to the floor. How could she help?

The revolver!

Kjell kept a gun in the bedroom. She would get it and defend her aunt. But Lydia had taken only two steps when another shot rang out, and Zerelda screamed. Lydia's legs felt like lead weights as one of the men's voices called, "Get the baby. Get him now."

Her breath came in rapid gasps as she hurried into her bedroom and closed the door. She frantically searched for some way to stop whoever it was from entering, but there was no lock, no bar. She thought of trying to slide the dresser against the door and went to give it a shove. It was too heavy. She only managed to move it a few inches.

She heard the doors to the other rooms being opened and closed. She felt bile in the back of her throat. What was happening? Why were they after Dalton? Then a hideous thought came to mind: Marston. This was his doing. He was trying to take the baby from her — to force her to return to Kansas City, where he could control her.

She again tried to push the dresser. With a strength she didn't know she possessed, she shoved it over before it caught on the rug. It now crossed the jamb by a small margin, blocking the door from opening at least for a bit. She went to get the revolver but it was gone. Kjell must have moved it. But where? There was no time to consider as someone began pounding on the door. The dresser began to shift. Hope faded.

Lydia frantically looked for a means of escape. The window was her only hope. She rushed to open it, wondering if she could ever manage to keep herself and Dalton safe on the slippery roof.

Struggling with the window, Lydia felt relief when it finally gave way and opened far enough for her and Dalton to make their escape. She was nearly blown backward by the wind and rain but gave it little thought. Instead she hurried to the bed and took up the quilt.

Lydia had barely made her way back to the cradle when the door finally gave way and the dresser was pushed aside. A large man came storming into the room.

"Give me the baby," he said. His Russian accent was thick, and his blue eyes seemed to stare right through her.

"Who are you? Why have you come here?"

"The child." He pointed to the cradle. "I want the child."

"No!" Lydia cried, putting herself between the two. Dalton began to fuss at the sound of his mother's frantic voice.

"You will wrap him warmly and give him to me."

She was nearly hysterical by this point. It didn't matter if he killed her — taking her baby would do that anyway. "Look." She took a step forward. "Whatever Marston Gray is paying you, I will double — no, triple."

The man's expression told her she'd touched a nerve. Lydia hurried to continue. "He doesn't have as much money as I do. I can get whatever you need."

The man seemed to consider this for a moment, then laughed. "Anatolli!" a voice called from downstairs. "Are you coming? I've killed this woman — have you taken care of the other one?"

Lydia knew then that Marston's plan was more hideous than she'd imagined. He didn't intend to urge her to follow him back to Kansas City at all. He intended to take the child and have Lydia put to death. That way she couldn't hurt him. She couldn't point a finger or put the law on his tail.

285

"Bring him now." The man's insistence was followed with the appearance of a revolver. "You will do as I say. Tell your son farewell."

"You can't do this. You mustn't," she cried. Tears rolled down her cheeks. "He's just an infant. He'll die in that storm if you take him out."

The man cocked the revolver. "Your time is up."

Lydia saw him point the revolver not at her, but in the direction of Dalton. She rushed to put herself between the baby and the gun. A shot rang out and she felt as if something had punched her hard in the shoulder. Then there was another hit and a burning sensation in her neck. She stumbled back and grabbed the bedspread as she sank to the floor.

She tried to speak, but the words wouldn't come. Looking up into the cold expression of the man, she could only watch as he lifted Dalton from the cradle. He cradled the baby awkwardly — not entirely sure what to do next.

The light in the room grew dim, and Lydia dropped her gaze to find the front of her blouse covered in blood. She was dying. She was dying and this man was stealing her child.

The darkness overcame her and she slumped over. "Kjell."

CHAPTER 19

Kjell felt exhaustion and cold permeate his bones as the horses made their way in the icy rain toward the house. He would have loved to leave the horses and run for shelter, but he couldn't be that cruel. The pair had served him faithfully for over five years and counted on him just as much as he did on them. Warmth and Lydia's sweet affection would have to wait until the animals were cared for.

He was about to drive the wagon around to the horse stable when he noted the front door was wide open. Reining back on the lines, he waited a moment to see if someone was coming from the house, but no one appeared. Something was wrong. He sensed it immediately and set the brake. Reaching under the wagon bench, he took up his revolver. He'd carried it with him since learning about the Sidorovs being hired to set the fire at his mill.

He carefully approached the door of the house and tried to peer inside. He could neither see nor hear anyone stirring. He edged just inside the threshold and caught sight of a woman's booted feet. Zerelda!

Throwing caution aside, he went to where the woman had fallen. Blood stained the floor beside her head. Kjell knelt and gently turned her face to see how badly she'd been injured. Zerelda moaned and struggled to open her eyes.

"Zee, what happened?"

She looked at him blankly for a moment.

"Can you hear me, Zee? What happened?" He patted her hand, hoping the contact might help bring her around.

She blinked hard several times. "I don't know. There was some commotion and . . ." She shook her head.

"Just rest." He jumped up and went to the kitchen drawer, where he knew he would find clean dish towels. Grabbing up several, he came back to Zee and pressed one against the wound. "Looks like somebody hit you hard upside the head. There's a pretty nasty gash and a lot of blood."

"Blows to the head always bleed badly. I'll be all right."

Kjell glanced around for Lydia. There was no sign of his wife or child. "Zee, where's

Liddie? Did she try to go for help?"

"I don't know." Zerelda's eyes opened wide. "Two men. They busted in. We were fighting, and I fired my rifle."

"Then what happened? Where was Lydia?"

"I don't know. I . . . everything went black." Her expression contorted. "They wanted the baby."

Kjell jumped up and ran for the stairs without another word. There would only be one man who would try to steal the child. Lydia would never allow for it, so he had probably taken her, as well.

The door to the bedroom was open and Kjell could see that the dresser had been pushed out of place. "Lydia? Liddie?"

Wind and rain rushed through the open window, giving Kjell hope. Maybe she had escaped. After all, there was no sign of either her or Dalton. Kjell rushed to the window and pushed it up all the way. He stuck his head outside but could see nothing. "Lydia!" he called out against the storm.

His heart raced and chest tightened. Where was she? Did Gray have her? He pulled back inside and closed the window. Wiping rain from his face, he turned back to survey the scene — and that was when he saw her. Crumpled there between the bed and the cradle, Lydia was covered in blood.

There was no time to react to the horror. He lifted her in his arms and carried her downstairs. He would load her and Zee in the wagon and get them to the hospital. Dr. Ensign would know what to do.

When he came down the stairs, Zerelda was already sitting on a chair. She held the towels to her head, but her eyes had cleared considerably. There was a noted look of shock when she realized that Lydia was lifeless in Kjell's arms.

"Oh, dear Lord. Is she dead?"

"No, but she will be if we don't get her help. I'm gonna put her in the back of the wagon, then I'll come back for you."

"I'll get some blankets," Zerelda said, trying to stand.

"Never mind. Just follow me if you're able." Kjell headed out the open door. "If not, I'll carry you, too."

"I'll manage just fine. I'll bring a lantern."

The storm had lessened, and while it still poured rain, the winds had dissipated. Kjell placed Lydia on the soggy floor of the wagon and turned to help Zerelda into the back. "Tend her as best you can, Zee." He took the lantern and tried to shield it from the rain, but even as he did, the flame flickered out.

"Can't see much in this blackness, but I'll do what I can."

"Kjell, what of the baby? What about Dalton? Where is he?"

The baby! Kjell had been so concerned about Lydia that he'd completely forgotten about the child. He put aside the lantern and raced back into the house. He listened for any sound of the child.

The silence was almost deafening. Kjell tore through all of the upstairs rooms, then made his way downstairs and searched the area. Dalton was nowhere to be found.

Kjell left the house and bounded up into the wagon and grabbed the reins. "He's not there." He nearly forgot to release the brake as he slapped the backs of the horses. The brake eased off just as the horses began to pull. Kjell glanced over his shoulder at the women but could see very little. "Dalton's gone."

"Gone?" Zerelda called back. "How can he be gone?"

Kjell clenched his jaw. There was only one way as far as he was concerned, but explaining it to Zerelda just now wasn't going to do any good.

"Just see to Lydia," he commanded.

It felt as if the ride into town took forever.

Muddy ruts caused the wagon wheels to slip and slide. In places the rain-soaked roadway threatened to engulf the wheels altogether, but somehow he managed to keep them moving.

Kjell took the last curve slightly faster than he should have and felt the wagon sliding away from the horses. Issuing a silent prayer, he reined back just enough to slow the animals and right the wagon. Up ahead, he could see the lights of the hospital. There were also several uniformed men standing outside. "I need help!" he yelled. The rain had finally stopped, but the temperature was dropping. Kjell worried that Zee and Lydia were probably frozen by now.

The soldiers approached and quickly recognized Kjell. "What's wrong?" one man called.

"My wife and her aunt have been wounded. Someone broke into the house." He stepped over the back of the seat and into the wagon bed. "They need a doctor!"

The soldiers helped Zerelda from the wagon. Seeing she could walk with help, the man in charge issued an order for one of the privates to aid her into the building. Next, he turned to help lift Lydia from the wagon, but Kjell pushed him back.

"I've got her. You lead."

By the time Kjell cleared the door, Mrs. Ensign, one of the doctors' wives, was there pointing the way. "They've taken Zerelda to the dispensary. Follow me."

They moved quickly down the west hall until they reached the end. Two orderlies followed behind with a long table. They assembled it in the middle of the room at the doctor's instructions. Mrs. Ensign quickly covered it with a sheet and motioned to Kjell.

With great care, he deposited Lydia on the table and then stepped back. The scene was terrible. Blood was caked and clotted on her neck and blouse. She was as white as the sheet upon which she lay, and there was only the tiniest hint of her breathing.

Dr. Ensign joined them. He turned to the orderlies. "Clean Miss Rockford's wounds while I see to Mrs. Lindquist."

The men nodded and immediately went to where Zerelda sat. Kjell turned his attention back to Lydia. Dr. Ensign began carefully pulling away the fabric of her blouse. "Bring the scissors." His wife went to fetch them while he cast a quick look up at Kjell. "Are you injured, too?"

Kjell followed the doctor's gaze to his chest. He was drenched in rain and blood.

"No. I'm fine. I wasn't there when it happened."

"And exactly what did happen?"

"I don't know. I came home to find them both injured. Zee remembers some men coming in. They were after the baby."

"The baby? Where is he?"

Kjell shook his head. He felt sick inside. "I don't know. He's been taken."

Disbelief rang clear in the doctor's voice. "Taken? You must be mistaken."

"I'm not. Whoever did this took my son." Water dripped down Kjell's face and he wiped it away with the back of his sleeve.

"Orderly, get this man some dry clothes. Kjell, you need to change or you'll catch pneumonia," the doctor insisted.

"I won't leave. I can change here."

The doctor nodded at the orderly and turned back to Lydia. Kjell had never felt so helpless in his life. He tried to pray but found that words escaped him. He tried to focus on anything but the sight of his wife.

The room was cold and sterile. It had been organized and arranged with all that the doctor would need for immediate care. There was a glass-front case with bottles neatly arranged. The shelves to the far side were just as well ordered. The room was probably the cleanest of any in Sitka.

He looked back to Lydia and felt a sensation of hopelessness wash over him. "Will she . . . live?"

"I don't know, Kjell. She's lost a lot of blood. The freezing air helped to slow the flow, however." He had removed her blouse and corset and was just cutting away the last of her chemise. "She's been shot, you know."

"I presumed as much, but I didn't know for sure," Kjell admitted. The orderly reappeared with a stack of dry clothes.

"Step behind the screen over there and get out of those things," the doctor ordered.

Kjell quickly did as he was told. He stepped out with only the dry trousers on. Clutching the shirt in his hand, Kjell came back to the table and finished dressing at Lydia's side.

"The wound on her shoulder isn't that bad. The bullet only grazed her." Dr. Ensign motioned to his assistant. "Hold this dressing in place while I assess her other injuries."

Kjell could see that the neck wound had begun to bleed once again. Dr. Ensign worked quickly to clean the site and survey the damage. "The wound is thawing. Kjell, you'll need to go. Wait outside."

"I won't leave her. If she's going to die, then I'm going to be at her side."

"Very well — just stay back over there." He cocked his head toward the door.

There was a chair not far from the counter. Kjell took a seat and watched and waited while everyone else bustled around as a team. They all seemed to know their duties and attended to his wife without having to be instructed.

When the doctor set the scalpel to Lydia's neck, Kjell nearly came up out of his seat. He calmed himself, however, realizing that the doctor knew what he was doing and only cared about saving Lydia's life.

But what if he couldn't? What if she died — died like Raisa? Kjell wasn't sure he could take another blow like that. Then he thought of Dalton. There was no telling where the child was. He wanted to go and search for his son, but he couldn't leave Lydia's side. Whoever had taken the baby had done it on the orders of Marston Gray — of this, Kjell was certain. And if Marston had taken the child, at least he would not be harmed. So for the time, Kjell reasoned, it was better to stay with Lydia.

He hadn't realized that Zerelda had come to join him until she touched his shoulder. The orderly set a chair for her beside Kjell, and she reached out to take hold of his hand. "We should pray," she whispered.

He nodded but felt completely helpless. "I don't have the words, Zee."

Zerelda, now sporting a bandaged head, bowed. "I believe God hears your heart."

CHAPTER 20

Evie Gray Gadston looked across the room at her husband. The man was surrounded by his friends and business associates and had no interest whatsoever in his young wife. She kept her feelings carefully masked so that no one would realize how miserable she truly was. She had been married for nearly a year — the twentieth of February would mark her anniversary. Evie had hoped with time, her husband would show more interest in her. So far, that hadn't proven true.

He was more married to his business dealings than to her. In fact, while he had consummated many new business arrangements over the last year, Thomas Gadston had failed to do the same for his marriage.

At nearly eighteen, Evie didn't know whether to be happy or sad about it. She hadn't wanted to marry the man in the first place — he was twenty years her senior, and they shared no common interest. From the first night she'd moved into the Gadston house as his wife, Thomas had shown her little regard. He hadn't even bothered to show her around the house — he'd left that to the housekeeper.

Her bedroom, appointed with everything a young woman could desire, had never been visited by her husband. Evie would spend many a long evening in the quiet confines of her suite while Thomas entertained businessmen in the rooms below. She had once approached him on the matter, only to be waved away with his reproach. "You are mine to do with as I wish," he had said, "and if I wish to preserve your chastity and virtue, it is of no concern to you."

"This is a wonderful party, don't you think?" Jeannette declared as she approached Evie.

"I suppose so. The men seem to have no interest in discussing anything but politics and financial interests, while the women stand idly, gossiping about whose family scandal is greater."

Jeannette frowned. "Honestly, I cannot understand you. You have everything. This glorious home — one of the finest in Kansas City. You're married to a man who was known to be the best catch in six states."

She giggled as she looked over her shoulder at Thomas. "And he is the most handsome by far."

"Maybe you should marry him," Evie said, rolling her eyes.

"As I said, I do not understand you. Look at you. You're wearing the very latest fashions, in the finest silk money can buy. You're positively dripping in jewels and —"

"And I'm miserable." Evie fingered one of her rings. "Thomas never talks to me. He never shows me the slightest bit of attention or affection."

"I wish I had it as good. Mr. Stone is already talking of wanting more children, and Jerrad is not but a year old. Goodness, but you would think two progeny would be more than enough for anyone."

Evie turned away. "Enjoy the party, Jeannette." She wasn't about to let her sister see how deeply her words had cut. Evie would love to have children. She longed for them, in fact. Jeannette spoke as if they were a curse.

"Genevieve, I heard you were just back from Europe. How did you enjoy your tour?"

Looking up, Evie found herself suddenly surrounded by several of the businessmen's wives. Mrs. Benedict, a particularly annoying woman, had posed the question.

"I found the Old World to be quite charming," Evie said with practiced ease.

"Did you sail on the Rhine?" Mrs. De-Hart asked. "We sailed the Rhine last spring, and it was divine."

"We visited the Alps but did not sail the Rhine, I'm sorry to say."

The women continued to ply her with questions, and even Jeannette joined in. "Mr. Stone says we will take the grand tour when the children are a little older."

"Oh, it is so difficult to travel with young ones," Mrs. Benedict admitted. "I find it much easier to leave them behind. A good nurse is all they need, anyway."

Evie had taken all she could. She scanned the room to see where Thomas was but couldn't find him. No doubt he had taken his cronies to another room for cigars and brandy. She sighed. It would be impossible to plead a headache and retire to her room if Thomas wasn't available to host their party.

"If you'll excuse me," she told the women, "I should see to my other guests."

She moved away before anyone could protest. Evie was glad when the small orchestra Thomas had hired began to play music once again. Several couples immediately began to waltz to the strains of "On the Beautiful Blue Danube." It was a wonderful piece that Evie had first heard in Vienna. She had specifically requested it for the evening's events. She had hoped to dance instead of stroll around the room, but at least she could enjoy the music.

"Might I have the honor?"

She looked up to find one of Thomas's secretaries. Trayton Payne was a tall, sleek young man, not much older than Evie. She smiled. "I would love to dance. This song is one of my favorites."

He took hold of her, careful to keep her a proper and very formal distance from himself. Evie stepped into the waltz as if she were a part of the music itself. She lost herself in its beauty for several moments.

"If I may be so bold, you look sad tonight. Are you all right?"

She looked up at Mr. Payne in surprise. "I'm fine, thank you for asking. I am surprised, however, that you aren't in the library with the others, enjoying bawdy talk and more masculine refreshments."

He smiled down at her, piercing her with his dark-eyed gaze. "I've wanted to spend time with you since first coming here tonight."

Evie couldn't hide her surprise. "Why me?

Thomas pays your salary."

He chuckled and pulled Evie just a bit closer. "Why not you? You are much more intriguing. In fact, I would venture to say you are the most beautiful woman here."

His comment was entirely out of line for a man of his position, but Evie couldn't be angry with him. His flattery was like food to a starving man — or woman, in this case. She lowered her gaze and smiled. What could it hurt to flirt with him a bit?

"I watch you all of the time, at any of the gatherings where you are both in attendance, and I can see how he neglects you."

"My husband is a very busy man," Evie replied. "And I'm quite capable of seeking my own entertainment."

"And might I be a part of that entertainment? At least tonight?"

"We are waltzing, are we not?" She felt a shiver run down her spine at the way he looked at her. His gaze was a mixture of appreciation and desire. It caused her heart to beat faster. Or was it just the pace of the dance?

When the last strains of the music faded and the couples were forced to separate and bow to each other, Evie found herself weak in the knees. She knew she'd put herself in a dangerous situation but didn't care. She was having fun, and for once, she felt desired.

"Come. Let me get you some refreshment. You seem rather . . . well . . . breathless." He grinned.

Evie knew she should tell him no, but seeing that no one else seemed to be watching, she could only nod. The man led her to a small alcove and bid her to sit.

"I'll be right back," he assured.

She stared after him as he walked away. He cut a dashing figure, to be sure. Thomas might have been considered one of the most eligible bachelors before their marriage, but this man carried a charm and essence of strength that Thomas could never hope to have.

When he returned, Evie had convinced herself that she would share one drink with him, and after that she would dismiss him and attend to her guests. Half an hour later, she was still trying to dismiss him.

"Why are you afraid to be with me?"

Evie shook her head. "I am not afraid. I am simply mindful of the fact that I am the hostess of this party. People will begin to talk if I allow you to take up any more time."

He laughed softly. "Let them talk. In fact, if you are the spirited and brave young woman I believe you to be, you would take a walk with me and give them something to really talk about."

She loved the way he looked at her. It made her feel truly pretty and wanted. Thomas had never made her feel that way. "I . . . uh . . . I can't," she said, trying to think clearly.

"Can't or won't?" He reached out and gently touched her cheek.

"Maybe it's better to say I shouldn't," Evie said, trembling as his fingers trailed down to touch her neck.

His eyes seemed to darken with amusement, and his knowing smile only served to intensify her desire to yield to his request.

"There are a lot of things we shouldn't do," he whispered against her ear, "but I find that most things have a way of working themselves out. Now, why don't we slip away for some air? I happen to know you have a lovely sitting room on the second floor. A very private sitting room."

Evie spotted her husband across the room. He had just emerged from the library and was completely engrossed in a conversation with one of his business associates. He didn't so much as cast a glance around the room for her. Anger coursed through her. Why did her own husband offer her no affection?

She returned her focus to Mr. Payne and nodded. "Maybe for just a little while."

CHAPTER 21

Kjell awoke slowly to find that Lydia was still unconscious. The doctor had done everything possible and had put her to bed in one of the hospital's empty wards, with Zerelda only a few beds away. Kjell had spent the night sleeping in the chair beside his wife, praying whenever he awoke that God would somehow set things right.

He reached over to gently stroke her hair. "Good morning, my darling." He was comforted that she continued to breathe steadily. The doctor had not held much hope for her recovery. Frankly, he hadn't thought she would make it through the night, but here she was.

Taking hold of her cold hand, Kjell rubbed it lightly. "Zee's doing very well. Her injuries weren't too bad. She was knocked unconscious for a time, but the doctor said she will recover. She's sleeping just across the room." He kept his voice low so as not to wake Zerelda. He glanced over to see that she was undisturbed before continuing.

"It's been a long night." He realized that the sun had already risen and reached for his watch. He had enough light to see that it was nearly eight. He should have already been at work. The army lumber order was expected today.

He needed to get word to Joshua at the mill. The poor man wouldn't have a clue as to why Kjell wasn't there. Getting to his feet, Kjell stretched and found his neck and back ached from his long hours in the chair. Dr. Ensign said he could take one of the empty beds, but Kjell had been afraid to leave Lydia's side. If she had called out, he might not have heard her.

Motioning for the orderly to come, Kjell explained the situation. "I need to get word to Joshua Broadstreet at the sawmill. Can someone take a message?"

"I'll see if I can arrange it," the man said. He left without another word just as Zerelda stirred and sat up.

"How is she?"

Kjell went to Zee and shook his head. "I don't know. She hasn't so much as moved all night. She's still breathing, though."

Zerelda reached up to touch her bandaged head. "Whoever he was, he sure gave me a wallop."

Just then, the orderly returned with a blue-uniformed private at his side. The man nodded rather formally to Kjell. "Captain said I was to make myself available to you," the young man declared. "He also said he wants to talk to you when you are able."

"Thank you. I need to get a message to Joshua Broadstreet at Lindquist Mill. Tell him my wife and her aunt were injured last night, and we're here. Tell him to come see me as soon as he can for instructions."

"Yes, sir. Anything else, sir?"

"Please tell the captain he can join us here."

"Yes, sir."

The young private pivoted and all but marched out of the room. Kjell turned back to Lydia, where the orderly was checking her dressings. He left Zee momentarily and went to his wife.

"How does it look?"

"The bleeding has stopped. That's good. She's lost a great deal of blood, and there's no telling if her body can withstand the shock. Hopefully, infection won't set in, but only time will tell."

Kjell nodded. "The odds are against us, aren't they?"

"It doesn't look good." He redressed the

wounds. "I need to report to Dr. Ensign."

"She's in God's hands, Kjell. We have to trust Him."

Surprised to find Zerelda by his side, Kjell turned to face her. "I can't lose her. I just can't, Zee."

She put her arm around his shoulder. "God is still the one to make those decisions. We have to trust that He knows what He's doing. Come over here with me for a moment."

Kjell let her lead him to the far end of the room. Zerelda's expression grew quite serious. "What of Dalton, Kjell?"

"My guess is that Marston Gray instigated that attack and kidnapping. It's what I told the authorities last night and still what I believe. I wouldn't be surprised if the Sidorovs had something to do with it, as well. I learned not long ago that they were probably the ones behind the fire at the mill."

Zerelda frowned and glanced over to Lydia's bed. "We can't talk about Dalton in front of her. Even as she is, she might hear something. If she realizes the baby is gone, she might give up hope."

"Mr. Lindquist?"

He turned to find the same army captain he'd talked to the night before. "Is there any news?"

"Nothing yet. We need to talk further with Miss Rockford if she's up to it."

"I am," Zerelda replied. "I'm happy to help in any way I can. I'm just afraid my memory isn't much better than it was last night."

"That's all right, ma'am. Why don't we sit so you can rest?" the captain suggested.

Zerelda made her way back to the bed and sat. Kjell pulled up two chairs and offered the captain a seat. He hadn't heard anything Zee had told the man before, and he hoped that she might shed some light on the attackers. It was apparent the captain wanted the same.

The soldier leaned forward. "I wonder if you could further describe the man who hit you. His size, hair color, clothes — anything at all would help."

"Well, I do remember the one that entered the house first. He was a good bit taller than me — maybe a whole foot. He had blond hair — not real pale, more the color of cornstalks." She paused for a moment. "Oh, he spoke with a thick Russian accent."

"Anatolli Sidorov," Kjell muttered.

"What is that?" the captain questioned.

"She just described Anatolli Sidorov. His brother is a bit smaller and his hair is darker — more of a brownish gold."

"Do you know this Anatolli, ma'am?"

Zerelda shook her head. "I've never met him or his brother."

"But you would know him if you saw him again?"

Kjell looked to Zerelda and awaited her answer. He was confident that the men responsible for the attack were the Sidorovs. He should have turned them over to the authorities when he caught them stealing from him.

"I think I would," Zerelda replied. "I never got a good look at the second man. Or if I did, it's all lost to me now. When the first man headed upstairs to find the baby, I tried to go after him. That's when the second man hit me from behind. I don't remember anything after that until Kjell woke me up." She cast Kjell a sympathetic glance. "I'm sorry."

"It's enough, Zee. I'm positive it was the Sidorovs. They were the only ones who had anything against us. They were also paid to burn the mill."

"Boss? You sent for me?"

Kjell looked up to find Joshua standing in the doorway to the ward. "Come in. I did send for you, but right now I need you to tell the captain here everything you heard about the Sidorovs being paid to burn the mill."

Seeing that the doctor had also arrived, Kjell dismissed himself and went to discuss Lydia's condition, but the doctor waved him away until he could finish examining her. After what seemed an eternity, he finally came to where Kjell stood.

"It's not good," he said, shaking his head. "She's incredibly weak and nearly unresponsive. There isn't any fight in her at all."

A quick glance at Lydia's pale, lifeless face left little doubt in Kjell's mind that the doctor was right. If she had been conscious when the Sidorovs took Dalton, she would have known it was Marston Gray's doing. And knowing how he and his family had bullied her in the past, Lydia probably knew there was little chance of fighting him. She would believe Dalton was lost to her forever.

"We have to find the baby," Kjell whispered. "That is the only hope we have of urging her to fight this."

"Perhaps if you talk to her about how needed she is," Dr. Ensign said. "Don't say anything about the baby being gone."

"Zee was just suggesting that, as well. I'll do what I can." He met the doctor's worried expression. "Please do anything necessary to save her. No matter the cost."

314

Dr. Ensign touched his shoulder. "Kjell, be assured we are doing everything humanly possible. We have our limitations here — we aren't a big city with a fancy hospital and surgery. Still, we have skilled individuals who know what they're doing. We will fight to restore her to you."

Thomas Gadston grinned as he held out a large stack of bills to Trayton Payne. "I presume you were successful last night. When I returned, Genevieve was nowhere in sight."

Trayton nodded and took the money. "I was. I seduced her, and she was eager to comply."

"How rich," Gadston said. "This is probably the best return for my money in ages. I don't know why I didn't think of it sooner."

Pocketing the money, Trayton shrugged. "I can't say that I understand, but I'm happy to help."

"I don't expect you to understand. It really isn't anyone's concern why I choose to do business the way I do. Suffice it to say I have no patience for this game of marriage. I never intended to take a wife. I married only for the purposes of making better business dealings. Unfortunately, those were lost to me when Gray had the misfortune of dying. Genevieve is unimportant to me now."

"So why not divorce her? Charge her with infidelity and be done with her."

Gadston's expression darkened. "My family would never stand for it. Divorce would cause a scandal, and I would be cut off from inheriting. There is far too much money at risk to merely walk away from my marriage. I will let the child have her interests, and I will have mine."

"And you've told her this?" Trayton asked in surprise. Most men would never tolerate their wives taking lovers, while Gadston seemed to encourage it.

Gadston laughed. "Certainly not. Half the fun will be watching her sneak around and try to avoid giving me any reason to believe she's having an affair. Her guilt will be amusing — especially if you should happen to get her with child."

"Excuse me?"

The shock of such a statement had Trayton doubting he had heard accurately. He watched Gadston for any sign of teasing, but there was none. Instead, the man crossed to his desk and took a seat. "We can discuss it at another time. Right now, I have work that needs my attention. You do, as well. Here are the figures that you need to take to Mr. McCarthy regarding the planned railroad."

Trayton took up the ledger being offered and held it for a moment. He felt confused by Gadston's comment and wanted to clarify the matter. Instead, the older man seemed unconcerned.

"Do what you can to keep her happy," Gadston said, as if reading the younger man's mind. "Do so, and I will increase your salary substantially."

Trayton Payne left the Gadston mansion and barely felt the pelting ice as he made his way to the enclosed carriage. He gave the driver the address and sat back to think on all that had just happened. He had always considered himself rather phlegmatic when it came to the eccentric ways of the rich. Rarely did any request or situation shock him. Still, he'd not witnessed any man being so nonchalant when it came to giving his wife over to another.

Still, it was a means to an end. Trayton intended to be one of those eccentric rich in his own right. He had long ago vowed that he would do whatever he needed to in order to earn the money that would allow him to rise to the top of society. Power and money were the most important things to him, and he intended to surround himself with plenty of both. If that meant he fathered a few children along the way in order to make a rich old man happy, then so be it.

He grinned and folded his gloved hands behind his head. "And Evie Gadston is definitely not hard on the eyes."

Evie had watched from her bedroom window as Trayton Payne left her house. She felt consumed with guilt. She had allowed him to take her from the party — to take her away from everyone else.

"You allowed him to do more than that," she admonished as she sat down to her vanity mirror. Picking up a brush, she stroked hard through the mass of golden curls. She could still remember allowing him to hold her. He had kissed her, too. Not just the quick, obligatory pecks that she'd had from Thomas. When Trayton's mouth had touched hers, she had forgotten everything except the man in her arms.

She met her reflection and frown. "It was wrong, and it cannot happen again."

But why not? Society certainly didn't look down on men taking lovers, so why should they be so hard on wives wanting the same benefit? Who was to know, as long as she was discreet?

If only Thomas would show her the slightest bit of love, it would change everything. Evie hadn't wanted to marry the man, but she had gone into the arrangement determined to be a good and faithful wife. Especially a faithful wife. But after nearly a year of not-so-wedded bliss, Evie was desperate to feel something other than lethargy. She had gone to Europe, hoping to stimulate her mind and heart. There had been museums and galleries to visit and wonderful parties where the latest fashions and foods had been presented to titillate the eye and tongue. She had spent copious amounts of money doing whatever pleased her, but nothing satisfied. What was missing?

Last night, Trayton Payne had given her insight into that question. Better yet, he'd given her an understanding of the answer. She couldn't replace her heart's longing for love by purchasing baubles. Trayton had awakened a hunger in her that she had managed to stave off until now.

"What am I to do?" she asked her reflection.

The last thing she wanted was to bring disgrace to her name or to her family. They had done a good enough job of that on their own, and she had no desire to add to it. Thomas was respected by his peers and society. If she were to cause him harm in such a way as to make him a laughingstock among that haughty group, it would certainly not bode well.

She put down the brush and continued to stare at her reflection. For a moment, she could see herself growing old and wrinkled. An image of her mother came to mind. Charlotte Gray hadn't been an old woman when she'd died, but the years had marked her face.

Even though Evie had been quite young, she'd sensed her mother's unhappiness. Then that awful day had come when her mother had fallen to her death. Evie wanted to tell everyone what had really happened, but she had been too afraid. Afraid that her father would throw her from the same rooftop. Afraid no one would believe her anyway. Maybe her memories were wrong.

"My life has been lived in fear," she said, shaking her head. She had even married in fear. Had she done anything to disturb the arrangement her father had made, Evie knew she would have suffered greatly for it. Her father had ways of making people suffer. Hadn't she learned that lesson from her mother and from Lydia?

Her anger resurfaced. "Why should I let them do this to me? Why should I care what anyone else says or does?"

She thought again of Trayton, and her guilt faded a bit. She had only kissed him. Nothing else had happened. He had been sweet to her. He had made her feel beautiful — alive. What was wrong with that? What damage could possibly come from a few kisses?

CHAPTER 22

"If she believes Dalton is lost to her forever," Kjell told Zerelda, "she may never come back to us." He had given the matter much thought and knew he needed to do whatever was necessary to find the baby.

"I don't want to leave her, but I don't know what else to do. If I scour the island and still come up empty, I'll have to go to Kansas City and confront Marston Gray."

"That family is pure wickedness," Zerelda said. "If they are responsible . . . well . . . I hope you can see them jailed for this."

Kjell hoped so, too, though he had his doubts. Liddie had always said the Grays were powerful people who were used to getting their own way. He took up his coat and cast one more glance at his unconscious wife. She looked so tiny and frail.

"I won't be too long. I'll scout out the grounds around the house and see if I can spot any tracks. I know the army has men looking, as well."

"I hope they can handle the job." Zerelda sounded unsure. "They've never managed to find the killers of those two Tlingit boys."

"I know, but this is a crime against whites. I hate to say it, but perhaps it will merit more attention — especially given that a child has been taken."

Kjell made his way downstairs and was surprised to find a gathering of army officers at the door. Dr. Ensign was also there.

"We were just coming to see you."

Kjell recognized the captain in charge. "Captain Briar, have you found anything? Have you found my son?"

"We haven't found the boy," Briar began, "but we do have news. We were able to find some tracks that lead down to the water's edge. We believe the attackers departed by boat." He motioned to one of the men.

"This blanket was found. Do you recognize it?"

Kjell took hold of the piece and immediately recognized it. Despite the mud, it was clearly the blanket Zerelda had given Dalton for Christmas. "Yes. It's his. Lydia's aunt made it for Dalton and gave it to us at Christmas."

"And what about this?" The captain took another object from the man and held it up.

"We found this knife not far from the blanket."

"That belongs to Anatolli Sidorov," Kjell replied. "I've seen him with it a hundred times if I've seen it once. He carved the handle, and you'll find his initials etched in at the top of the blade."

The captain nodded and handed the knife back to the soldier. "We assumed as much. The initials are there, just as you say. It would seem we have good proof that at least Anatolli Sidorov was involved in the attack."

Kjell balled his hands. "And if he's involved, his brother, Ioann, is involved. They always work together."

"I had my men tear apart the Double-Decker, but there was no sign of them. One man told us they had departed some weeks back. He thought they had taken up living with someone on the far west side of the island. We've sent men to investigate."

"I'll go, too," Kjell declared.

"We'd rather you not," Captain Briar responded. "It's better if you leave this to us. Believe me, Kjell, we're leaving no stone unturned."

"There's more you should know," Kjell said. He thought carefully for a moment. He needed to explain Marston Gray's part in this. At least what he presumed the man's part to be. "Is there somewhere we can sit and talk privately?"

Twenty minutes later, Captain Briar rubbed his chin and considered the details of Kjell's explanation.

"If what you say is true — if this Gray fellow took your son — then we need to get word to the authorities in Kansas City. We can wire the information from Seattle or San Francisco. It might even beat Gray back if we act quickly. I'm going to speak to General Tidball. Since this is now his post, he needs to be notified and kept apprised."

"Whatever it takes. Whatever it costs." Kjell met the man's gaze. "This man will stop at nothing. He's a danger to everyone, but especially to my son. I wouldn't put it past him to have the child put to death rather than see him returned to Lydia."

"I believe you, Kjell. Let me talk to the general. We'll decide how best to get word to Kansas City. Meanwhile, we'll continue to search the island."

Kjell nodded with a heavy sigh. Here was yet another situation where all he could do was wait. It made him feel helpless. He couldn't help Lydia recover, and he couldn't search for his son. If he didn't have some task to keep his mind on, he would go mad.

■ ■ ■ ■

Zerelda held Lydia's hand and stroked it gently. "Liddie, I do wish you would wake up. We miss you, dear heart. I know you've suffered greatly, but we need you. Dalton needs you."

She hesitated to say more. Looking at her niece, Zerelda could see no sign that she'd heard or understood. She wanted to have hope that Lydia would survive but felt her faith beginning to falter.

Oh, Father, she prayed silently, *I don't want to give up. I know you have the power to bring life back from the brink of death itself. I ask you to do that with Liddie. Bring her back to us, Father.* Tears streamed down her face. *Please.*

Hearing the ward door open, Zerelda wiped her face and turned. It was the doctor. He nodded at Zerelda and went immediately to Lydia's side.

"Have you seen any change?" he asked her.

"No. I've been talking to her, but there hasn't been any response — no sign that she hears."

Dr. Ensign frowned but continued to examine his patient. "I had hoped to see her regain consciousness by now."

Zerelda knew the longer a patient remained unconscious, the less hope there was of their recovering. And while it had not been that long since the attack, it would have boded better had Lydia shows signs of awakening.

"She feels feverish." He checked her breathing. "I'm worried about pneumonia setting in."

"I can keep an eye on her," Zerelda said. "I can keep turning her."

The doctor nodded. "Just don't overdo it. You're recovering, too. I'll send my orderly to check on her in an hour."

As he left the room, Kjell returned. He stopped and talked briefly with the doctor, then joined Zerelda at Lydia's bedside. "I need to talk to you."

Giving Lydia's hand a squeeze, Zerelda leaned over. "I'll be right back, Liddie. You just rest."

Kjell's expression told her this would most likely be bad news. Zerelda squared her shoulders and drew a deep breath. "What is it?"

"They found Dalton's blanket by the water. Apparently, the Sidorovs took him out in that storm — probably to meet up with Gray. He was probably on a larger boat waiting for them."

"Do you think he already left the island?"

"That's my guess. Gray didn't have many friends here. Someone at the Double-Decker thought the Sidorovs had moved out to live with someone on the west side of the island. The army has men checking this out even as we speak, but I doubt they will find anything."

"So you are confident that it was Marston and the Sidorovs?"

"I am. Especially now. Captain Briar showed me Anatolli's knife. Apparently he had dropped it near the baby's blanket by the water. There was no other knife like that one. The Sidorovs were known to have been paid to burn my mill, and the only one who would have benefited from that would have been Gray. He held me a grudge for my interference and marriage to Lydia."

Zerelda felt a bit lightheaded and reached for Kjell's arm. "I should sit."

"I'm sorry, Zee. What was I thinking?" He led her to the bed and helped her to sit.

"So now all we can do is wait." It was more statement than question. Zerelda knew that there was little else to be done. Besides that, she didn't want to leave Lydia's side.

"And that's the part I'm no good at," Kjell

admitted. "I feel like I should be doing something more." He glanced across the room to where Lydia slept. "I can't help her, and I can't help Dalton. I offered to go search, but the army doesn't want me in the middle of it. They feel they have the investigation under control, but I would feel better if I had a hand in it, as well."

"We can have a hand in it by praying," she suggested. "I know it seems like such a small thing, but it's not. Jesus promised we could bring our needs to Him. God already knows what they are anyway."

"I've been praying, Zee. As best I can. It seems sometimes the words just won't come."

"But God understands that, too. He hears the unspoken prayers of our hearts through His Spirit. He knows our longings, even when we can't form the words."

With a sigh, Kjell sat in the chair beside her bed. "Don't you ever struggle in keeping your faith?"

She smiled. "Of course I do. But I know that there is no one who could possibly love me more than God does. I trust Him, even when I don't understand Him. Of course, I wish He would see things my way more often."

This brought a hint of a smile to Kjell's

face. "Me, too. Especially where Lydia is concerned."

"I'm glad you love her so much. She deserves that. She's had such a hard life, and the one thing she always longed for was love. You've made her a very happy woman over the last couple of months."

"I just want to go on loving her. I want to have a future with her and more children. I can't even imagine her happy, though, unless Dalton is returned to her."

"Then we have to pray that he will come home. God alone knows where he is and who is caring for him. God alone can bring him back to us."

Kjell awoke the next morning to the sounds of rain against the window. He had taken the doctor up on his offer of a cot and had pulled it close to Lydia's, just to be near her. Many times through the night he had awakened to check on her. He just needed to know that she was still breathing — still with them.

Swinging his legs over the side, Kjell sat and wondered what the hours ahead would hold. Would this be the day Lydia would wake up?

He reached for her hand. "Please wake up, Lydia. I can't bear being without you. I need you more than I ever thought possible." He slipped off the bed and knelt beside his wife. "I went to the house yesterday, and nothing was the same. It will never be the same without you. You have to get better."

Tears blurred his vision as he kissed her hand. "I love you more than life, Liddie."

Kneeling there, Kjell prayed as he had never prayed before. He pleaded with God for Lydia's life, careful to say nothing about the missing baby. Silently, he added his petitions for the child, knowing full well that the mother and son were so tightly connected that each would suffer without the other.

He felt someone touch his shoulder and thought it was Zee, but when he opened his eyes and looked up, he found Dr. Ensign instead.

"How are you doing, Kjell?"

He got to his feet and rubbed the back of his neck. "I feel like I'm just marking time."

"I feel the same. I wish there were something we could do to change the situation, but all we can do is wait." He left Kjell's side and went to Lydia. He put his hand upon her forehead and smiled. "The fever is gone. She doesn't feel hot to the touch — not like yesterday." He listened to her heart and lungs and nodded. "The lungs sound clear, and the heart is strong. I think it's possible she's turned a corner, Kjell. She's fighting again — fighting to live."

The words were all Kjell had hoped to hear, but doubt lingered. "Then why doesn't she wake up?"

The doctor shook his head. "I don't know. I can't know. The body is such an unpredictable science. Just when you think you have it all figured out, it throws you yet another symptom or problem. So much depends on the patient."

Dr. Ensign completed his exam, then motioned Kjell to follow him out of the ward. "Captain Briar is downstairs. He said when you have time, he'd like to speak to you."

"Did he say if he'd found something — the Sidorovs or Dalton?"

"No. He showed up just before I came up here and said he'd wait downstairs in my office. Mrs. Ensign has coffee waiting for you, as well. When you finish with the captain, feel free to join us for breakfast."

Kjell hurried downstairs ahead of the doctor and made his way to the small office. Captain Briar was waiting inside, standing rather formally at the window.

"You wanted to see me?"

The man turned and nodded. His expression was grave. "Please sit."

A vise tightened around Kjell's chest. He reached for the nearest chair but didn't sit. "What is it? Something isn't right."

"No, it isn't. I'm afraid things don't look good. My men located the cabin that the Sidorovs were using. It's on the water and . . ." He pressed his lips together as if unable to say another word.

"Tell me. Tell me now. I have to know what you found."

Captain Briar cleared his throat and hesitated a moment longer. "We found Anatolli Sidorov. His body washed up on shore, along with debris from a small boat and other things."

"What other things?"

"There were articles of clothing — baby clothing."

"No. You're wrong."

The captain moved to where Kjell stood. "We didn't find the baby, but we feel . . . that is . . . with the boat destroyed . . . well, it's just a matter of time."

"Until what? What are you saying?" Kjell heard his own frantic words and knew the answer without asking.

"We believe all of them were lost at sea in the storm," Captain Briar finally said. He

reached out to grip Kjell's arm. "Since Anatolli's body washed ashore, we're hoping
the remains of the others will, as well."

Kjell shook his head. "You're wrong. You
have to be wrong. My son can't be dead."

"I'm sorry. I just don't think he would
have survived. Even if the Sidorovs were
taking him to the Gray man as you suggested, they had to battle the storm. You
know yourself that was one of the worst
we've seen in a long while. They were simply
unable to keep off of the rocks."

Kjell sank into the chair and buried his
face in his hands. How could he ever tell
Lydia that their child was dead? At least if
he were with Gray, there was hope of getting him back safely.

His shoulders shook as deep sobs made
their way up from his heart. *God? Where
are you? Why is this happening? How can we
bear it?*

The captain stayed at his side, his hand
still on Kjell's arm. He offered no words of
consolation. There were no words. Nothing
spoken could make sense of what had happened.

Kjell thought of the tiny boy — of his love
for this child. *He might not be flesh of my
flesh,* he thought, *but Dalton is my son, just
the same.*

■ ■ ■ ■

Zerelda was waiting for Kjell when he finally emerged from the office. She could see for herself that the news hadn't been good. Kjell's red-rimmed eyes bore clear evidence that the worst thing possible had come to pass.

"Did they find Dalton?" she asked, terrified to even ask the question.

Kjell took hold of her and led her to a wooden chair. He sat down beside her. "No. Not yet."

Zerelda felt a sense of hope. "Then what has you so upset? I thought for sure —"

"They found Anatolli Sidorov and . . . and . . . wreckage."

"Wreckage?"

Kjell met her gaze and nodded. "The boat was ripped apart by the storm. There was debris, along with Anatolli's body. Some things belonged to Dalton."

She put her hand to her mouth and shook her head. She knew in her heart what Kjell was trying to tell her, but she couldn't fathom that it could possibly be true.

"Captain Briar believes that in time, Ioann and Dalton may be found, as well. He believes them all to have drowned."

Zerelda's eyes filled with tears as she continued to shake her head. She couldn't bear the thought. Dalton could not be dead. He simply couldn't be.

Kjell put his arm around Zerelda to hold her close, and this was her undoing. She wept softly into her hands. *Dear Lord, please don't let this be true. He's just a baby. Please, Lord.*

CHAPTER 23

Evie made her way downstairs. She was due at a meeting of the Kansas City Orphans and Widows Association, where she and many others of society's finest would share refreshments and determine how best to help those in need.

She sent for the carriage and allowed the butler to help her with her coat. Evie was just doing up the buttons when Thomas crossed the hall and spotted her.

"My dear, where are you headed on this cold afternoon?"

"I'm going to my meeting for the widows and orphans. Remember? I told you about it at breakfast this morning."

He considered her statement for a moment. "Yes, I suppose I do recall that." He gave her a disinterested nod, then said to the butler, "Miles, don't forget to have the carriage brought round for me at eleven."

"Yes, sir," the man replied with a curt nod.

Evie pulled on her gloves. "If anyone comes to call, tell them I'll be receiving later today — after two."

"Very good, madam." He opened the door for her and offered to assist her. "Shall I see you to the carriage?"

"No thank you, Miles. I'll be just fine."

Evie felt the bite of the February air and buried her face in her coat. The coachman opened the door of the enclosed carriage and helped her aboard. Evie settled into the leather upholstery with her face still tucked low as the door was secured.

"I can help keep you warm," a voice whispered.

Startled, she looked up to find Trayton Payne sitting opposite her. He quickly came to her side just as the driver put the carriage in motion.

"What are you doing here?" She saw his serious expression turn to one of amusement as he pulled her close.

"What do you suppose?" He silenced any reply by kissing her.

Evie tried to push him away at first. Trayton, however, would have no part of that. He only tightened his hold and pressed kisses against her jaw and ear.

"I've missed you," he whispered.

"Stop this," she said, although she hardly

sounded convincing.

"You don't really want me to stop," he said matter-of-factly.

Evie knew he spoke the truth. The worst of it was that he knew how she felt. She didn't want him to stop. She thrilled to his touch, his attention.

"You are the most beautiful woman I've ever laid eyes upon." He gently fingered a wisp of hair at her temple. "Beautiful and intelligent. Most women cannot boast of both. Some cannot even claim one or the other. How unique to find it all in you."

"Why are you here?" she said, her voice barely audible.

"I heard that you were going out this morning. I slipped into the carriage when the driver was otherwise occupied." He eased his hold and grinned. "Are you sorry that I did so?"

She didn't move from his embrace. For a moment, she considered lying, but then shook her head. "I regret only that I am not free to receive your attention." She looked away immediately, realizing she'd said too much. Embarrassed by her words, she hurried to change the subject but chose the wrong topic. "It's certainly cold today."

"I can make you feel warm," he said with a low chuckle. Trayton took up a lap blanket and spread it out slowly, leaning over to tuck it around her snugly.

Evie trembled at his nearness. This was madness. She was a married woman, and despite the fact that her husband showed her no attention or affection, adultery was still frowned upon by those in society. Of course, it wasn't frowned upon for men — just women. A woman could be lonely and as desperate for love as she was, and still an affair would be scandalous news. She would be ostracized — rejected completely — and her only guilt would be that she desired to feel loved. Well, maybe not her only guilt.

"I seem to have lost your attention. I must try harder to keep your thoughts on me," Trayton said, pulling her back against him.

A very small part of her wanted to fight him — to say no and demand he leave her alone. But one look into his dark eyes and Evie knew the situation was hopeless. She was being seduced, and she felt helpless to stop herself.

"I have a wonderful plan. Thomas is sending me to Chicago on business. Why don't you come with me? I can act as your chaperone, and we can be together without worrying about the ever watchful eye of busybodies."

Evie's mind whirled with a thousand

thoughts. "How would I ever explain my going to Chicago?"

"You love to travel, and you're bored. It's winter, and you need to get away for something different. If we plan it right, you can ask him while in my presence, and I can suggest you travel with me."

"I don't know." Evie put her hand to her head. Things were moving too fast.

"Oh, Evie, you deserve better than what Thomas gives you. I see the way he ignores you. I see the hurt in your eyes when he passes you by without much more than a single glance."

"You do?" she said in disbelief.

His hand caressed her cheek. "I do. I see that and more. He truly has no regard for anyone or anything except his money and business affairs. He doesn't understand your needs."

"And you think you do?"

He grinned. "I suppose you could best answer that. For example, how does this meet your need?" He kissed her again.

Evie shivered from the intensity of his touch. She felt him pull her onto his lap, and she did nothing to stop him. Cradled in his arms, she lost all rational thought. There was only this moment and Trayton. Nothing else mattered.

■ ■ ■ ■

Kjell wandered down Lincoln Street, desperately trying to figure out how he would tell Lydia about Dalton. She was still unconscious, but the doctor was seeing signs that she was starting to come back to them. The army had found no other wreckage or sign of Ioann or the baby but remained confident that they were lost. Captain Briar saw no reason to send word to Kansas City authorities, as they had no proof that Marston Gray had been involved.

He made his way back to the hospital as a gentle rain started to fall. The slate-colored skies meant it would most likely rain off and on all day. There was no sign of a break in the clouds for as far as Kjell could see, and the heaviness of the sky only served to deepen his sadness.

"There you are," Zerelda said as he entered the hospital's foyer. "Were you able to manage things at the mill?"

Kjell had told her that he was going to the mill in order to finish out several invoices, but in truth he'd never made it that far. "I lost track of time and never got there," he admitted. "What did the doctor say about your wound?"

342

"He told me I have a hard head and that I'm doing just fine." She took hold of his arm. "I'm going to head home and make us a nice supper. When do you plan to be there?"

Glancing around the entryway, he shook his head. "I don't know, Zee. I hate to leave Lydia."

"I know you do. Just come home for supper and then you can come right back."

Kjell looked past her to the stairs. "I suppose."

Zerelda reached out and took hold of his arm. "What's wrong?"

He shook his head. "I just don't know what to tell her about Dalton." Zerelda nodded and Kjell met her gaze. "I just don't think he's dead. The army has found no definitive proof. I have to believe that Gray was behind all of this."

"But what can you do to prove it one way or the other?" Zee asked. "How can we keep clinging to hope when there is no evidence that Dalton is still alive?"

"That's why we have to find out for sure."

"But how?"

Kjell squared his shoulders. "I'm not sure, but —"

"Kjell! Zerelda!" Dr. Ensign called to them from the top of the steps. "It's Lydia.

343

She's waking up."

Kjell bounded up the stairs, taking the steps two at time. He completely forgot about Zerelda and rushed past the doctor and into the ward. He could see Lydia stirring and went to her side.

"Liddie? Darling, I'm here. Talk to me," he pleaded.

Slowly, Lydia opened her eyes and blinked hard several times. She looked at him oddly, obviously confused by her state. "Water." She croaked the word.

Kjell reached over to the pitcher and poured a glass of water. "Here, let me help you." He put his arm around her and lifted her just a bit to drink. She grimaced in pain but said nothing.

By now the doctor and Zerelda had joined them. As Kjell eased Lydia back against the pillows, she looked from one person to the next. "Where . . . am I?"

"You're in the hospital," the doctor answered as he came to her side. "How do you feel?"

"I hurt," she said, reaching up to touch the place where her shoulder and neck connected. "What happened?"

Kjell and the doctor exchanged a glance. Everything in Kjell tensed. "What do you remember?" he asked.

Lydia shook her head. "I don't remember anything."

Her face seemed to contort, but whether from confusion or pain, Kjell couldn't be sure. He reached out and took hold of her hand. "It's all right, Liddie. You don't have to remember it all right now."

She looked at their entwined hands and then back to Kjell's face. "Who are you?"

Looking at Zerelda and then to the doctor, Kjell felt his throat close up. "What do you mean — you know who I am."

Lydia studied him for a moment, then looked at Zerelda, and finally Dr. Ensign. "I don't know any of you."

The doctor frowned. "You don't know your aunt — your husband?"

"Husband?" Lydia stared at Kjell. "You're my husband?"

"I am." Kjell could barely speak.

Zerelda stepped closer. "Sweetheart, do you know who you are?"

Lydia seemed to consider this question for a moment, then shook her head. "No." She frowned and pulled her hand away from Kjell. "I have no idea." She tried to sit up.

"Don't," the doctor warned. "You'll tear your stitches and start bleeding again."

"I don't want to be here. I don't remember what happened." Lydia's tone took on a definite sense of fear. "What's wrong with me?"

"There was a storm, and you were injured," the doctor said softly. "You were brought here to the hospital. Your wounds and the shock of their infliction have caused you to temporarily lose your memory. Don't be afraid. It sometimes happens."

"Who are you?" she asked.

"I'm Dr. Ensign. I've been taking care of you."

She seemed to accept this and nodded ever so slightly before looking to Zerelda. "And you . . . you're my aunt?"

"I am, although you have become much more like a daughter to me."

"Where is my mother?"

Zerelda bit her lower lip and looked to the doctor. Kjell saw the man nod as if encouraging her to explain. "Your mother passed on a long time ago."

"She's dead?" Lydia questioned, putting her hand over her eyes. "Why can't I remember?"

"Don't fret, child. I've seen this kind of thing before. It will pass in time. You need to rest for now." Dr. Ensign motioned to Zerelda and Kjell to come with him. "I'll send the orderly in with something to calm your nerves."

Lydia said nothing. She studied Kjell as he stepped away from the bed. He could feel her gaze upon him even as he exited the room. He wanted to scream in despair and cry for joy all at the same time. Lydia was alive and awake. It was a miracle that she had survived the attack. But her memory was gone. She didn't know him — didn't realize that she loved him or that he loved her.

They made their way to Dr. Ensign's office in stunned silence. Once they were seated, it was several minutes before the doctor addressed the situation.

"The mind is quite delicate," he told them. "It often cannot process shock. The circumstances of the attack, not to mention the blood loss, would be enough to cause her brain to . . . well, not function as it had before. We know so little about the way the mind works, but as I said, I've seen this before."

"What can be done?" Kjell asked.

"Nothing. We must be careful not to give her further shock. We mustn't lose patience with her inability to remember. We cannot try to force her knowledge of the past."

Kjell focused on the wooden floor. He felt like he was on a boat that had suddenly lost its buoyancy. Water was rushing in and would soon sink his vessel, but there was no understanding of how to stop it — how to fix the situation.

"There is one thing we must be extremely cautious about," the doctor continued. "Say nothing of the baby. I'm afraid in her delicate state of mind, it would cause her to lose her grip on reality altogether. I doubt she could withstand the truth."

Zerelda nodded and took hold of Kjell's hand. "Perhaps we should accept this as a blessing in disguise. It gives us and Lydia time."

Kjell's anger got the better of him. "Time for what? What possible hope can we give her?"

The older woman's expression softened. "Time for healing, Kjell. Maybe Lydia will never remember us or the baby, but she can learn to know us again. She lived with such a painful past, maybe it's best she not remember any of it. Maybe that's God's gift to her."

"Some gift. He allows her child to be taken, along with her memory." Kjell couldn't fight the bitterness in his tone. He got to his feet. "I can't sit here any longer."

He stormed from the room and out of the hospital. He had no idea where he would go, but for now, he couldn't be there. Lydia took no comfort in his presence. Once again, he was unable to help.

Lydia tried to force her mind to clear. No matter how hard she tried, nothing of her life came back to her. She felt alone and afraid. Her wounds left her weak and in pain, but she felt overwhelmed by the blank slate of her memory.

"Who am I? Why can't I remember?"

The woman who called herself Zerelda came into the room. She smiled as she approached. "Am I disturbing you?"

She studied the woman, trying hard to place her.

"Do you mind if I sit and talk with you for a few minutes?"

Lydia shook her head. "No. That would be fine."

"I know you're confused right now. Probably scared, too. I know I would be if I couldn't remember who I was or who anyone else was, for that matter."

"It's very frightening. I know I should be able to remember things — that I should know you . . . but I don't."

The woman had such compassion in her expression that Lydia immediately felt at ease. This person obviously cared a great deal about her. Lydia could sense that much.

"Tell me about my past. Tell me who I am. Who you are."

"Well, I'm your aunt Zerelda Rockford. Some folks call me Zee. I am your father's sister."

"And where is my father?"

Lydia sensed the woman felt uncomfortable with her question. "Is he dead, too? Like my mother?"

Zerelda nodded. "Yes. He passed on almost a year ago."

"How?"

Again the woman shifted and seemed to consider her words. "There was a carriage accident. He was injured and died shortly afterward. You moved up here to be with me shortly after that. Do you remember anything about the move?"

Lydia thought for a moment. "No. Nothing comes to mind."

"Well, this is the town of Sitka in Alaska. We're on an island in the far northwest. It's not a big town by the standards of most American towns, but by Alaska standards, it's very large."

"Are you my only family?"

Zerelda couldn't hide a momentary look of surprise. Lydia figured it had to do with the man that had been there earlier. "I know I'm married to that . . . that . . . man."

"Yes, to Kjell Lindquist." Lydia saw the woman's face light up. "He's a good man, Lydia, and you loved him quite dearly. You two made the perfect couple."

"So we were happy?"

"Oh, very much so and in love." Zerelda laughed. "You haven't been married that long. Just since last November. Kjell's been so worried, he hasn't wanted to leave your side."

Lydia considered this for a moment. The man did seem very kind, and he looked at her with such concern. He must truly love her if he'd spent so much time watching over her. "How did we meet?"

Zerelda seemed amused by this question. "When you arrived you were exhausted. The travel had made you . . . seasick . . . and . . . well, you were extremely weak. You walked up the wharf and promptly fainted into Kjell's arms. When you came to, you explained who you were and that you were looking for me. Kjell knew me and brought you to my cabin."

Lydia tried to absorb the information, but it was proving too much. In fact, instead of offering comfort, it only served to make her more frustrated. Why couldn't she remember? "I think I should rest now."

Zerelda patted her hand. "Yes, I'm sure that would be best. Just know that I love you, Liddie. I love you dearly and always will. We'll get through this with God's help."

Lydia nodded. "I'm sure you're right." But even as her aunt got up to leave, Lydia felt overwhelmed with doubt. Would she ever remember the past? Would she ever have memory of her husband and what had caused her to fall in love with him?

And if she didn't, could she be a wife to him?

CHAPTER 24

In the end, it wasn't Evie or Trayton who suggested she travel to Chicago. It was Thomas himself. Evie was stunned when her husband brought up the topic.

"You seem to be rather melancholy, my dear," he announced as Evie looked up from a book. She found Trayton and Thomas had entered the library as if on some important business.

"I'm fine," she replied, uncertain of what else to say.

"Well, I had a marvelous idea. I'm sending Trayton to Chicago. I think it would work well for you to travel with him. There is a great deal to do in that marvelous city. A few days away would do you good, and with Trayton along, I wouldn't have to worry about your safety."

Evie glanced at Trayton and felt her heart pick up its pace. He was very nearly smirking at her, as if he knew she was helpless to refuse him.

"Trayton assures me it won't be a bother to him. He's a good man — probably the best on my staff."

Swallowing hard, Evie found she couldn't speak. She looked again from her husband to his secretary. She could still feel his lips upon hers, smell the scent of his cologne.

Trayton held her gaze with smoldering passion in his eyes. Evie wanted to turn away, but she couldn't.

Thomas was already busying himself with a stack of papers. "I'll make all of the arrangements. I'll see to it that two of your maids accompany you, as well. Now run along and see to your packing, my dear."

His voice broke the spell, and Evie quickly got to her feet. "I don't . . . think . . . I really shouldn't go. My sister hasn't been feeling well of late, and I should probably stay close to home in case she takes a bad turn." Evie knew Jeannette had nothing more than a cold, but it gave her a reasonable excuse.

"Nonsense," Thomas replied, not even bothering to look up from his papers. "Your sister will be just fine, and you won't be gone more than a fortnight, at the most. Now go and pack."

Evie moved across the room as if under a spell. She felt helpless, unable to keep the situation from tumbling out of control. As she passed Trayton, he reached out and touched her fingers. She pulled her hand to her breast as if burned. He smiled in amusement.

Nothing about the situation made any sense. Evie had been prepared to ask her husband to allow her to accompany Trayton to Chicago, but when the suggestion came from Thomas, it felt awkward. It was odd that he had brought up the trip. Had she truly seemed melancholy? And even if she had, when had Thomas ever given her more than a passing glance?

Her stomach churned at the thought of being alone with Trayton. There was a part of her that very much wanted to be with him, and another part that wrestled with the impropriety. She had not been raised to be a religious woman, but she knew that it was wrong to commit adultery. Still, there was no real conviction on her part. She lived in a world where her father and brothers made their own rules, and morals were never considered important unless they came with a monetary value attached.

Starting up the grand staircase, Evie realized she didn't know when they would leave. Thomas had only told her to pack. She drew a deep breath and went back to the library. Hopefully Trayton would have the good sense to ignore her.

Evie reached for the door and paused as she heard her husband laugh heartily. "If you impregnate her," he told Trayton, "I will give you a bonus of one thousand dollars."

Her eyes widened as Thomas continued. "There is already enough talk about me, and a child or two might put such gossip to rest."

"Why not simply deal with the task yourself?" Trayton asked.

Again Thomas laughed. "Because I have no interest in . . . her. I married her only for her father's fortune and the connections he promised. When he died, much of that was lost. I cannot divorce her without risking my own inheritance. So I play this game. She is kept very nicely here, and now with your help, she will receive the romantic attention she desires. I will continue to pay you well, but that money also ensures your silence and discretion."

"But of course," Trayton replied. "I wouldn't dream of disgracing either of you."

Evie was sickened by the conversation. She backed away from the door. Never had she felt so betrayed, so used. Trayton didn't care at all for her; he was simply playing a part. Her own husband had hired him to seduce her.

Running up the stairs, Evie nearly knocked the housekeeper off her feet. She didn't bother to apologize to the woman but escaped to the solace of her room. Locking the door behind her, Evie felt hot stinging tears come to her eyes.

Of all the nerve! How dare he do this to me? How dare they? She went to the bed and threw herself down.

It was so wrong, so unfair. She had very nearly yielded her body and soul to a man whose only interest in her was the money he was getting from her husband. She wanted to vomit. *How could I have been so stupid? How could I have been so taken by Trayton Payne's act?*

She hated herself. Hated that her loneliness and longing had nearly robbed her of her wisdom. Pounding her fists into the mattress, Evie wanted to scream. She didn't, however. She knew she couldn't say a word about this. The embarrassment was far too great.

As the evening wore on, Evie refused to go to dinner. Instead, she insisted her maid help her to dress for bed. "Tell Mr. Gadston I am feeling unwell. Tell him I will not be traveling to Chicago."

"Yes, ma'am," the girl said with a curtsy.

Evie dressed quickly for bed and once the girl was gone, relocked her bedroom door so that no one — especially not that sneaky Trayton — could gain entry to her quarters.

She remained awake until well after midnight, trying to figure out what she would do. Many times she had contemplated asking Thomas to release her — to annul their marriage on the grounds that it had never been consummated. He would never agree to it, of course. No man wanted to admit that he'd not preformed his husbandly duties. But now Evie had something to threaten him with. She could expose him to the whole world and tell everyone of his schemes with Trayton.

But what if Trayton lied? What if he merely laughed at her announcement and called her mad? Evie shook her head. No doubt Thomas would pay the man well to keep silent.

"I'm trapped. I'm really and truly trapped." Despair crept over her, crushing her, leaving her struggling to breathe. "What am I going to do?"

CHAPTER 25

March 1871

"It seems like a very nice house," Lydia said.

"I'm glad you felt comfortable enough with us to come home," Zerelda replied. "After over a month in the hospital, I would think any place would feel better."

Kjell watched his wife evaluate their home. She walked around the parlor looking at the various pieces of bric-a-brac. Some were things she'd acquired after coming to Sitka, but most belonged to Zerelda.

She walked to the rocking chair and ran her hand across the back. "I've always liked rocking chairs."

The comment surprised everyone. Even Lydia looked up in shock. "I'm not sure how I know that, but it just came out. I know it's true." She sounded excited, and Kjell couldn't help but smile.

"It is true," he told her. "You have always enjoyed sitting by the fire, rocking."

Her smile broadened. "What else do I like?"

Zerelda laughed. "Well, maybe it will come to you as you explore, but you like a great many things."

"What was my favorite food?" Lydia asked, looking back and forth between Kjell and Zerelda.

"You've always loved peaches. We can't get them very often up here — they spoil too easily on the trip. But sometimes I make you peach pie with canned peaches, and you think that simply grand."

"Peaches," Lydia said, as if weighing the truth of the statement.

"You seem fond of deer roast," Kjell offered. "And fresh bread."

"That's true," Zerelda said. "You always love to eat it hot out of the oven."

"I'm looking forward to getting my memory back," Lydia said. "Dr. Ensign assured me there was no reason it wouldn't return in time."

Kjell watched her move around the room. She stopped and looked down at the violin case. She studied it a moment and cocked her head back and forth. No one said anything. Kjell knew it was important she try to remember it for herself.

"Is this mine?"

"Yes," Zerelda replied. She came to stand close to Lydia. "You've played since you were a child."

Lydia turned and looked at her aunt. "Do you suppose I will remember it if I try again?"

"You might."

Kneeling, Lydia reached for the case, then paused. Without touching it, she stood up. "I think I'll wait. I feel so good about remembering that I like rocking chairs, I wouldn't want to spoil the moment if I couldn't remember what to do."

Kjell thought her quite practical. He couldn't help but wonder if the music would come back to her. Music had a powerful way of reaching people. It was like a bridge from the heart to the mind, providing a means of expressing what words could not.

"Would you like to see upstairs? There are two bedrooms there."

Lydia nodded. "Yes, show me."

Zerelda led the way up the stairs. Lydia followed, touching the polished wood rail with great interest. Kjell walked silently behind, praying that Lydia would find peace in their home.

"My room is the first one," Zerelda said. "There's an indoor bath in the next room. See, there's a small tub and wood-burning stove with a large receptacle for water. You can heat water here and bathe in privacy."

Lydia seemed pleased. Kjell thought she might even ask to take a bath right then and there. She looked as if she were about to suggest just such a thing when Zerelda pressed on. "This is the sewing room."

Lydia stepped inside and Kjell couldn't help but wonder if she would remember that it was to be Dalton's bedroom. She looked back rather puzzled and questioned, "Do I sew?" Kjell nearly gave an audible sigh of relief.

"You were learning to," Zerelda replied. "I had been teaching you." She continued down the hall. "And the last room is yours and Kjell's."

Kjell watched Lydia hesitate for a moment before entering. For the past weeks he had tried to help her know him better — to court her in a sense. They had laughed and talked about many things — especially Kjell's past and life in Sitka.

Now, coming back to the house — to the very room where she'd been shot — Kjell couldn't help but wonder what Lydia might remember. He'd taken away any reminders of the baby. He'd stored the clothes and cradle outside in one of the large sheds and figured if Lydia ever found them there, he would plead ignorance. The idea of ever telling her the truth was more than he could imagine. How could it benefit her to know that she had once had a child and now he was dead?

"It's a pretty room," Lydia said, looking around. "I like it very much. It's so big."

"Remember I told you that you and Kjell purchased this house from the man I used to work for, Mr. Saberhagen? He spared no expense in making his wife comfortable. Most of the furnishings were ones he left here when he moved back to Germany."

Nodding, Lydia touched the oak headboard of the bed. Kjell thought she might be trying to imagine lying in it — perhaps even resting there with him. She moved across the room to the window and pulled the curtain aside. "It's so pretty here. I can see why I would want to live in this house."

"Well, today is exceptional for the season. We haven't had a sunny day like this in quite a while, but you're right," Zerelda offered. "The view is incredible. That was one of the reasons Mr. Saberhagen built the house here. You can see the water from here, but in the other direction are glorious views of the mountains."

"I like the fireplace, too. The blue and white tiles are pretty." She pointed to the white mantel. "They really look nice against the painted wood."

"Mr. Saberhagen brought them from Holland. That's the country where his mother was born and raised."

"How nice." Lydia continued to look around the room.

Kjell had been silent since coming upstairs. He couldn't help but reflect on a conversation he'd had with Lydia only a few days earlier. She had told him that she was resolved to be a good wife to him — that she could sense in him a compassion and love that was genuine. He had told her they could live separately upon her return to the house, especially since she was still weak from her injuries. She had thanked him and added that she felt confident her memory of him would soon return, and she would be comfortable again sharing his bed.

The thought of living in the house so close to Lydia — and yet so distant — was going to be trying. Kjell knew there would be times of sorrow when he couldn't help but think of Dalton, as well as moments of anger when he remembered all that had happened. It was Zerelda who had asked him if it would be easier if she returned to the cabin so that he and Lydia could share the house alone. He had told her no, then realized that perhaps it would be best if he stayed in the cabin instead. Moving his things there had been one of the hardest, most discouraging things he'd ever done, but he felt it was the right thing to do. Lydia needed time, and he might be tempted to press her recovery if he had to see her so intimately day in and day out.

"Everything is so bright and cheerful," Lydia said, finally coming to stand in front of Kjell. "It seems so fresh and clean, too."

"Kjell did a lot of work in here while you were in the hospital," Zerelda said. "He wanted to make it nice for your return."

Lydia looked into Kjell's eyes and smiled. "Thank you so much. You are so considerate of me."

Oh, how he wanted to take her in his arms and kiss her! He wanted to stroke her long brown hair and tell her that everything would be just fine, but of course he couldn't do either one. He stepped back a pace to set an even wider distance between them.

"You're very welcome. I was glad to do it," he told her. "I would do anything for you."

After weeks of contemplating what she would do, Evie had come to the conclusion that she would push for a divorce. She would suggest an annulment but be prepared that Thomas would never want to admit to his failings as a husband. Divorce would be the last thing he'd want — she knew his family would be staunchly opposed. Perhaps, however, if she approached his parents, explaining that it was entirely her desire — that he was without fault — then they would not disinherit their son.

After a great deal of thought, Evie decided that she would say nothing about Trayton. Just thinking of the man made her angrier than she could bear. Keeping away from him had been like trying to avoid mosquitoes in summertime. He always seemed to be at the house, and he always seemed to be looking for a way to be alone with her. Evie had triumphed, however, even dashing up the servants' stairs one evening when he followed her into the kitchen.

Now Trayton was away on a trip. She had heard Thomas say he would be gone for at least a month, and that suited her just fine. It would give her plenty of time to plead her case with Thomas and perhaps even find a small house for herself.

With careful consideration to her wardrobe, Evie dressed in a dark plum- and pink-striped dress. The bodice was delicately pleated and embroidered with the finest designs in black silk thread. It was one of her newest gowns and had cost a small fortune, but Evie knew her husband could afford it. He owed her far more than a mere gown.

Sweeping across the foyer and past the stairs, Evie made her way through the large sitting room. At the far end of this, she passed through another large room, this one devoted to music. It had been where she had danced with Trayton on that fateful evening so long ago. At least it seemed long ago — a lifetime in the past. She had grown up a great deal in a few short weeks.

Thomas's office could be accessed off of the music room. It had another entrance from the main hallway, but Evie had purposefully chosen this path to remind herself of her anger. She spied the small alcove where Trayton had first tried to seduce her. It was here that he had convinced her to adjourn upstairs with him to share a private moment.

Evie squared her shoulders. She was now sufficiently ready to face Thomas. She would be firm with him, but reasonable. Reaching for his office door, she was surprised to hear the voices of her brothers. She had thought Marston was still traveling.

"Ah, Evie. How good of you to join us," Thomas said, seeing her at the door.

Evie nodded. "I didn't know my brothers were here."

"You are positively grown up," Marston said, crossing the room. "Look at you. You've become a very beautiful woman."

She frowned. "It isn't like you to flatter, Marston." She allowed his embrace. "Welcome back. Where did you go?"

"Well, it's a long story. But I'm glad to be back, and there is something of great importance that I wish to discuss with you."

"With me?" she looked at Mitchell and then at Thomas. "What could you possibly want to discuss with me?"

Just then a baby began to cry. Evie's forehead furrowed as she tried to see around Marston's broad shoulders.

He took her arm and led her across the office. "That is what I wish to discuss." They crossed to the door and into the hall. Marston motioned to an older woman dressed in black.

The woman got to her feet and turned away from them. Reaching into a perambulator, she pulled out a crying baby.

"What is this all about? What child is this?"

The woman came to deposit the baby in

Marston's arms. He grinned. "This, Evie, is your little brother, Dalton. Dalton Gray."

CHAPTER 26

April 1871

"I've decided to hire a detective to look into whether or not Marston Gray has Dalton," Kjell told Zerelda as they drove into town. Overcast skies above looked heavy with rain.

"How will you find one?" Zerelda asked him.

Kjell pushed back his hat a bit. "Not long after the attack, I sent a letter to the mayor's office in Kansas City. I could see that the army believed the case closed — that Ioann and Dalton were lost at sea — but I just can't rest when I know Gray might well have my son.

"I explained that there was a matter of great importance that required a bit of investigation. I asked if he or his people could recommend a detective agency. I got a reply back just the other day with the name of a reliable company. I plan to write to the man in charge and seek his hire."

"What will you say? What will you ask him to do?"

"I'll tell him the truth. I'll explain that I know Gray is a powerful man, but that this involves kidnapping and attempted murder. I'll play to his ego and explain that seeing this man in prison will likely bring him positive notoriety. Which in turn could bring him additional cases."

Zerelda considered this for a moment. "But what if he's a friend of the Gray family?"

"I remember Lydia telling me that the Grays were rapidly falling from grace with the powers around town. She said that her lawyer, Mr. Robinson, had explained all of this, which gave her hope that she could make a new start without their interference."

"You know who her lawyer is? Why didn't you write to him for the name of a detective? As a lawyer, he surely must have known such men."

"I did write, but I never got a response. I don't know if the man is still alive or if he's moved from the area. Lydia never mentioned it. I know he was handling some business affairs for her, however. I figure we'll get something from him or his colleagues sooner or later in regard to that."

Zerelda motioned to the side. "This is where I get off. I'm meeting new missionaries. A Reverend John Brady and Miss Fanny Kellogg. They are said to be quite excited about working with the Tlingit people. I'm to help facilitate introductions."

Kjell brought the wagon to a halt and got out to help Zerelda down. "Do you think Liddie's getting any better, Zee? I mean, you're with her day and night. Have you seen any sign that she's recovering her memory?"

She looked at him with an expression of motherly compassion. "I can't help but think she is, Kjell. Sometimes she asks me questions about the past, and it seems to me that something must have triggered a memory."

"What about her music? Has she . . . is she playing?"

Zerelda shook her head. "She attempted it once, but after holding the instrument for several minutes, she simply put it away. But don't worry. I believe God will restore what is needed in time. Like I said before, it might be best that she never remember the past — especially if Dalton is truly lost to us. If he's not with Gray, then we will have to accept that he drowned at sea."

"But no one has ever found anything to

suggest that. Ioann's body was never recovered."

"Kjell, you know very well that people are lost at sea and never recovered. Hire your detective and see what he says. It will put our minds at rest once and for all."

He clenched his teeth. Nothing of the sort would bring peace or rest to his mind. He would always feel that he had failed Liddie and Dalton. If he hadn't been working late that night, and if the storm hadn't delayed him, none of this would have happened.

Lydia sat in the sewing room attempting to pin together the pieces of a shirt Zerelda was helping her make for Kjell. She liked doing things like this — things for Kjell. He'd been so considerate of her, and she'd appreciated his gentle courtship. In fact, she'd found such pleasure in his tenderness and affection that she felt the time had come to be a wife to him in full. The idea made her nervous and happy, all at the same time. She felt she could trust this man. Somewhere deep in her heart, she knew that she had loved him sincerely. She was tired of trying to battle her recovery on her own. Zerelda was wonderful to help her and give her insight into the past, but Lydia's heart longed for Kjell, and she didn't want to deny that any longer.

As she worked on the shirt, she tried to figure out what would be the best way to invite Kjell back into their home. Should she simply say that she was at ease with the idea and wanted him to return? Maybe she would be better off to ask him if he was comfortable with the suggestion.

She smiled to herself. Of course he was comfortable with it! He had told her many times of his love for her and his longing to be with her again. His love was evident, and Lydia couldn't help but love him in return.

Rain began to fall outside. The steady beat of the drops against the window suddenly made Lydia feel uncomfortable. She put down her sewing and got up. Something akin to panic rose up in her. Her chest tightened, and she felt as if her throat were closing up.

She paced back and forth for several minutes. The feeling refused to abate, however. Lydia thought perhaps she would find solace in her bedroom. Stepping through the door, her focus was immediately drawn to the window and then to the far corner of the room, where a dresser stood.

Something wasn't right, but she couldn't figure out what it was. She stood frozen, almost paralyzed with fear. It dawned on her that she had been injured the night of a storm. Maybe it was nothing more than that realization that was making her uneasy.

"But I've been through many other showers. This is hardly a storm."

Going to the window, Lydia reached out to touch the glass. A fleeting image passed through her mind. She had come here to open the window that night. But why? Why would anyone open a window during a storm?

Lydia pulled away and hurried downstairs. Maybe it was best if she didn't remember. She got the distinct feeling that something very bad awaited her in her memories.

Lydia stoked up the fire. The flames greedily accepted the logs she offered and soon the room seemed much cheerier. Lydia sat down by the fire and began to rock. She hummed a song, not knowing why she knew it or what it was.

Kjell had said music was very important to her, and she looked at the violin case now and frowned. Lydia had been sadly frustrated the times when she had picked up the instrument. She wanted to play it, but she had no idea how.

"It's not fair," she said, gazing at the ceiling. Zerelda had told her to talk to God when she felt overwhelmed. "Are you listening to me, God?" She didn't ask the question out of anger but of desperation. It was so hard to consider that the God of the universe would give her needs even the slightest consideration, but her aunt had assured her it was true. Every Sunday when they gathered as a family to read Scriptures, Kjell would lead them in prayer. Lydia felt that God was very real — that He did care — but she couldn't really understand much else.

"I want to remember. Oh, Father, why can't I know the truth?" Tears began to form in her eyes. She hugged her body and rocked. "I just want to know who I am."

She continued to rock, hearing the rhythmic creak of the chair on the floor. Tears streamed down her face. Lydia stared into the glow of the fire and wondered if she would ever be able to fill the void in her mind.

"Liddie?"

She startled and turned. It was Kjell. He saw the tears on her face and hurried to her side.

"What's wrong?" He looked almost fearful.

"I don't really know. I felt frightened for no reason. It's silly," she admitted.

Kjell took out a handkerchief and knelt

beside her. He wiped her tears so gently. "It's not silly. You have endured a great deal."

"I just want to remember. I was working upstairs, and when the rain started to hit the windows . . . well, it scared me. For just a moment, I thought I remembered opening the window the night of the storm. But then it was gone, and I couldn't remember anything else. I still feel afraid."

He stood and pulled her into his arms. Holding her for several minutes, Kjell said nothing. The warmth of his embrace made Lydia feel safe, and she realized that now was the moment to tell him to come back to her — to come home.

"Kjell," she whispered. "Please come home."

Pulling away, Kjell looked into her eyes. "What are you saying?"

"I want you here . . . with me. I want us to be together. I feel so much better when you're here. You've been so patient to wait for me, but I don't want to wait anymore."

He gently touched her face. "Lydia, I want that more than anything, but I don't want to do it simply because you're afraid."

"It's more than that," she assured. Reaching up, Lydia put her arms around his neck. "I was already convinced of it before the rain came." She smiled. "I was even trying to figure out a way to suggest it without seeming too forward."

Kjell laughed. "Be as forward as you like, wife of mine."

"In that case, perhaps you would like to see to the fireplace in our bedroom."

"Is there a problem with it?"

Nodding, she smiled and moved away from him. "Yes. It wants for a fire."

Evie cooed at Dalton and shook a rattle in front of his face. "See here. See how pretty."

He tried in his uncoordinated manner to reach out. Evie helped him take hold of the toy and for a moment, Dalton gripped it and flailed his arm. Then just as quickly he dropped it.

Evie picked him up and smoothed her hand over his dark brown hair. He looked very much like Lydia, she thought. She remembered Marston's sad story of finally finding where their stepmother had gone, only to get there as she was dying in child-birth.

"Poor baby," she whispered against Dalton's cheek.

She had agreed to take her little step-brother and raise him as her own, but she couldn't help but think of Lydia. In fact,

Lydia was the reason she had decided against seeking a divorce from Thomas. She would focus on raising Dalton for his dead mother.

Evie had always liked Lydia and had secretly longed to spend time with her — to feel the connection to a mother figure once again. Jeannette, however, had threatened Evie on more than one occasion. *"Don't you dare like her,"* Jeannette had said. *"If you like her, it means you hate our mother."*

That had caused a battle to ensue in Evie's heart. Could her sister be right? She couldn't understand why doing one thing meant the other must happen, as well.

Frowning, Evie struggled to forget the past. She focused, instead, on the baby in her arms. Dalton didn't make up for the lack of love in her life, but at least with him here, she had someone to care for — someone who needed her.

"Oh, my sweet boy, your life has started so tragically, but I promise to be a good mama to you." She kissed his nose, and he reached to take hold of her face. Laughing, Evie whirled around gently, holding Dalton high in the air. "You will see. We will have a good life together. I will love you just as Lydia would have loved you."

"Mrs. Gadston, your brother is here,"

Miles announced from the arched entryway.

Evie turned and lowered the baby as Marston entered the room. "What brings you here?"

"I wanted to see my little brother." He crossed the room with a box in hand. "I've brought him a gift."

"That was very considerate," Evie declared. "Would you like to hold him?"

Marston shook his head. "That's quite all right. I really have no use for him at this age, but when he's older . . . well, things will be different then."

Evie was puzzled at her brother's statement, but she said nothing. Instead, she kissed Dalton's cheek, then put the sleepy baby to her shoulder. "I do wonder, though . . ."

"Wonder what?"

"Shouldn't we make some attempt to bring Lydia's body back to Kansas City and bury her properly in the family plot? I mean, Dalton may one day wish to visit her grave."

"It was completely impractical. I would have done it had it merely been an issue of the cost. However, her aunt wished for her remains to be buried there in Sitka. I didn't want to grieve the old woman further — after all, I was taking Dalton from her."

Evie considered this a moment. Just then,

the nurse came to put Dalton down for his nap. Already the baby was starting to nod off. Evie handed him over reluctantly.

"I suppose you did the right thing. We can always journey with Dalton when he's old enough and wishes to see where his mother was buried."

He shrugged. "Perhaps, though I doubt he will care." Marston seemed to dismiss the idea. "I'm glad to see you getting along so well with him. I wasn't certain that you would be comfortable, but knowing that Jeannette has her hands full with the two she already has, I haven't even told her about the baby."

"You haven't told Jeannette? I fail to see what harm it would do." Evie saw Marston frown and decided not to press him further. "Would you care for refreshments?"

"No, I can't stay. I have several meetings this afternoon." He came to where she stood. "It's important that we say nothing about Dalton being here. I hope you will remember to keep your promise concerning that."

She shook her head. "But why? It doesn't make sense."

He took hold of her shoulders and tightened his grip. "It doesn't have to make sense to you — you just need to adhere to my desire in this matter."

Evie frowned. She knew her brother was up to something, but for the life of her she couldn't understand what. "Does this have something to do with the will and Lydia's inheritance?"

Marston appeared to consider her question for a moment. "Yes. It has to do with that in part. There are other reasons that I cannot disclose at this time. Suffice it to say, we need to keep things quiet. It's really for Dalton's best interest."

Evie, however, didn't believe him. He didn't seem sincere. But why would he feel the need to conceal whatever the situation was from her? Why would it matter if people knew about Dalton?

"Now I must be off," he told her. "I do hope you enjoy the gift. I had it sent from Chicago. Our little brother deserves only the best of everything."

Evie waited until Marston's carriage had pulled down the drive before opening the package. Inside she found a silver cup. The name Dalton Gray was engraved along with the date of his birth. No wonder Marston had ordered it from Chicago. If he was determined to keep folks from knowing about the baby, he couldn't possibly have risked the questions that might have come from a local merchant.

She turned the cup to see it from every angle. This was something of a tradition in the Gray family. There had been such a gift to commemorate each of them, and Jeannette had carried the tradition on with her children.

Evie couldn't help but wish this were a piece to celebrate her own child. She felt the old familiar longing for love rise up in her and pushed it back down. Replacing the gift in its box, Evie drew a deep breath and lifted her chin.

CHAPTER 27

May 1871

As the weeks passed, Evie found great joy in caring for Dalton. Nevertheless, she felt a growing emptiness inside. Thomas rarely spoke to her. In fact, he was often gone from home for weeks at a time. She had no idea if he was caught up in his business affairs or if he'd taken a mistress. Added to that was Marston's decree that she allow no one to know about Dalton. He promised a better explanation as time went on but insisted she trust him for the time being. It seemed senseless but Evie complied, knowing that if she didn't, Marston would take Dalton away from her. Her misery only mounted as the weather warmed, however. She would have loved to have taken long walks with the baby, even to share the company of her shallow friends. Instead, she was nearly a prisoner in the house. It wasn't that she couldn't leave the baby and go out, but frankly, Evie worried that she might say something that would reveal the truth of the child's existence.

Evie couldn't shake the sense that there was something underhanded in the way her brother demanded she keep the baby out of sight. She'd tried to approach Thomas about it on the rare occasions he was home, but he wanted no part of it. "This is a problem within your family; let your brothers handle it."

She walked toward a thick arrangement of climbing roses and noted that there were already buds. Soon the plant would spill glorious blossoms in abundance. Gently, she fingered one of the flowers and sighed.

"You've gone out of your way to avoid me, and I can't help but wonder why."

Evie looked up to find Trayton Payne had followed her into the gardens. She moved away. "Please leave me alone."

"Evie, we need to talk."

He called her by her family's nickname, and it irritated her that he presumed upon such an intimacy. "Don't call me that." She walked away at a fast clip. He followed her deeper into the elaborately landscaped lawn.

She finally stopped under the cover of several large oak trees. "What do you want?"

"I think you know the answer to that."

Shaking her head, Evie decided to be blunt. "I know about the arrangement you had with my husband. I'm not interested."

Trayton was unmoved by her declaration. "I'm glad you know. I hated using his request as an excuse to be near you. I hope you know me better than to think I was only interested in you because of his arrangement."

"Why should I believe anything you say?" She narrowed her eyes. "You completely lack integrity or honor." He took a step toward her. She held up her hands. "Stop right there."

"Eve — Genevieve, I am not without honor. I care for you. Thomas's requests to entertain you were just a means to get closer to you. With his blessing, I could feel free to court you."

"I am a married woman, sir. You have no right to court me." Evie shook her head, her anger mounting. "The fact that you do not respect the institution of marriage leaves me without respect for you."

"Eve, that isn't fair." He moved closer, ignoring her extended hands. He took hold of her even as she backed up. "Please hear me out."

"There is nothing you can say that will interest me."

"Eve, you're lonely. I know that you are. That baby doesn't take care of your womanly desires. A baby can't hold you in the night or assuage your fears. Those are the things a husband might do, but not a child."

"Then you hardly qualify." She felt her body come in contact with the trunk of a tree. She could move no farther.

Trayton smiled and surrounded her with his arms. "Eve, I played the game so that I could be with you. I want to help you. I want to make you happy."

She wished she could think clearly. Evie had never been one to have quick retorts or the ability to counter with witty sarcasm. She looked at Trayton for a moment. She simply couldn't deny there was something so appealing about this man, so enticing.

"Evie, you are important to me."

"If that is so," she replied softly, "then leave me alone."

He shook his head. "I can't do that." He tried to kiss her, but Evie turned away. "Don't resist me. You know you feel as passionately about me as I do you. You belong to me."

The words angered Evie and broke any remaining spell. She pushed hard against Trayton's chest, catching him off guard. He stumbled back, and she darted past him.

"Don't ever touch me again."

Hurrying to the house, Evie decided she'd had enough. Her mind raced with thoughts. She had contemplated asking Thomas to send her and Dalton elsewhere — somewhere she could live freely and openly with the child. Perhaps he could set her up in her own house far away — even Chicago. Thomas had enough money, that much was certain. She would even offer to make this a permanent arrangement, if that was to his liking. Whatever it took, she desired only to leave Kansas City and the complications of her marriage and this madness behind.

She stepped through the open French doors into the music room. The aroma of spring lilacs drifted in on the breeze, the scent sweet and heady. Evie paused and drew a deep breath as she glanced around for her husband. There was no better time than now, she decided. She would go to him and tell him that she knew everything about Trayton.

Evie walked with determined steps toward the sound of voices in Thomas's office, but she halted when she heard Marston's rather loud comment. "I didn't know until today. I just got word."

"You should have been more thorough," Mitchell declared.

Frowning, Evie pressed against the wall just outside the doorway. Her husband added, "It doesn't need to cause us trouble. They believe the child to be dead, don't they?"

"But Lydia is alive. And she will not rest until she knows where Dalton has gone — to know if he's truly dead or alive."

Evie gasped and covered her mouth with her hand. Lydia was alive? What was Marston talking about?

"Sitka is a great distance away, and Alaska is a very primitive land. I cannot imagine that she would come all the way to Kansas City to ascertain whether you have her child," Thomas said. "I mean, think of the difficulty."

"You don't know her like we do," Mitchell countered.

"Mitchell's right. I would not put it past her to show up here. When I arranged for her to be taken care of, I thought the men I hired had accomplished the job. I should have known better. They couldn't handle setting a simple fire in a lumber mill. This is the exact reason I swore everyone to secrecy regarding the child. If anyone decides to send the authorities to investigate, we cannot let them know the baby is here."

Evie could scarcely believe what she was

hearing. Her brother had tried to have Lydia killed. He had stolen her child and returned to Kansas City as if nothing had happened. No wonder he didn't want the child seen in public. It all made sense now.

She didn't need to hear any more. Evie moved away from the office in a daze. Making her way upstairs, she couldn't even begin to comprehend the situation. Marston in his selfish cruelty had stolen Dalton from his mother. He'd tried to murder Lydia, just as their father had killed their mother. Evie was heartsick. Had the Gray men not done enough to hurt the innocent?

Lydia walked alongside her husband, enjoying the quiet of the afternoon. They were searching for chocolate lily, which Zerelda had requested. Kjell pointed to a patch. "There, see the green stems with the dark red flowers?"

"They look like brown flowers to me," Lydia said, leaning closer. "So this is it?"

"Yes. The Tlingits call it *koox.* Actually, it has lots of names. Some people call it the Kamchatka lily or even wild rice. It's a part of the lily family." Kjell squatted down. "You pull the plant out, and you'll find a bulb with white kernels. This is the rice." He demonstrated. "You have to be careful or the bulb will fall apart and sprinkle the rice everywhere. I always like to put down a cloth beside the stems and hope for the best."

The stem held tight for a moment despite the damp soil. Kjell finally loosened it and the bulb came out in one piece. "Success!" he declared proudly.

Lydia immediately followed suit and began gathering plants. The area was well shaded by large spruce and cedar trees. The ground was marshy and damp, a perfect environment for the much-loved dish. She was glad Kjell and Zerelda had insisted she wear her sturdy boots. Even now, she could feel the wetness of the ground seeping into the leather.

"There is so much here that can be utilized," Lydia commented. "If you know what you're looking at, that is. I would have simply thought these were lovely flowers, and I never would have considered that the roots might offer something to eat."

"The Tlingit have learned to use much of the vegetation on this island. My mother would take the rice and mix it with the rhubarb that grows wild here. With a little sugar and cinnamon, it was quite a treat. I'll bet Zerelda knows how to do the same."

"I've enjoyed getting to know her better."

"Zee is well respected in Sitka. The people here know they can count on her for help. She's a wonderful midwife; she's helped deliver quite a few babies in her time."

Lydia looked up rather shyly. "I think I'd like to have a baby one day."

Kjell responded with a shocked expression.

She laughed. "I suppose I have spoken too boldly."

"Not at all. I'm sorry if I seem surprised." He looked away and turned his attention to the rice once again.

Lydia, however, sensed he was uncomfortable. "Have we ever talked about having children?"

"Of course. I hope one day we will have many, but . . ."

"But what?" Lydia frowned. "What's wrong?"

Kjell shook his head. "Nothing, sweet." He smiled. "I simply want to make sure you are healed from your wounds. The doctor said it would be wise to keep your activities limited while you recuperate in full. Having a baby now would be hard on you."

"I suppose you are right. Still, I find that I long for a child. I sometimes dream about having a baby. It's strange, but it seems so real." Lydia rose to her feet, but she winced at the pain in her neck and shoulder.

"Are you all right?" Kjell asked. "We can return to the house. You need to take it slow and easy."

"Perhaps we should go back." Lydia didn't want to admit to how quickly she tired.

Kjell nodded and gathered their collection of rice. "We've probably been gone too long as it is."

"It was so enjoyable," Lydia said as he came to her side. "I love how quiet and peaceful it is here."

He put his arm around her. "And I simply love you."

"I know you do. I'm so grateful for that love." Pausing, Lydia looked deep into his eyes. "You would tell me the truth if I asked for it, wouldn't you?"

Kjell frowned. "What do you mean?"

"I know that you and Zerelda know a lot more about my past than you are telling me. I also know the doctor said to not push myself and let time heal my body and mind. But, Kjell, you wouldn't try to keep things from me, would you?"

She studied his expression as he considered her question. It was obvious that he was hesitant to reply.

"Do you remember the verses we studied this morning?"

Nodding, Lydia reflected on their devotions. "It was about forgetting the past."

"I chose those verses because I thought God was leading me to share that with you. The past has its place in our life, but the present is so much more important. Living here and now, with a heart for what's truly beneficial and important."

"But you have all of your memories, so it's easier for you to say that." Lydia started toward home and found Kjell quickly keeping step with her.

"It's not that it's easy," Kjell declared, "but I have come to a better understanding. All through the Bible you will find verses that speak of forgetting the past. The past isn't something we can change or enhance. It cannot be rearranged or made over to better satisfy our current state. I firmly believe that God wants us to put the past to rest — as if it has died and we are burying it. Once a person dies and you bury them, you have no means by which you can bring them back to life. Even in memory, they are still gone. In the same way, the past is still gone, even when you dwell on it."

"It's so hard not knowing who I really am. I find that every day I must confront that reality. Do you realize how many things we react to purely based on our experiences? I would venture to say that nearly everything is that way. I have no experiences for many of the things I confront."

His expression grew sympathetic, and with great tenderness he touched her face. "In many ways I think you are the blessed one of us all. You have the ability to forget the pains and sorrows of the past and start anew. You get to make choices and plans based on nothing more than how you perceive them at this point in time. I find that rather refreshing . . . but I also respect that you feel overwhelmed at times."

Lydia grew thoughtful. "I'd never really thought to see it as a blessing. I've only focused on the grief of not knowing — of feeling lost. But I have you and I have Zerelda." She smiled. "And you have both given me such love. I suppose eventually, should my memory not return, I will find a way to put it all away from me and enjoy what I have. I am trying to let it go, you know."

Kjell nodded. "I do, and you have done a wonderful job." He kissed her gently. "No one could expect more."

CHAPTER 28

"I really love this time of year," Lydia said. She and Zerelda were working together to prepare the garden soil. "Everything seems so alive and fresh."

"Spring goes rather quickly up here," Zerelda explained, "but if you are wise and willing to work, you can use the lengthening hours of sunshine and grow a wealth of food. Then later in the summer, all the berries will ripen and we'll go picking. That's always fun but dangerous, too. The bears like to gather them, as well. The two most important things about berry picking are to remember you aren't alone out there, and never pick any white berry. White berries are always poisonous."

Lydia nodded. "I'll remember." Then she frowned. "Well, at least I hope I will. I've probably said that about other things and now I can't remember them at all."

"Maybe in time you will," her aunt encouraged. "The doctor said it wasn't impossible. He's seen folks recover their memories after enduring trauma. He's hopeful for you."

"If God is all-powerful, Zerelda, why doesn't He give me back my memories?"

The question took the older woman by surprise. Lydia could see that she wanted to speak on the matter but hesitated. Finally Zerelda leaned on her hoe and answered.

"I suppose there are always things we want to ask of God. Why does He seem to tarry when people are sick? Why does He seem to favor one people and not another? Why does He allow bad weather, evil, and death? I don't pretend to have the answers, Liddie. I do believe, however, that He has the power to make all things yield to His authority, and one day He will do just that."

"And until then I will just have to content myself with starting over," Lydia said with a sigh. She had known this was the direction her aunt would take. "I want to have faith — to trust Him — but it's so hard. Kjell told me the other day that it's best to put things behind us. He reminded me of that verse in Philippians 3 where it says, 'But this one thing I do, forgetting those things which are behind, and reaching forth unto those things which are before.' I've read that passage in the Bible over and over."

"So much so that you've memorized it," Zerelda declared. "See there, you're filling your mind with things that will help you over and over." She smiled. "Dwelling on God's Word is wonderful. It's an important part of our inheritance."

The last word permeated Lydia's thoughts. Inheritance. Something about that was important to her — but what?

"Inheritance," she murmured.

Zerelda was already back to work and looked up. "What was that?"

"Inheritance," she said again. "For some reason that word seems important to me." Lydia closed her eyes as if that might help her to recall the meaning. "Why would I think this?"

"Ah . . . well . . . perhaps because your father left you an inheritance. That's how you came to live here. You took some of that money and moved to Alaska."

Lydia opened her eyes and considered Zerelda's explanation. She tried to put a memory with it, but nothing came to mind. "Was my father a wealthy man?"

"Yes. I suppose he was. He was a prudent businessman and knew how to practice restraint when it came to spending. I believe he thought it important to leave you with something."

"Did I live with my father?" Lydia asked, leaning on her hoe again. "You said that I'm twenty-nine. Was I a spinster living under my father's care? Had I decided to stay with him and take care of him after my mother died?" But the moment the words left her mouth, she noticed an ache settle in behind her eyes. She rubbed her forehead. "Never mind. I need to take a walk. I can't bear this right now."

"Pitkae and Nicoli have brought us a new order of logs like you asked, and Captain Briar is here to see you," Joshua declared.

Kjell looked up from the log he'd been peeling. He hadn't seen or heard much from the army officials since they'd decided to close Lydia's case. Putting aside the spud bar he used for stripping the bark from the logs, Kjell went to the office to see what the man wanted.

"Captain, I didn't expect to see you here," Kjell said as he extended his hand.

"I know." Briar shook his hand. "But something has developed in your case."

A rush of fear washed over Kjell. "What is it?"

"We found Ioann Sidorov. He's alive."

"And the baby?" he asked hesitantly.

"We haven't found him," the captain replied. "But we may know where he is."

"Tell me everything."

The captain gave a hint of a grin. "We thought you might like to come over and be in on the interrogation."

"Ioann is here?" Kjell asked in disbelief.

"Yes. They arrested him in Wrangle; then one of the men realized who he was when he recognized his name. They contacted us, and we had him brought here."

Kjell was already heading for the door. "Let's not waste time."

It wasn't a far walk to where they were holding Ioann, but Kjell thought it seemed like miles. Questions flashed through his mind as he joined several other men at a large table. Within moments, Ioann Sidorov was brought in. They had shackled his arms and legs, making his ability to walk more strained.

Ioann had lost a great deal of weight. His once-muscular body seemed almost skeletal, and his expression was void of emotion. Meeting Kjell's gaze, Ioann didn't so much as blink.

The desire to beat the man to a pulp nearly sent Kjell flying across the room. He wanted to punish this man for what he'd done. Kjell gripped the seat of the wooden

400

chair, however, and stayed in place. It was all he could do to concentrate on what was being said.

"Mr. Sidorov, as we have already explained, you are here to answer questions regarding an attack last February on Mrs. Lydia Lindquist and her aunt, Zerelda Rockford, as well as the subsequent kidnapping of Dalton Lindquist."

Kjell watched the man carefully.

"I'll talk," Ioann said, "but only to help myself. I want to go home to Russia. Otherwise, I will not talk."

"You'll talk all right," Kjell said in a threatening manner. He narrowed his eyes. "I'll see to that."

It was the first time Ioann showed any emotion. Fear clearly marked his expression as he turned to Captain Briar again. "If you let him harm me, I will never tell you anything."

Briar looked at Kjell. "I would suggest you let us handle the investigation. We extended this courtesy to you because you are known to be a man capable of great control. Can you adhere to our rules?"

Nodding, Kjell forced himself to ease back in the chair. "I can and will."

"Very well." Captain Briar motioned to the man at his left and received a stack of papers. "The only arrangement we can offer, Mr. Sidorov, is this: If you will tell us everything you know, we will spare your life. If you refuse, we will hold a trial and then carry out the sentence immediately."

"That's hardly fair," Ioann said. "I want to return to Russia. I cannot do that in prison."

"You should have thought of that before breaking the law." Captain Briar fixed his stern, unyielding eyes on the man. "I have already discussed this with you. We have enough evidence to tie you to the crime. We know you were involved, and now all that is left to do is find you guilty and hang you."

Kjell watched Ioann wrestle with his options. It was obvious that he knew he was defeated. There was no other chance to save his life. Clenching his jaw tightly, Kjell pierced the man with his angry glare.

"All right. I do this thing," Ioann agreed. He looked in defeat at the captain. "What do you want to know?"

The captain led the man back in time to the days just before the attack. "We want to know why you and your brother participated in such a heinous act."

Ioann began to detail how Marston Gray had come to them after learning they'd been fired by Kjell.

"First he came to us because he heard we knew Kjell and held him a grudge. He was angry with him, too. He said Kjell had threatened him and that he wanted revenge. So he paid Anatolli and me to burn down the sawmill. Of course we tried, but the fire was put out before it got too bad."

"What about Aakashook and Keegaa'n?" Kjell asked.

"I didn't kill them. Anatolli did."

Kjell shook his head. "That's easy to say now. Your brother is dead and can't dispute you."

"It is true. They saw us lighting the fire. Anatolli told me to finish up and he would deal with them. He took them away, and I did not see what he did to them. He told me later he had killed them."

"Did he say where he had taken them?" the captain asked.

Ioann shook his head. "He said very little. He was not happy to have done such a thing."

"Then he shouldn't have done it," Kjell muttered. Captain Briar fixed him with a stare. Kjell drew a deep breath and swallowed his rage. He wasn't helping matters.

"We did not see Mr. Gray for a long time, but when he found us again, he said he would pay us a lot of money for helping him reclaim what belonged to him. He wanted us to take the baby and bring it to him on the far side of the island.

"It was raining hard, and the storm was very bad," Ioann continued. "We barely got our boat to shore when the worst of it hit. Anatolli told me to let him go first. He was bigger and thought this would scare the women — make them . . . cooperate."

"But they didn't, did they?"

Ioann shuddered. "No. When we came in the older woman shot at us. Anatolli knocked the gun from her hand. She was not seeing me, as I was behind her. When Anatolli went up the stairs, I hit her hard over the head. I did not want to kill her, or I could have shot her."

"Why didn't you want to kill her? You were there to do just that, were you not?" Captain Briar asked.

"I was not there to kill. I wanted to help Anatolli get the baby so that we would get the money. Mr. Gray promised us a thousand dollars."

"And you believed him?" Briar questioned in disbelief.

"We did. He had a great deal of money."

"What happened next?"

Ioann frowned. "After I hit the woman, I saw the blood and got scared. I told Anatolli to hurry and get the child. I thought I had killed the woman, and I wanted to run before someone found out. I heard some gunfire from upstairs and knew Anatolli had probably killed Mrs. Lindquist. He came down with a bag of things and the baby wrapped up in some blankets. He told me the baby's mother was dead, and we left."

Kjell found himself gripping the sides of the chair even tighter. The man spoke of his actions as though they'd been nothing more than accounts of a day spent fishing. How could he be so callous in regard to human life?

"Where did you go?" the captain asked.

"Back to the boat. The storm was bad, though. We had much trouble and only got a little ways at a time. Anatolli finally decided it was too much, and we put to shore and walked instead. We knew it would be only a short time before Kjell would get home, and we had to get to the cabin where we had promised Gray to meet."

"We found your cabin. We also found the body of your brother not far from it, as well as debris. What happened?"

Ioann frowned. "Mr. Gray shot Anatolli and would have shot me, but I ran. He tried to find me, but I hid very well."

Briar leaned toward the man. "And what

of the baby?"

"Gray took him. He always planned to take him back to where he lived. He had a boat and supplies waiting to take him south. He knew the mail ship would come that way, and he would board it and go home."

"And you are certain the baby was alive?"

"Yes. Gray wouldn't harm him. He seemed quite pleased to have him."

Briar looked to Kjell. "I suppose it's time to send the authorities to find Marston Gray."

"It was time for that months ago," Kjell said, not even attempting to hide his ire with the man. "I told you that Gray was behind this and that he would have the child — if at all possible." He got to his feet. "Now it's time to get my son back."

Lydia found herself humming a song and wondered how she knew it. It was a lovely melody — soft and sweet, gentle like a lullaby. She couldn't help but wonder who had taught her the song and whether or not she could play it on the violin.

A glance across the room drew her attention to the idle case. She hadn't tried in a long time to play the instrument. The few times she had attempted it, the only sounds she could draw from the strings reminded her of screeching jays.

She heard the wagon approach and knew
that Kjell was home. After checking on supper, Lydia pulled off her apron and went to
greet him. Lydia waved at her husband, but
he barely acknowledged her. His mind was
clearly preoccupied. She could see that
much.

Making her way back to the corral, Lydia
watched as Kjell unharnessed the horses.
He hadn't yet realized she was there. His
hands went quickly to the work at hand,
but Lydia could see that he was muttering
the entire time.

"Is something wrong, Kjell?" she asked.

He startled, which in turn caused the draft
horse to sidestep and knock him against the
rail fence. Lydia gasped and covered her
mouth to keep from crying out. If Kjell was
injured, it would be her fault.

The horse calmed as Kjell spoke sooth-
ingly. He nudged the beast back and slipped
from between him and the fence. Kjell offered her a smile. "I'm all right. Really."

Lydia waited in silence while he finished
with the horses. Kjell led the animals to
their stalls and gave them ample food and
water before coming to join her. He tried to
make light of the situation, but Lydia knew
he was concerned about something else.

"I'm sorry to have spoken out like that," Lydia said.

He put his arms around her. "It's all right. My mind wasn't on my work as it should have been." Pulling her close, he kissed her and buried his face against her hair for a moment. "I missed you today."

Lydia thought there was almost a sound of desperation in his voice. "Kjell, what's wrong?"

He pulled back and looked at her. "Why do you ask?"

"You aren't yourself. I can see that much for myself."

Offering her a smile, he reached up and smoothed back her hair. "It was just a very busy day."

She stepped back and frowned. "You're lying to me. I asked you not to keep the truth from me, but I can see that you are."

His expression changed. "Liddie, please listen to me. I want to tell you everything, but I just don't know what it might mean to your getting well."

"I am well. My memories are the only thing missing, and maybe if you and Zerelda would be honest with me, my memory would come back."

He studied the ground for several minutes. Lydia thought to leave, but something kept her fixed to the spot. "Why won't you just tell me? I'm stronger now," she told him. "I can deal with whatever it is."

The silence stretched between them and when Kjell did finally look up, Lydia saw there were tears in his eyes. Panic spread through her like a wildfire. What was he upset about? What was so troubling that he would cry?

She stepped back another pace. Maybe she didn't want to know the truth. Maybe she should leave well enough alone.

Kjell seemed to sense her fear. "Lydia, please just trust me a little longer. It's not all bad — in fact, it might well be something very good."

Nodding, Lydia wrapped her arms to her body. She felt so alone, but there seemed no other choice. "All right, I'll trust you."

CHAPTER 29

Marston Gray bounded out of his carriage and into the three-story brick house that he called home. He longed for a drink to calm his nerves. All day long, he'd been on edge, and when finally his worst fears were confirmed, Marston knew he would have to act quickly.

Word came to him through a business associate, who told Marston in no uncertain terms that someone was snooping around, trying to get information about him. They were asking all sorts of ridiculous questions about whether Marston was married and had recently had a child born to him. The man had laughed it off as assuming it was someone with a case of mistaken identity, but Marston knew better.

"Lindquist." He nearly choked on the name. Stalking through the house and ignoring his staff, Marston secluded himself in his study and locked the door.

He considered the brandy for a moment, then instead poured himself a liberal amount of whiskey and took a seat behind his desk. He tossed down a good portion of the drink, all while trying to figure out what he should do. If Kjell Lindquist had contacted authorities, then why didn't they simply come to the house and question him?

If only Lydia would have died, none of this would have been an issue. As the child's true next of kin, Marston could have easily explained his decision to take the child. He could have even fabricated some sort of story as to how he came to be in possession of the baby. But now all of that was impossible.

Nursing the remaining amber-colored liquor, he tried to think of what he should do. Obviously, he'd been cautious about letting anyone know of Dalton's existence. As far as he knew there were only a handful of people who were even aware that the child was in Kansas City. Still, if the authorities were truly investigating the situation, they would be watching.

It would probably be best to go see Thomas and Evie and discuss the matter. He would have to either tell Evie the truth or create another fabrication. But what story could he give his sister to gain her sympathy

411

or support? He could only hope that her time with the baby had caused a tight bond to form. Maybe if she was sufficiently attached to the child, she would be willing to lie in order to keep him with her.

Marston finished the whiskey and stared at the empty glass for several minutes. He wanted another drink, but he had to keep his wits. Nothing was going right. Nothing at all. They had not been successful in ridding themselves of Dwight Robinson, nor of obtaining his records concerning Lydia. The casket business continued to run successfully without them, headed instead by an appointed group of officials, who were only too happy to keep the Gray family out of all matters.

His own investments were suffering, and Mitchell declared the same to be true for him. They needed the casket business and the steady money it brought. Without it, Marston wasn't certain they could reestablish their financial footing.

A knock sounded on his door, disrupting any further thought. Marston drew a deep breath and went to see who had come to disturb him. He was surprised to open the door to find his twin on the other side.

"What brings you here?"

"There is trouble afoot," Mitchell declared. "Someone has been checking into my affairs."

Evie found it impossible to look at Dalton and not be consumed with guilt. She had suffered nightmares every night since learning the truth about Lydia. How could her family be so corrupt and evil? She had hoped that sinister side would have died with their father.

Sequestered in her private sitting room with Dalton and the new assistant nanny, Evie tried to figure out what she would do about righting this wrong. She longed to get Dalton back to Lydia, but how? What possible action could she make and not find herself up against her brothers and husband? Perhaps she could write to Lydia and tell her to come to Kansas City. If Lydia knew exactly where Dalton was and how to reunite with her son, surely that would resolve the situation.

She glanced across the room where the young woman played with Dalton. The girl was new to the household, hired only the week before to assist the much-older nanny.

"Ellie, how old are you?"

The young woman turned. "I'm sixteen, ma'am."

Evie nodded. "And how did you come to

be hired?"

The dark-haired girl looked away. "My mother died when I was quite young and my sister took charge of me. Then she went west with her husband last year. My sister's mother-in-law is Mrs. Shevlin."

"My housekeeper?"

"Uh-huh. She knew I needed work."

"Why did your family not take you with them?"

"It was too costly. My sister arranged for me to stay with friends, but that didn't work out. The husband . . . well . . . he was . . ." She fell silent, her face turning several shades of red.

"I think I understand," Evie said softly. "There's no need to go into detail."

Ellie repositioned Dalton on the blanket and handed him a toy. "My sister cried and cried when she left. They really didn't want to leave me, and they had plans to send for me."

"Where are they now?" Evie asked.

"Sacramento. My brother-in-law, Bill, got work with the railroad there. My sister cleans house for one of the wealthy families in the area. She said as soon as they have enough saved up, they will arrange for me to take the train west."

"So you don't plan to be long with us?"

Ellie looked up with an expression of horror. "I didn't mean it that way. Please don't dismiss me."

Realizing how much she'd upset the girl, Evie shook her head. "I have no desire to dismiss you." Evie didn't want to say too much, especially since she really wasn't sure what she was going to do.

Nanny Hubble entered the room as silent as a mouse. She glanced at Evie and then Ellie. "Bring him along. It's time for his bath," she instructed.

Ellie picked up the baby and brought him to Evie for a kiss. It was their routine every evening. "Sweet boy. You be good now." She kissed his chubby cheek and laughed when he grabbed her nose.

Once Ellie and Mrs. Hubble had gone, Evie began to consider what she could do. She heard the clock on the mantel chime and knew her maid would soon appear to help her dress for dinner.

Crossing into her bedroom, Evie went to her wardrobe and pulled out a beautiful gown of green silk. She placed it carefully atop the bed. It was only moments before her maid knocked upon the bedroom door.

"Are you ready to prepare for dinner, ma'am?"

"Yes, come in. I'll wear that." She pointed

to the bed.

The young woman gave a curtsy and helped Evie out of her day dress. Once she'd finished disrobing, Evie accepted the additional petticoat offered by the woman.

"Oh, Mr. Gadston said to tell you that your brother would be joining you for dinner."

"Which one?" Evie asked.

"Mr. Marston."

Her heart skipped a beat. Why had he come? Were there already problems with someone learning about Dalton's presence? Was he coming to take the child? Evie realized she would have to act very quickly. It might only be a short time before the authorities stepped in.

"Is my brother already here?" she asked as the maid did up the buttons to the gown.

"Yes. He arrived a few minutes ago."

Evie waited impatiently for the woman to finish. Once done, Evie quickly checked her hair. It was still sufficiently arranged. She put on a touch of perfume and waited while the maid brought her a change of shoes.

Contemplating Dalton's circumstances, Evie was resolved to settle the matter in the most amicable way. She would tell her husband and brother that she would like to travel with the child. Maybe suggest going abroad. If she mentioned England, rather than a westerly destination, perhaps no one would be the wiser.

She made her way downstairs and found Thomas and Marston enjoying drinks in the large formal sitting room. They stood in an obligatory manner and nodded. Smiling, she joined them.

"This is a surprise," she declared. "But I must say I am pleased."

Marston eyed her curiously. "And why would that be?"

"Well, I'm hoping to convince Thomas of something, and thought you might well help me, since in a roundabout way, it involves you."

Her husband looked at her suspiciously. Evie took a seat in the high-backed rococo chair. "Please sit down, and I'll explain everything."

The men did as she suggested but appeared quite uncomfortable. Evie would have laughed had the situation not been so serious. She lightly fingered the dark walnut wood of the armrest. "I have a request to make. It pertains to Dalton, as well, thus my happiness to have you present, Marston."

He frowned, looking rather upset. "Do tell."

"I would like to travel to England for the summer and take Dalton with me."

Thomas choked on his brandy, but Marston's focus never left her. Evie grew uneasy. She'd never been good at lying, but she reminded herself that this was for the sake of reuniting Dalton with Lydia.

"England?" Marston said, looking to Thomas. "Why England?"

"We have friends there," Evie announced. "I was invited last year to visit this summer but hadn't given it serious consideration. I think, however, I would very much like to go — and show off Dalton, as well. It will be a nice distraction."

For a moment no one said anything, then finally her brother nodded. "I think that sounds marvelous." Marston looked to Thomas but addressed Evie. "How soon would you plan to leave?"

"The sooner the better," Evie ventured. "I thought perhaps to leave in a matter of days. Packing won't be an issue, for I plan to take only a minimal amount of clothing and buy myself a new wardrobe. That is, if Thomas approves."

Thomas was now edging up on his seat. "You could travel to New York, and I could wire ahead to secure tickets for the remainder of the trip."

Marston nodded. "I think traveling would be beneficial to everyone. England is lovely this time of year."

"I would like to take Ellie with me. She's not been in our service long; however, I like her very much, and she is quite good with the baby. Nanny Hubble is simply getting too old to manage — at least with all her ailments."

"Who else would attend you?" her husband asked.

"No one. The trip to England is not that difficult, and I can utilize staff aboard the ship. Ellie can act as my maid as well as nanny to Dalton. I believe we will travel quite comfortably together."

"The last time you went abroad you traveled with at least five people," Thomas reminded her.

"I know, and everyone was forever stumbling over each other. It seems easier to hire people as I go," Evie assured him.

Marston got to his feet. "You know that friend of mine in Chicago — George Pullman? We made his acquaintance when he was still making caskets. Now he makes private railcars. I'm sure I could wire to have a private car available for Evie. He's offered me the use of one on many occasions. Once she gets to New York, we can arrange for them to be picked up and escorted to the ship."

Evie smiled. "That sounds lovely."

"Dinner is served," Miles announced from the doorway.

Marston extended his arm. "Come. We can further determine your plans."

"I have so many thoughts about the trip, and I knew I wouldn't be able to rest at all until we came to some conclusion."

After the meal concluded, Marston bid his sister good-night, then followed Thomas into his office.

"That neatly resolved itself," Thomas said, lighting up a cigar. He offered one to Marston.

"No thank you," he said, shaking his head. "I must say I am greatly relieved. I am, however, uncertain as to how to get the baby out of Kansas City without someone noticing."

"Yes, it is imperative that no one know Dalton is here. However, I think I might just have an answer for that problem," Thomas replied. "It actually came to me while you two were discussing England and mutual friends." He puffed away for a moment then lowered the cigar. "I believe we should tell Evie that Dalton's life is in danger and that we've only become apprised of this."

"But what excuse will you use?"

Thomas rubbed his chin. "We will tell Evie that we've heard rumors of an epidemic spreading in the poor sections of the city. She will understand the need to sneak Dalton away from Kansas City if she believes his health is in danger."

"Then what?"

"We will suggest she and her girl journey by private carriage to say, Omaha, for example. From there she can easily get a train to Chicago."

"I see what you mean. It could work."

"Of course it will. It also allows us to get them out of here sooner. I will tell her this evening of the situation and that they will leave before dawn. That should keep anyone from even noticing her departure, and we can definitely hide the fact that a baby is in attendance on the trip."

Marston liked the way his brother-in-law thought. "I will leave it in your hands, then."

Thomas nodded. "I will ensure they're well cared for. Evie will have everything her heart desires and plenty of available cash. In fact —" he glanced at his pocket watch — "I will get a letter of credit from our bank."

"At this hour?" Marston asked.

His brother-in-law put out the cigar. "I, too, have my friends."

CHAPTER 30

Evie found the constant jostling of the carriage a comforting reminder that they were well on their way to safety. She knew, however, that it was time to explain everything to Ellie. The girl had been stunned at the sudden departure for Europe. With wide-eyed wonder, she had agreed to go and act as maid and nanny. Now with Dalton sleeping soundly, Evie made her decision to be honest with the girl.

"Ellie, there is something we need to discuss."

The young woman straightened in her seat. "What is it, ma'am?"

"I need to know that I can trust you. If I can, I will see to it that you join your sister in Sacramento."

"Truly?" The girl's expression showed her surprise.

Evie nodded. "There has been a grave injustice done, and I am trying to right it.

This will, however, require your absolute cooperation. You must do as I say and offer no other comment if questioned. Otherwise, we might find ourselves in danger — Dalton, too."

The girl's innocent expression grew serious. "I promise to do whatever you ask, ma'am."

"Very well." Evie felt confident she could count on the girl to keep her word. "We aren't going to Europe. Instead, we are going to catch the train in Omaha and head west to San Francisco. We will send a wire along the way to your sister. The train route passes right through Sacramento, so it should be easy enough for her to meet you there. If not, you are welcome to continue with me."

Ellie looked at the sleeping infant. "But what about you and the baby? Won't you need help?"

"I will only be on my own for a short time. The injustice I spoke of is this: My brother tried to have the child's mother killed."

Gasping, Ellie shook her head. "But that would be murder."

"Yes. He wanted her dead so that he could steal Dalton and bring him back to Kansas City. However, Dalton's mother survived the attack. I only just learned this, and it is my ambition to return the baby to her."

"She must be so upset that he's gone," Ellie said. "He's such a good baby."

"And he's been gone for months now," Evie said sadly. "I'm sure Lydia's heart is broken in pieces. But we, hopefully, shall mend it again."

"And this is why we left so quickly?"

Evie looked out the carriage window. "I believe the authorities are after my brother. He didn't say anything, but he was anxious to see me on my way. I wanted to keep Dalton from being given over to strangers, so I suggested the trip abroad. I felt if my brother were being pursued, he would be supportive of getting Dalton out of town. And by suggesting the trip abroad, no one will anticipate hearing from me for some time."

"That was quite cunning," Ellie said in admiration. "You are very smart."

"I hope I am smart enough. If my brother knew what I was doing, he would track me down and take Dalton back. I won't rest until I have that baby in his mother's arms, however, even if it costs me my life."

Ellie looked at her in shock. "Why should harm come to you?"

"My husband and brothers are powerful men. They may even come after you and seek answers. You must do exactly as I say or Dalton may never see his mother again."

"I will. I promise. I will help you however I can," the girl promised.

Ellie's enthusiasm to aid Evie was still evident two days later when they boarded the westbound train. Ellie posed as a young mother with child, while Evie traded in her finer clothes and bought two simple ready-made gowns. Once she topped them with a traveling cape and bonnet, she looked no different than many of the other women passengers. She and Evie boarded the train separately, then found their way to the same car. They didn't approach each other or even attempt to sit together. Evie had told the girl that somewhere along the way they would change trains and then they could travel together.

When the train pulled out of Omaha, Evie breathed a sigh of relief. The first part of their deception had come together. Was it wrong to pray for a lie to go undiscovered?

Evie had spent nearly every Sunday for the past year sitting beside her husband in the large Episcopalian church where he'd been raised. Thomas, like her father, saw attending church as a means to gain social acceptability. Evie had tried to understand some of the things spoken of, but when questions arose, she had no one to ask. Even the priest had suggested she not worry about it. But Evie wanted to know more — especially about prayer. She thought of the wordy prayers the priest had espoused during services. Could she do the same? What if she prayed in her own words? Common, ordinary, everyday words. Would God understand?

Marston was glad to know that Evie was well on her way to England with Dalton. This relief was even more of a blessing when the butler announced that there were men who wished to see him.

He had just finished breakfast and was enjoying a cup of coffee when the butler ushered the men into the dining room. One was a police official he recognized, and the other two were in plain clothes. Perhaps these were the detectives who had been asking about him.

"Good morning, gentlemen." He nodded to the uniformed man. "Davidson, good to see you. How's your family?"

"Doing well." The man turned to introduce his companions. "This is Mr. Wilson and Mr. Kloosterhof."

Marston nodded. "Gentlemen, will you

join me for coffee?"

"No thank you, Mr. Gray," Mr. Wilson responded. "We're here on official business. I've been hired to locate a missing child."

"And what child would that be?" Marston tried to act confused but curious. "One of the neighborhood children?"

"No, sir. A baby. The child would be your brother."

Marston laughed. "I have no baby brother. I'm sorry to say someone has led you on a merry chase. I hope they are paying you well for this joke."

Wilson looked to Kloosterhof and then back to Gray. "I suppose you had no idea that your stepmother, Lydia Gray, gave birth to a child?"

"Truly?" Marston touched a napkin to his lips. "Now, that is amazing news. My father died over a year ago. I hardly see how she could have given birth to his baby."

"The child was born last December," Kloosterhof said matter-of-factly.

"I see. Well, that is news to me. I had no idea when Lydia left us that she was expecting. We've heard nothing from her and presumed she'd started a new life elsewhere."

"That much is true, but you were known to have visited her. It was believed you were there when the child was born, and later you took that child and brought him back to Kansas City."

"And exactly where was it I was supposed to have gone to do all of this?"

"A town called Sitka in Alaska," Wilson replied.

Marston pushed back from the table. "I can't say I've ever heard of it."

"There are witnesses who will testify to your being there."

"Gentlemen, I don't know how I can possibly help you. Goodness, Davidson, you know I'm a single man without a child anywhere in the vicinity. My sister and brother have children, but I am happily without."

"Can we search your home?" Wilson asked.

"That's uncalled for," the uniformed officer stated. "This man is an honorable gentleman. If he says he knows nothing, he knows nothing."

"That's all right, Davidson." Marston turned to the two detectives and got to his feet. "You are free to look through my home if you'd like. I, however, have several meetings to attend to. I will let the butler know that you will be conducting a search." He

429

paused at the end of the table. "Will that be all?"

"For now," Wilson said, frowning. "We will be in touch, however."

"Very good. If indeed I have a little brother who has been taken from the bosom of his mother, I would very much like to aid in his recovery."

Marston then left, the men staring after him.

Evie stared out the window of her hotel room and watched the sun set over the ocean. It was a glorious sight, as the rich golds and oranges reflected back on the water.

California had captivated her. San Francisco was quite a town to behold. It was even bigger than Kansas City — at least, there seemed to be a great many more people. Turning away, she glanced at the sleeping baby. Dalton had been such a good traveler, and for this Evie had been greatly relieved. Especially now that she was on her own.

She had left Ellie in Sacramento only days before. Her sister had cried and fussed over the poor girl until Evie thought Ellie might want to get back on the train. The woman had thanked Ellie over and over, offering to have her stay with them before heading on to San Francisco. Evie had been touched by her generosity but had refused. The sooner she was on a ship bound for Alaska, the better.

Now, however, she sorely missed Ellie's company. Constant baby care was something Evie was not used to, and at times, she found herself overwhelmed. The changes and feedings alone were enough to keep her busy, but sometimes the child cried for seemingly no reason at all.

Not only that, but Ellie had been a fine companion, easy to talk to. And, if she were to be completely honest with herself, Evie was scared. She wasn't sleeping well, fearing that at any given moment Marston would break down the door to her room and demand she give Dalton back.

Plans were progressing well, however. Evie had managed to secure passage on the regular mail ship, *The Constantine,* and she would leave in a matter of days. It seemed God was clearing the way for her, although Evie was still struggling to wrap her mind around who He was — and that He might truly care for her. They hadn't suffered a single problem during their trip west. Everything had gone so smoothly, in fact, that Evie was beginning to believe that prayer truly worked.

Lydia awoke screaming. The nightmare had been so real that she could still feel the piercing fire in her neck. She had been shot. A man had come into her bedroom. She could still see him.

"Liddie, are you all right?" Kjell asked. He lit the lamp beside their bed and looked back to see what was wrong.

"It really happened, didn't it?" she asked, quivering.

"What are you talking about?"

"The night of the storm. Tell me what happened," she pleaded.

"I wasn't here. I don't know exactly."

"I was shot, wasn't I? My wounds weren't from the storm at all."

"You remember, then?"

She shook her head. "Not completely. I know I stood over there." She pointed to the corner. "I don't know what happened, but a man came into the room and shot me. That really happened, didn't it?"

His hesitation in answering spoke more than any admission.

"Kjell, who shot me?"

"His name was Anatolli Sidorov."

"Was? You mean he's dead?"

He nodded. "He is. He had once worked

for me, and I had to fire him and his brother for deceptive business dealings."

"Why didn't you tell me this before? Why did you let me believe I was injured during the storm?"

"You *were* injured during the storm — I just never said how it happened. The doctor didn't want us to burden you with a lot of memories. He felt it would be too much for you all at once. Liddie, you have to understand. Everything we've kept from you has been for your own good."

She put her hands to her head. "Stop it! I don't believe it helps me at all. Maybe it's really been for your good — yours and Zerelda's — but it's not for mine. I need to know the truth. I need to hear what really happened."

Kjell reached for her, but she pushed him away. "Don't you see, Kjell? I want to know. I need to know, even if it's bad." She fixed him with a questioning look. "It was very bad, wasn't it? That's why you don't want to tell me."

"Yes," he admitted.

"Bad enough that it scares you, too." She could see the fear in his eyes.

"Yes."

She knew she had a choice to make. She could continue and hear the truth of what had happened that night. It was obvious Kjell would tell her, if she wanted him to. But what if it turned out to be more than she could handle? Lydia suddenly wasn't at all sure that it was better to know. A rising tide of terror rose inside her. She knew that whatever awaited her in those damaged memories was powerful enough to have caused her to hide them away in the first place.

"I don't know what to do," she said, tears streaming down her face. "I need to know, but I'm afraid."

Kjell reached for her again, and this time Lydia allowed him to hold her. "I'll do whatever you ask, but please know that I have only remained silent in the hope that you might not suffer more than you already are."

What could be worse? She couldn't imagine that it was even possible to hurt more than she already did, but something deep inside convinced her that Kjell was speaking the truth. There was something much worse, much more horrific than she could even imagine. A monster awaited her. A monster that very well might devour her.

CHAPTER 31

The next morning Lydia sat at the table with Kjell and Zerelda and contemplated all that had happened the night before. She had warred within herself trying to figure out whether it was better to know the truth and deal with the pain or to continue to block out the memories. Something terrified her about knowing the past. She knew it would change everything . . . but then, whatever had happened had already reordered her life.

Not only that, but she couldn't even hide behind the excuse that by not knowing, she was somehow saving Zerelda and Kjell from suffering. That couldn't be — they knew what had happened. She had often come across her husband in prayer, tears rolling down his face, and knew he was hurting.

She put her hands around her untouched cup of coffee and made up her mind. "I think I need to understand what happened that night — what you are both trying to save me from knowing. I realize it's bad. I know there will be pain. And I know that your telling me won't change that I don't remember; however, it might allow me to stop fighting against those memories."

Zerelda looked at Kjell and nodded. "I think she's right. I think it's time to explain everything."

"Where do we start?" he asked.

"Start with that night. You told me about the man who came and shot me," Lydia said. "Why did he shoot me? Was it a robbery?"

"In a sense," Kjell replied. He let out a heavy breath and rubbed his temple. "Lydia, you were a widow when you came to Sitka. You had been married to a man named Floyd Gray back in Kansas City."

Lydia struggled to remember any part of that life. There had been fleeting images of people she didn't recognize, but nothing solid. "What happened to make me a widow?"

"Your husband and father died in a carriage accident. They were together when it happened," Zerelda explained. "Your husband died instantly, and your father — my brother — passed on two days later."

"All right. What does that have to do with

me being here?"

"You wanted to leave Kansas City because the family — your stepchildren — were cruel to you. You inherited money from your father," Zerelda continued. "Remember when you mentioned the word *inheritance* being important to you, and I told you about the inheritance from your father?"

Lydia nodded. "Yes."

"It left you quite wealthy, but it also took away some of the fortunes of the Gray family. Apparently your late husband's will was closely tied to your father's. I don't know all of the details, but your lawyer could tell you better than I."

"So I came here to live with you, and they were angry at me?"

"Yes, because they hoped to recover their fortune."

"But why didn't I just give it to them? It doesn't sound like it would be worth the battle and animosity to keep hold of something like that."

"You were pregnant," Kjell said matter-of-factly. "You were expecting your late husband's baby and decided that the baby was entitled to part of the fortune."

"A baby?" Lydia shook her head. She stood and pushed away from the table. The chair fell to the floor. "What baby? What are you talking about?"

Zerelda stood and reached out for Lydia. "Try to remain calm about this, Lydia. It won't serve you well to get upset."

"But you're telling me . . ." She looked at them in confusion. "What are you telling me? Are you saying I have a child?"

"Yes. A son named Dalton. Our son."

Lydia felt as if the room were spinning. She had so often dreamed of a baby. Even now she could envision the child crying in his cradle. She longed to hold him and comfort him. Was this the child of whom Kjell spoke? Why couldn't she remember her own son?

"Where is he? Is he dead?"

Kjell shook his head. "I don't think so."

Hysteria edged her voice. "What do you mean? Don't you know whether he's dead or alive?"

Zerelda turned Lydia to face her. She gripped Lydia's shoulders almost painfully tight. "Lydia, you have to calm down. It isn't healthy. Please sit back down."

She considered her aunt's words for a moment. Her breath caught in her throat, and for a moment, Lydia felt as if she might faint. Zerelda picked up the chair while Kjell reached out to take hold of her hand.

"Here. Sit." His face was so full of loving

compassion that Lydia continued to clutch his hand even after she returned to the chair.

The memory took hold. Though nothing more than a wisp of images, at that moment Lydia was transported back to the night of the attack. She could see the man again — the raised gun. Then glancing to her side, she saw the cradle and Dalton. With a gasp and cry, she looked at Kjell, shaking her head.

"They took him. They took my baby, didn't they?"

The Constantine harbored overnight in Sitka Sound, much to Evie's dismay. When morning came and the launches were readied to carry the mail and passengers to Sitka, she and Dalton were the first in line.

"We will send your things over in the next launch," a man assured her.

Evie truly didn't care. She longed only to find Lydia. She stared across the harbor at the town and wondered how she would ever locate her stepmother. The town appeared larger than she'd expected. Would someone there know Lydia?

Dalton settled into her arms and went to sleep after a great deal of fussing. She knew he sensed her tension, and she wished she could calm herself. The best thing she could do for him was being done; aside from that, she had nothing to offer. For a moment, Evie dreaded finding Lydia. Dalton had been a comfort to her, and she had grown very fond of the boy. When she had thought Lydia dead, Evie was perfectly happy to become the boy's mother. However, when she learned what her brother had done, something inside her changed. She knew she couldn't let things continue as they were . . . but oh, how she loved this little one. What if Lydia wanted her to leave and never return? Evie didn't know how she'd bear giving up the child altogether.

"The weather is perfect," someone was saying, but Evie didn't acknowledge the conversation. "What a beautiful day."

She sat in quiet contemplation, wondering what her future might hold. During her trip north, Evie had practiced what she would say to Lydia. If things went well, Lydia would know it wasn't Evie's fault that Dalton had been taken. Maybe she would even allow Evie to remain with her there in Sitka. Otherwise, Evie wasn't sure what she was going to do.

Ellie and her sister had assured Evie she would always be welcomed in Sacramento, but that really wasn't where she wanted to be. The thought of being with Lydia offered her great comfort, and Evie could only pray that somehow her stepmother would welcome her.

She shook her head at the irony of it all. She longed to remain with Dalton, but even more so, she longed to be close again to Lydia. Would the one act negate the possibility of the other? Would Lydia send her away, simply for being related to the wrong family?

Once on shore, Evie glanced around the docks. She had hoped there might be a cab to hire, but most folks seemed to be on foot. The smell of fish and other unpleasant aromas wafted on the air, but otherwise the day was, as the man on the launch had said, quite perfect.

"You look lost. Might I be of some assistance?"

Evie turned.

The older man smiled. "Your baby is a handsome one."

She returned the smile. "I'm looking for someone. I need to find Lydia Gray."

The man laughed. "Ain't Gray no more. The name is Lindquist. And I know her husband well. In fact, his foreman is just over there. Josh! Josh, come here." He turned back to Evie. "That's Joshua Broadstreet."

Evie watched as a young man fixed his brown eyes upon her. He seemed momentarily mesmerized, making her feel uncomfortable. Then he smiled.

"What's the problem, Briney?" he asked, crossing to where they stood.

"This young lady would like to get out to the Lindquist place. She's looking for Lydia. I told her you worked with Kjell."

"I do." He seemed to notice the sleeping baby for the first time. Evie saw a frown cross his lips before he spoke. "I can drive you out there — that is, if I can borrow a rig."

"Thank you." Evie looked back at the man called Briney. "And thank you for your assistance. I'm afraid I came a bit unprepared."

The man laughed. "Ain't no problem. Most everyone knows everyone else around here. I'll just stay with you until he gets back. You'd probably be safe enough, but we have our share of unsavory characters."

She nodded, thinking of Marston's words about hiring someone to take care of Lydia. Shivering, she pushed aside the thought. It would only be a short time until she could rectify the hideous wrong her brother had done.

Joshua finally returned with a small two-wheeled cart. It was pulled by a stout-looking gelding that seemed far from interested in attending to their needs.

"Come on, get up there." Josh guided the poky beast into place, then set the brake. He grinned as he climbed down. "Patches is about a hundred years old, but he'll do the job."

He looked at Evie for a moment and sobered. "I can take the baby, if you like, while you climb aboard. I'd be hard-pressed, however, to help you up at the same time."

"It's no bother. I'm capable." Handing Dalton to him, she admonished, "Don't drop him."

He met her gaze and grinned again. "I wasn't planning to."

Evie hiked her skirts, unconcerned about showing her ankles, and hoisted herself onto the cart seat. Reaching down, she took Dalton from Joshua and waited while he climbed aboard. He released the brake and slapped the reins lightly on the back of the horse.

"Pick it up there, Patches."

The horse moved out onto the road and gently plodded past the shops and businesses that lined the waterfront.

"What's your name?" Josh asked.

"Evie. Evie Gadston."

"How do you know Lydia?"

She considered this for a moment. "Through my family." The last thing she wanted was to have to explain herself. "Is it far?"

She was anxious for this matter to be resolved. The horse's painfully slow pace almost made Evie suggest they walk.

"It's a ways. More than you'd want to hike," he said, as if reading her thoughts. "So what brings you to Sitka? Is Lydia a friend of yours?"

Evie nodded. "I hope so. Tell me — it's been a long time since I've seen her — how is she?"

"Well, she has good days and bad. You know about the accident?"

"I knew something had happened, but I don't know the details," she admitted.

"She was shot a couple of times. Nearly died. It left her with a long recovery period and no memory."

"No memory? None at all?"

"Well, Kjell tells me she's getting it back in tiny bits. She doesn't remember much, though. She probably won't remember you." He smiled at her. "But don't take it personal-like. She's a good person, and she'll still welcome you."

"I hope so. I mean, I think once she realizes why I've come, she'll be more than happy to see me." Evie didn't really expect Josh to reply. What could he say? Obviously the situation had changed from what she had anticipated. It had been her hope that she would come, and Lydia would be so overjoyed about Dalton's return that she would welcome Evie with open arms. But now she wouldn't even know who Evie was. This could complicate everything considerably.

"You still with me?" Josh asked.

She shook her head. "What? What do you mean?"

"I asked you a question, but you didn't seem to hear."

"I do apologize. My thoughts were preoccupied." She stared at the evergreen trees and glanced up at the mountains beyond. It was a beautiful island.

"That's all right. I simply asked why you'd come."

"It's . . . well . . . difficult to explain."

He shook his head. "That family doesn't need any more difficulties. I'm sure if you know about the accident, then you heard about her baby, too."

Evie hugged Dalton a little closer. "I did."

"We don't know what happened to him. I was a little bit alarmed when I saw you were bringing a baby to visit. I don't know if Lydia will remember her boy or not, but you might be prepared for her to be upset. She gets that way when she thinks about things and can't remember.

"Fact is," he continued, "they don't know what ever happened to the baby. Kjell's been trying to find out, but so far there's been no luck. He thinks Lydia's stepson took him or at least hired someone to take him."

Evie felt the intensity of the moment unlike anything she'd ever known. "He did," she blurted out.

Joshua pulled back on the reins and looked at her oddly. "What?"

She met his dark eyes and hoped he wouldn't hate her for what she was about to say. She just needed to declare the truth. "Mr. Broadstreet, my brother did take Dalton." She pulled back the lacy blanket that shielded the baby from the morning sun. "But I'm bringing him back."

Lydia sat on the porch in her rocking chair. The tightness in her chest threatened to rob her of breath. How could she have forgotten her own son? No matter how traumatic the attack, it seemed unthinkable that she would have lost her memory of him.

Kjell had explained everything, but very little made sense. She tried to remember more about that night, but nothing came to her. Perhaps in time it would, but then again, did she really want it to?

In his account of the story, Kjell had told her that he'd hired a detective, and that the authorities were finally involved in investigating Marston Gray. This was the man — her stepson — who had taken Dalton away. At least they believed he had. Some other man — a brother to the man who had shot her — had testified that this was what had happened.

She buried her head in her hands and rocked. Where was her baby? Why couldn't they find him?

Oh, God, she prayed, *please help me — help us. Please let us find Dalton. Let me know him again.* The empty feeling of not remembering — of not knowing even now where her baby might be — was more than she could bear.

The tears came as they had earlier, and still she rocked.

Lydia had begged Kjell and Zerelda to leave her alone — to let her have time to consider all that they'd told her. Now, however, she wished for Kjell's presence. He had a way of making her feel at peace, even in the midst of despair.

She was just about to go inside to find Kjell's comfort when the sound of a wagon approaching caused Lydia to look up. She didn't recognize the horse as it rounded the bend, but the driver appeared to be the young man who worked for her husband. There was a woman at his side, but Lydia couldn't see who it might be. She was carrying something, so perhaps Zerelda had arranged a delivery of goods.

Lydia dried her eyes on the edge of her apron and drew a deep breath. She got to her feet and was just about to go inside when for some reason she felt compelled to look once again at the passenger beside Josh. There was something familiar about her. As the wagon drew closer, Lydia felt as if she recognized the blond-haired woman.

Unable to move, Lydia waited by the door as Josh brought the wagon to a stop. He reached up to take hold of the woman's bundle. That was when Lydia realized the stranger was holding a baby.

The young lady climbed down from the wagon and took the infant back in her arms. She saw Lydia and approached ever so slowly. Smiling, she spoke.

"Lydia? It's me, Evie. Evie Gray — remember?"

Shaking her head, Lydia felt bile rise in her throat. She studied the woman again. She knew those eyes. Those haunting blue eyes. A passing memory of a painting came to Lydia. A woman who looked very much like this one stared down at her with those same eyes.

She took a step away from the door and scrutinized the young woman. She said her name was Gray. Just like the name of the stepson who had taken away her child.

"I know this must be a shock to you," the woman continued. The baby began to fuss, and she shifted him to her shoulder. When she did, the blanket fell away.

Lydia looked at the child and then at the stranger. "Evie," she repeated the name.

"Yes. And this is your son. I've brought him back to you."

A scream filled the air, but Lydia didn't realize it had come from her own throat until Kjell bounded out the door and took her in his arms.

"What's wrong?" he asked.

Lydia felt herself falling as darkness engulfed her vision. "Dalton," she whispered and then knew nothing.

CHAPTER 32

Lydia opened her eyes to find everyone watching her. There were tears in Zerelda's eyes, and Kjell's expression was concerned. She shook her head, trying to clear away the confusion in her mind.

"Let me help you sit up," Kjell told her. "Zerelda, get a cold cloth."

He gently eased Lydia up against the back of the davenport. She spied the young woman and suddenly remembered why it was she'd fainted. The baby began to cry, and Lydia extended her arms.

"Bring him to me . . . please."

It was only a moment before mother and son were reunited. Lydia stared down in wonder at the boy and put him to her shoulder to comfort him. "There, there." She patted his back and he calmed.

Lydia breathed in the scent of him and felt a rush of emotions. The smell evoked a feeling of happiness and calm. She marveled at the wonder of the moment. The child she had forgotten was now home in her arms.

"I am so sorry for what Marston did to you," Evie said, kneeling down beside Lydia. "When I learned the truth, I did what I could to bring Dalton back to you."

Lydia looked at the young woman. She had the vaguest recollection of knowing her. "It wasn't your fault," she said, somehow knowing the truth of her statement.

Evie nodded. "But my family — they've never treated you right. I care for you, however, and I hope my actions here today have proven that."

"It goes without saying," Lydia assured her. "I wish I could remember the things from the past, but after I was injured, I lost most of my memory."

"There's a part of me that's actually glad about that. I was beside myself with grief, imagining you suffering over Dalton's disap-pearance," Evie confessed. "I couldn't bear to think of you sitting here crying for him and having no solace." Tears formed in her eyes.

Lydia reached out and patted Evie's hand just as a knock sounded on the door. Kjell got up and went to see who it was. Lydia heard muffled talk and then saw the man she'd been introduced to as Captain Briar enter the room.

"Ma'am." He looked at the baby and then at Kjell. "I came with word from Kansas City, but perhaps it is unimportant now."

"Nonsense," Kjell declared. "Tell us what you know."

"It seems rather moot in light of your son being returned to you. The authorities have sent a letter. It came today on *The Constantine.* They've investigated Mr. Gray as you suggested but found no sign of your son. Obviously, if he is here with you now, he wasn't taken by Gray."

"That's not true," Evie interrupted. She got to her feet and looked from Lydia to the men. "I am Marston Gray's sister. He brought me the child several months ago and told me that Lydia was dead. He asked me to raise Dalton, and I agreed. He is guilty of having taken this baby and of trying to murder Lydia."

Briar's eyes narrowed. "And how do you know all this for a fact?"

"I heard him admit it." She glanced down at Lydia. "My husband and brothers were talking. They didn't know I could hear them." She turned back to Briar. "When I learned the truth, I took Dalton and came here immediately."

Briar looked at Kjell. "I find this all rather

confusing."

"There's no confusion at all," Evie declared. "My brother is guilty, and I will testify to that. I will tell you everything I know, just as I should have years ago when my father threw my mother off the roof to her death."

Lydia gasped. "Floyd killed her?" The name came back all at once. She remembered the angry face of her husband as he stood over her with a whip. He had just beaten her and his first words to her were, *"Charlotte never learned to obey me, either, and you see where it got her."*

The scene passed just as quickly as it had come.

Evie came back to Lydia. "He did. I saw the whole thing, but I never told anyone. I'm sorry now that I didn't. Maybe things would have been different. Maybe you would never have had to suffer under his hand."

"It's not your fault, Evie," Lydia said, reaching up to take her hand. "It's not your fault. You were just a child."

Captain Briar cleared his throat nervously. "I suppose now that we have a witness more reliable than Sidorov, we can hardly ignore Gray's part in this crime. I will contact the authorities immediately and see what can be done. Where can I locate you, Mrs. . . ."

"Gadston. Genevieve Gadston."

"She'll be here," Lydia interjected. "She'll stay with us, if that's all right with you, Evie."

"Truth be told, I was going to ask you for just such a favor. You see, I can't go home. None of them will have me back after this."

"What of your husband?" Kjell asked.

"Thomas has never cared about me. He'll probably be relieved to have me out of his hair. With any luck at all, he will give me a quiet annulment, and if not, then I'll simply live out my days apart from him."

Kjell nodded. "Then stay with us, by all means."

"It's settled," Lydia said, looking into the inquisitive face of her son. Somewhere deep inside her there was a sense of recognition — a certainty that he belonged to her. "It's settled."

Watching her sleeping baby, Lydia marveled at the way the child seemed undisturbed by all that had happened. He slept so easily, so peacefully. She stroked his fine hair and somehow knew she'd done this a hundred times before.

"Is he asleep?" Kjell asked.

"Yes." Lydia straightened but refused to

leave the side of the cradle. "He settled right down after I fed him."

Kjell smiled and came to pull her back against him. He nuzzled Lydia's neck and kissed the lobe of her ear. "It's a miracle, to be sure."

Lydia glanced back at him. "Do you really think so? Did God bring him back to us, Kjell?"

"I'm certain He did. I don't believe in coincidence or luck. I think God plans our steps and then guides them. Sometimes others interfere with what He would have, but even so, God is able to make it all work to His glory." He leaned his cheek against hers. "I can't begin to understand why this had to happen or how it is glorifying to Him, but, Lydia, I do believe He has His hand upon us and upon Dalton."

She turned in Kjell's arms and reached up to touch his face. "I want a wonderful future with you and Dalton, and any other child we are given."

He stroked her hair. "I want that, too. It doesn't matter to me whether you know me from before, only that you know me now and that you love me forever."

"Oh, you can be certain of that," she said, pulling back enough to see his face. "Just as I am certain of your love."

In the glow of firelight, Lydia smiled and pulled his face toward hers. Kissing him lightly, she knew more joy — more content-ment — than she had ever thought possible. When he lifted her in his arms, she could only sigh in satisfaction. No matter where the future took them, no matter the trials they would face, this moment would be the prelude to a new dawning of life and love that they would face and share together.

ABOUT THE AUTHOR

Tracie Peterson is the author of over eighty novels, both historical and contemporary. Her avid research resonates in her stories, as seen in her bestselling HEIRS OF MONTANA and ALASKAN QUEST series. Tracie and her family make their home in Montana.

Visit Tracie's Web site at *www.traciepeter son.com.*

Visit Tracie's blog at *www.writespassage .blogspot.com*